SMOOTH CRIMINALS ™

CRIME HEALS ALL WOUNDS

LUSTGARTEN • SMITH • ROY • RIDDEL • PEER

SERIES DESIGNER
MARIE KRUPINA

COLLECTION DESIGNER
CHELSEA ROBERTS

ASSOCIATE EDITOR
SOPHIE PHILIPS-ROBERTS

EDITOR
SHANNON WATTERS

BOOM! BOX™

SMOOTH CRIMINALS: CRIME HEALS ALL WOUNDS, August 2019. Published by BOOM! Box, a division of Boom Entertainment, Inc. Smooth Criminals is ™ & © 2019 Kiwi Loves You, Inc. and Kurt Lustgarten. Originally published in single magazine form as SMOOTH CRIMINALS No. 5-8. ™ & © 2019 Kiwi Loves You, Inc. and Kurt Lustgarten. All rights reserved. BOOM! Box™ and the BOOM! Box logo are trademarks of Boom Entertainment, Inc., registered in various countries and categories. All characters, events, and institutions depicted herein are fictional. Any similarity between any of the names, characters, persons, events, and/or institutions in this publication to actual names, characters, and persons, whether living or dead, events, and/or institutions is unintended and purely coincidental. BOOM! Box does not read or accept unsolicited submissions of ideas, stories, or artwork.

BOOM! Studios, 5670 Wilshire Boulevard, Suite 400, Los Angeles, CA 90036-5679. Printed in China. First Printing.

ISBN: 978-1-68415-463-0, eISBN: 978-1-64144-580-1

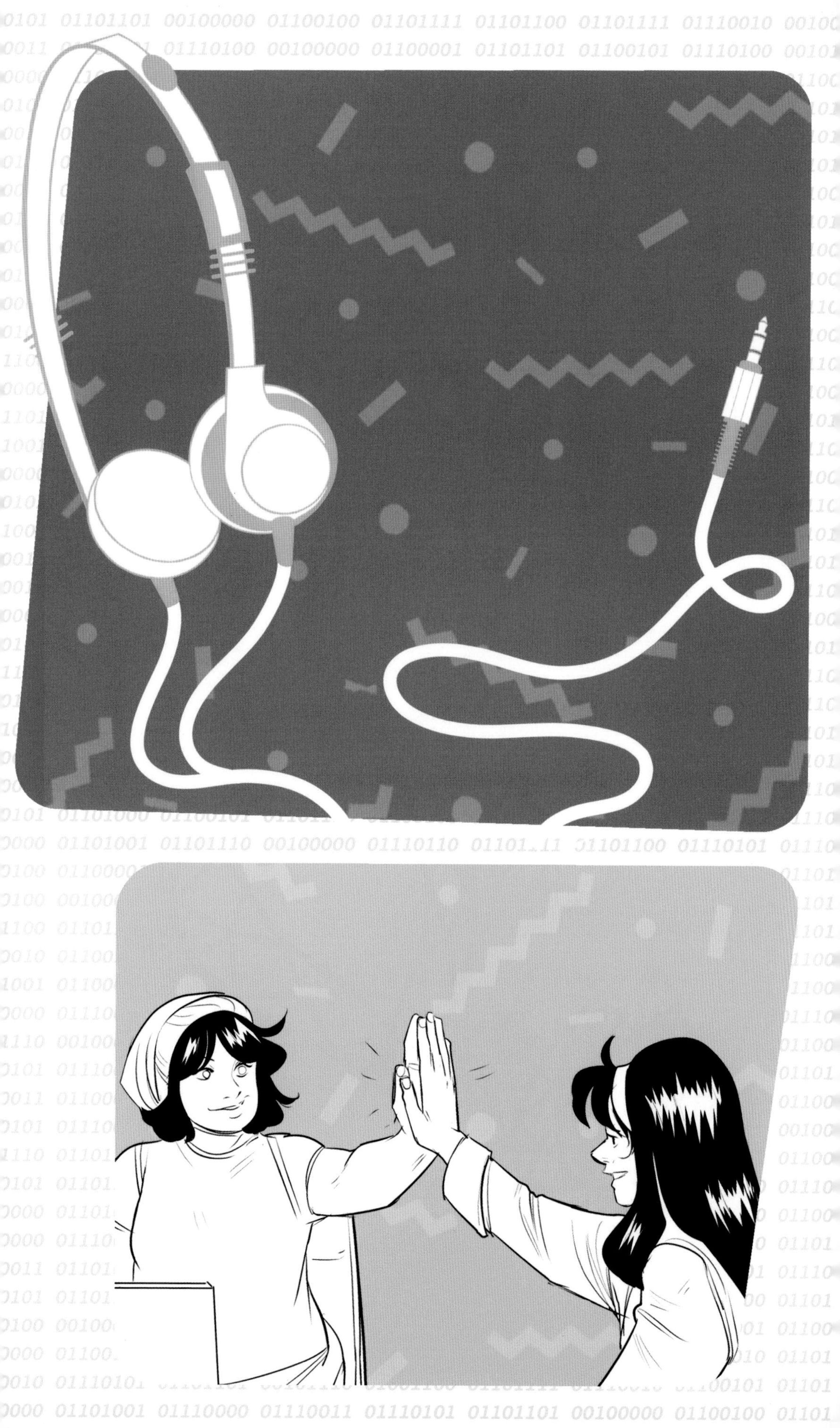

SMOOTH CRIMINALS

CREATED BY KURT LUSTGARTEN & KIRSTEN 'KIWI' SMITH

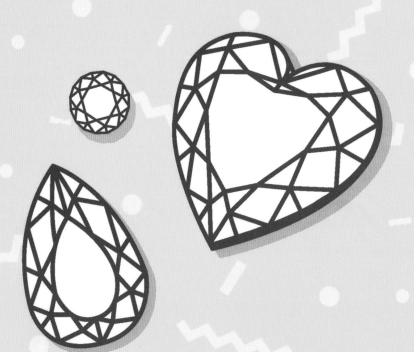

WRITTEN BY
KURT LUSTGARTEN, KIRSTEN 'KIWI' SMITH & AMY ROY

ILLUSTRATED BY
LEISHA RIDDEL
WITH ADDITIONAL INKS BY **RAVEN WARNER** (CHAPTER 5)

COLORED BY
BRITTANY PEER (CHAPTERS 5 & 6)
JAMIE LOUGHRAN (CHAPTER 7)
JOANA LAFUENTE & GONÇALO LOPES
(CHAPTERS 7 & 8)

LETTERED BY
ED DUKESHIRE

COVER BY
AUDREY MOK

CHAPTER FIVE

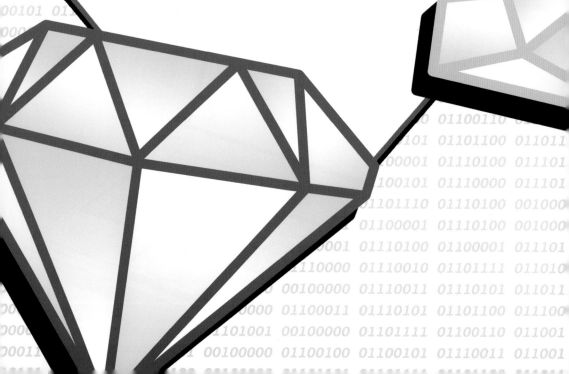

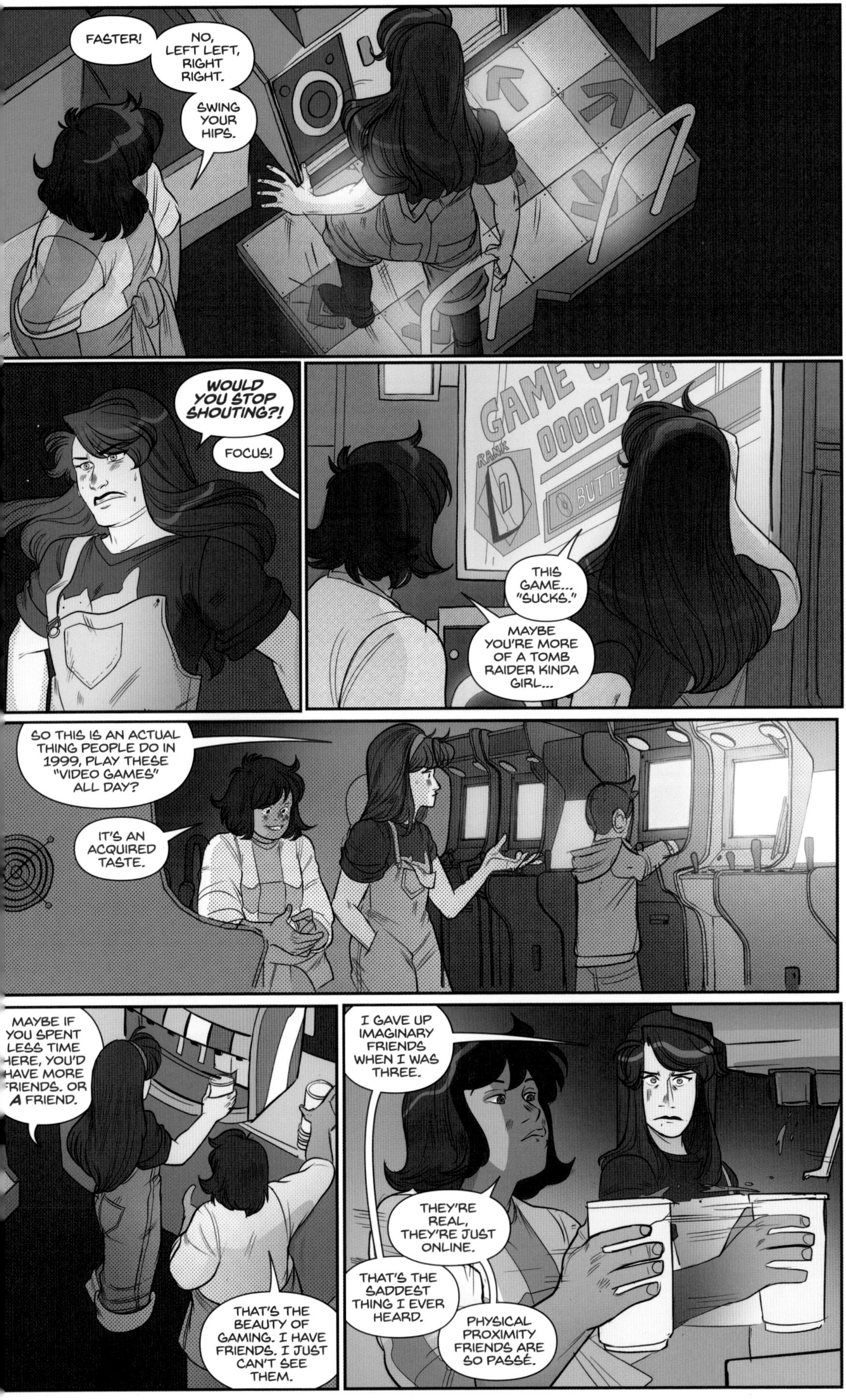
FASTER!
NO, LEFT LEFT, RIGHT RIGHT.
SWING YOUR HIPS.
WOULD YOU STOP SHOUTING?!
FOCUS!
GAME O
00007238
RANK
D
BUTTE
THIS GAME... "SUCKS."
MAYBE YOU'RE MORE OF A TOMB RAIDER KINDA GIRL...
SO THIS IS AN ACTUAL THING PEOPLE DO IN 1999, PLAY THESE "VIDEO GAMES" ALL DAY?
IT'S AN ACQUIRED TASTE.
MAYBE IF YOU SPENT LESS TIME HERE, YOU'D HAVE MORE FRIENDS. OR A FRIEND.
THAT'S THE BEAUTY OF GAMING. I HAVE FRIENDS. I JUST CAN'T SEE THEM.
I GAVE UP IMAGINARY FRIENDS WHEN I WAS THREE.
THEY'RE REAL, THEY'RE JUST ONLINE.
THAT'S THE SADDEST THING I EVER HEARD.
PHYSICAL PROXIMITY FRIENDS ARE SO PASSÉ.

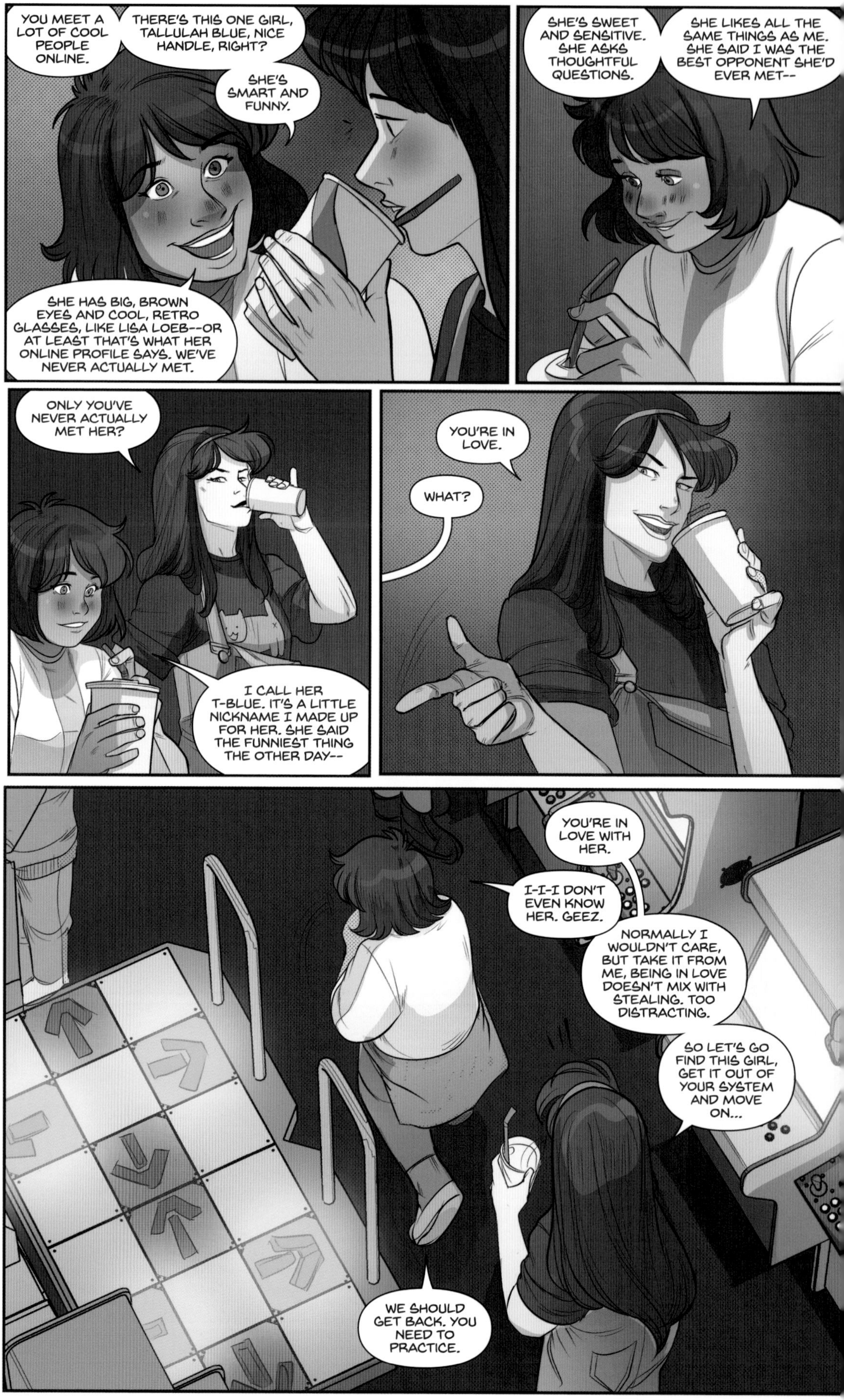
YOU MEET A LOT OF COOL PEOPLE ONLINE.
THERE'S THIS ONE GIRL, TALLULAH BLUE, NICE HANDLE, RIGHT?
SHE'S SMART AND FUNNY.
SHE HAS BIG, BROWN EYES AND COOL, RETRO GLASSES, LIKE LISA LOEB--OR AT LEAST THAT'S WHAT HER ONLINE PROFILE SAYS. WE'VE NEVER ACTUALLY MET.
SHE'S SWEET AND SENSITIVE. SHE ASKS THOUGHTFUL QUESTIONS.
SHE LIKES ALL THE SAME THINGS AS ME. SHE SAID I WAS THE BEST OPPONENT SHE'D EVER MET--
ONLY YOU'VE NEVER ACTUALLY MET HER?
I CALL HER T-BLUE. IT'S A LITTLE NICKNAME I MADE UP FOR HER. SHE SAID THE FUNNIEST THING THE OTHER DAY--
YOU'RE IN LOVE.
WHAT?
YOU'RE IN LOVE WITH HER.
I-I-I DON'T EVEN KNOW HER. GEEZ.
NORMALLY I WOULDN'T CARE, BUT TAKE IT FROM ME, BEING IN LOVE DOESN'T MIX WITH STEALING. TOO DISTRACTING.
SO LET'S GO FIND THIS GIRL, GET IT OUT OF YOUR SYSTEM AND MOVE ON...
WE SHOULD GET BACK. YOU NEED TO PRACTICE.

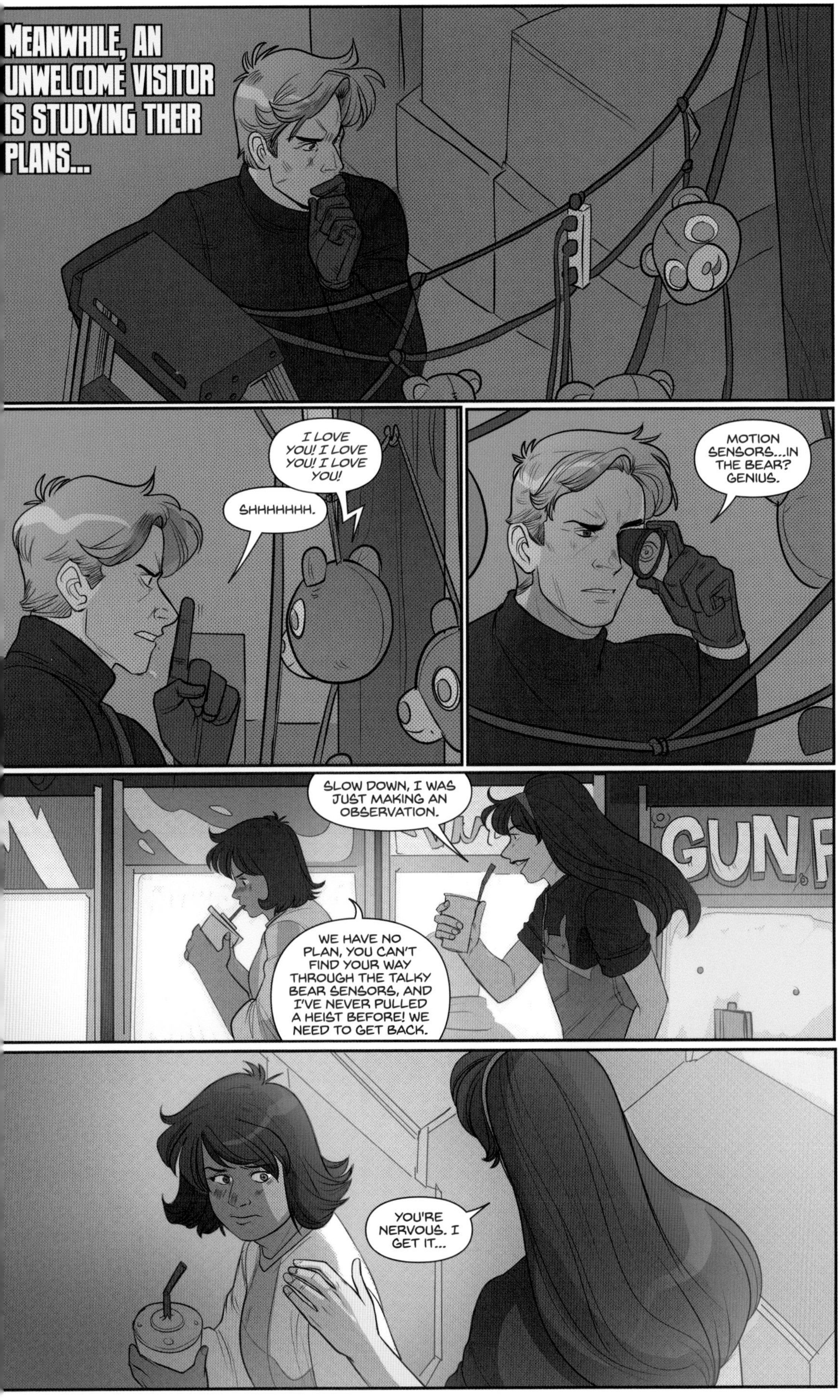
MEANWHILE, AN UNWELCOME VISITOR IS STUDYING THEIR PLANS...
I LOVE YOU! I LOVE YOU! I LOVE YOU!
SHHHHHHH.
MOTION SENSORS...IN THE BEAR? GENIUS.
SLOW DOWN, I WAS JUST MAKING AN OBSERVATION.
WE HAVE NO PLAN, YOU CAN'T FIND YOUR WAY THROUGH THE TALKY BEAR SENSORS, AND I'VE NEVER PULLED A HEIST BEFORE! WE NEED TO GET BACK.
GUN
YOU'RE NERVOUS. I GET IT...

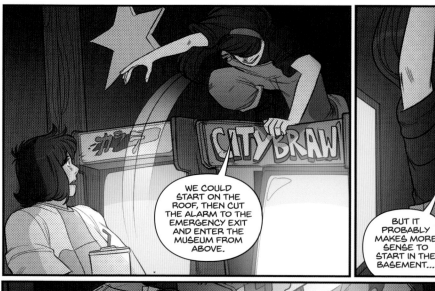

WE COULD START ON THE ROOF, THEN CUT THE ALARM TO THE EMERGENCY EXIT AND ENTER THE MUSEUM FROM ABOVE.

BUT IT PROBABLY MAKES MORE SENSE TO START IN THE BASEMENT...

...AND EITHER A.) HITCH A RIDE ON THE ROOF OF THE FREIGHT ELEVATOR, UNDETECTED, TO THE SECOND FLOOR.

OR B.) FIND OUR WAY TO THE HEATING/COOLING FACILITY, DISRUPT THE THERMA-SHIELD, AND CRAWL THROUGH THE VENTILATION TUBING. AGAIN, UNDETECTED.

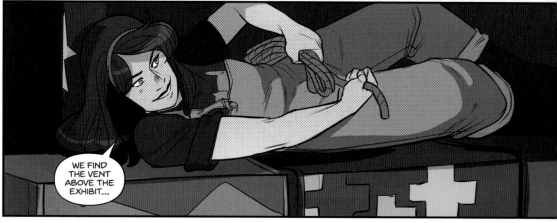

WE FIND THE VENT ABOVE THE EXHIBIT...

...AND...

...AND...

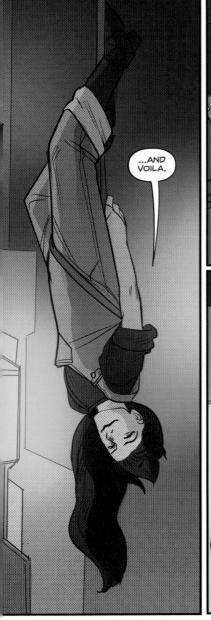

...AND VOILA.

YO! LARA CROFT IS *REAL.*

DUDE.

SEE? HANDLED.

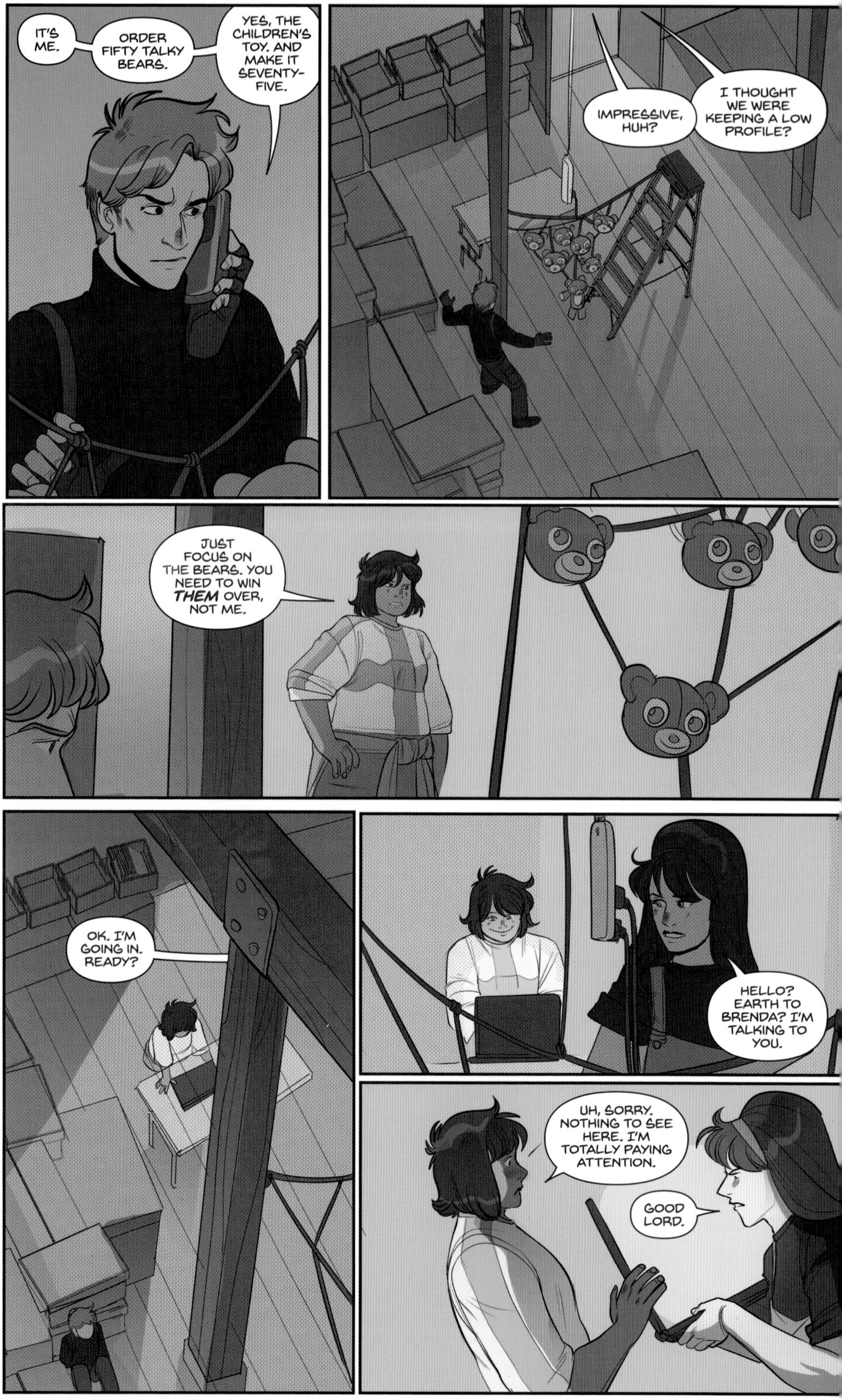
IT'S ME.
ORDER FIFTY TALKY BEARS.
YES, THE CHILDREN'S TOY. AND MAKE IT SEVENTY-FIVE.
IMPRESSIVE, HUH?
I THOUGHT WE WERE KEEPING A LOW PROFILE?
JUST FOCUS ON THE BEARS. YOU NEED TO WIN *THEM* OVER, NOT ME.
OK. I'M GOING IN. READY?
HELLO? EARTH TO BRENDA? I'M TALKING TO YOU.
UH, SORRY. NOTHING TO SEE HERE. I'M TOTALLY PAYING ATTENTION.
GOOD LORD.

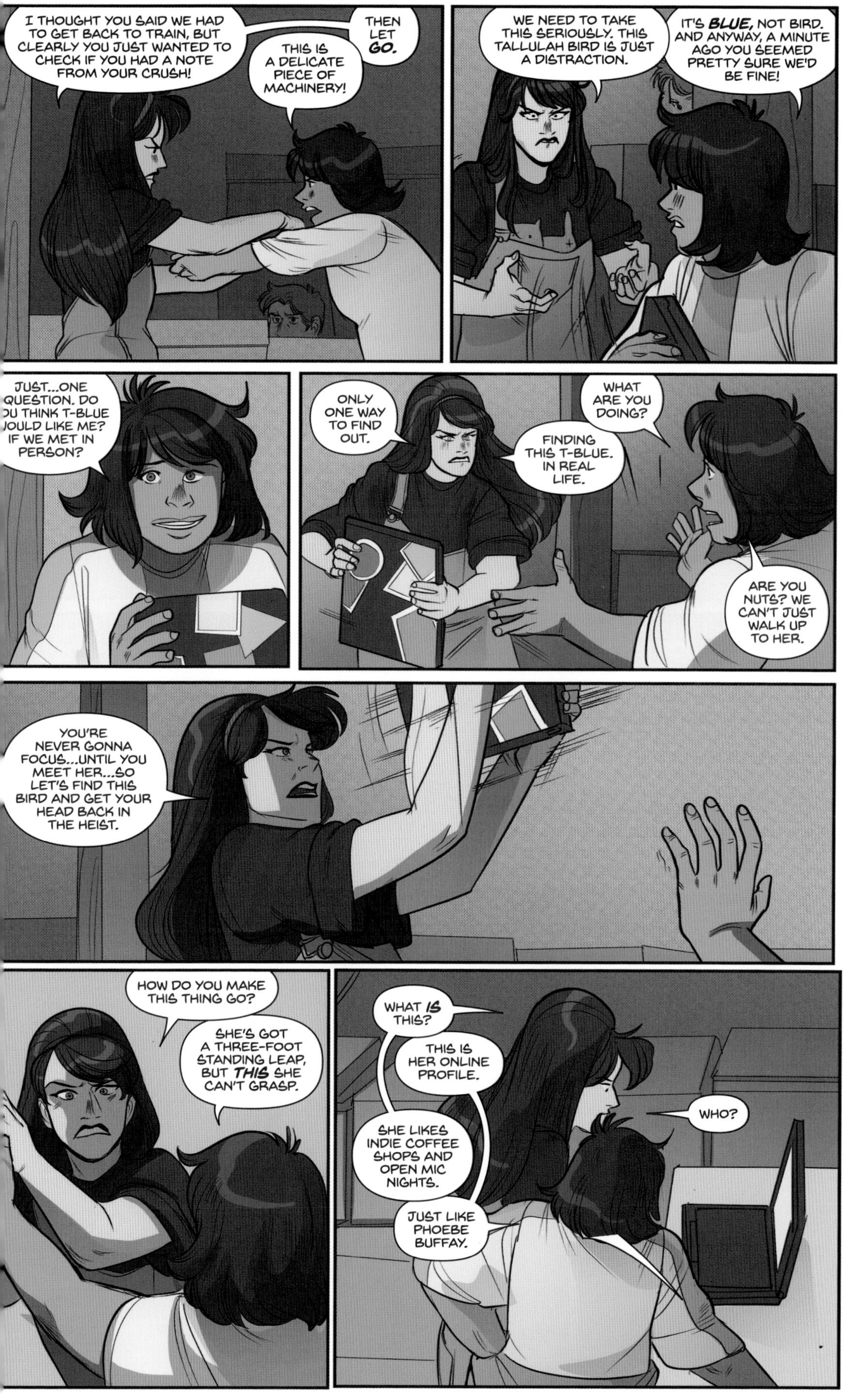
I THOUGHT YOU SAID WE HAD TO GET BACK TO TRAIN, BUT CLEARLY YOU JUST WANTED TO CHECK IF YOU HAD A NOTE FROM YOUR CRUSH!
THEN LET GO.
THIS IS A DELICATE PIECE OF MACHINERY!
WE NEED TO TAKE THIS SERIOUSLY. THIS TALLULAH BIRD IS JUST A DISTRACTION.
IT'S BLUE, NOT BIRD. AND ANYWAY, A MINUTE AGO YOU SEEMED PRETTY SURE WE'D BE FINE!
JUST...ONE QUESTION. DO U THINK T-BLUE OULD LIKE ME? IF WE MET IN PERSON?
ONLY ONE WAY TO FIND OUT.
WHAT ARE YOU DOING?
FINDING THIS T-BLUE. IN REAL LIFE.
ARE YOU NUTS? WE CAN'T JUST WALK UP TO HER.
YOU'RE NEVER GONNA FOCUS...UNTIL YOU MEET HER...SO LET'S FIND THIS BIRD AND GET YOUR HEAD BACK IN THE HEIST.
HOW DO YOU MAKE THIS THING GO?
SHE'S GOT A THREE-FOOT STANDING LEAP, BUT THIS SHE CAN'T GRASP.
WHAT IS THIS?
THIS IS HER ONLINE PROFILE.
WHO?
SHE LIKES INDIE COFFEE SHOPS AND OPEN MIC NIGHTS.
JUST LIKE PHOEBE BUFFAY.

LUCKY FOR YOU, I HAVE THE *FRIENDS* BOX SET, SEASONS 1-5.

AND? WHAT AM I SUPPOSED TO DO WITH THIS?

THEY'RE VHS? MOVIES YOU CAN RENT AND WATCH ON YOUR TV?

FRIENDS

WHERE ARE YOU GOING?

TO FIND AN OPEN MIC NIGHT.

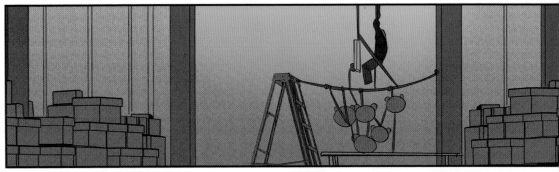

YOU GIRLS GONNA PAY FOR THAT?

IT'S *FREE.*

BINGO.

PERK IT UP

COMING TO THE PERK IT UP STAGE... *TALLULAH BLUE.*

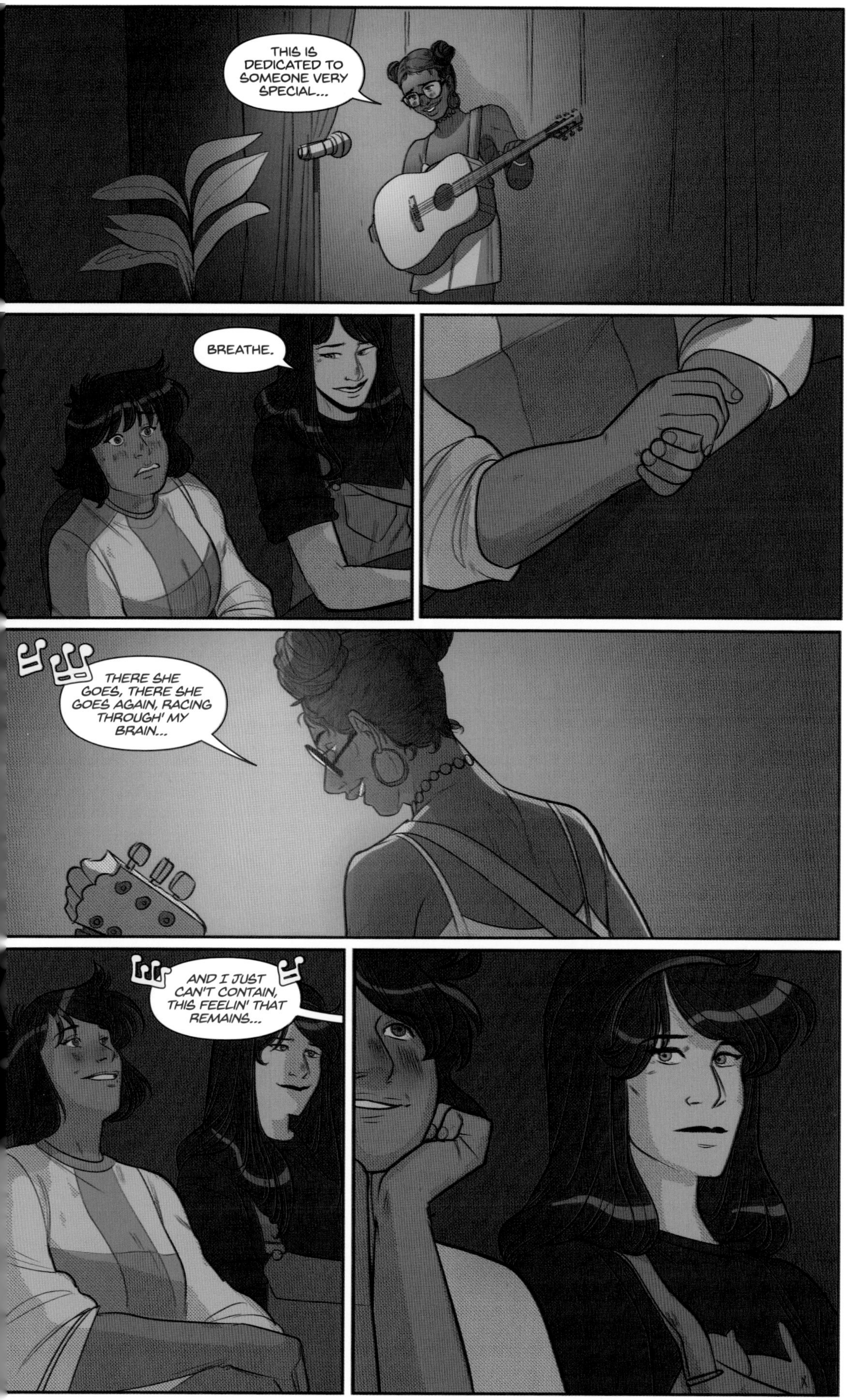
THIS IS DEDICATED TO SOMEONE VERY SPECIAL...
BREATHE.
THERE SHE GOES, THERE SHE GOES AGAIN, RACING THROUGH' MY BRAIN...
AND I JUST CAN'T CONTAIN, THIS FEELIN' THAT REMAINS...

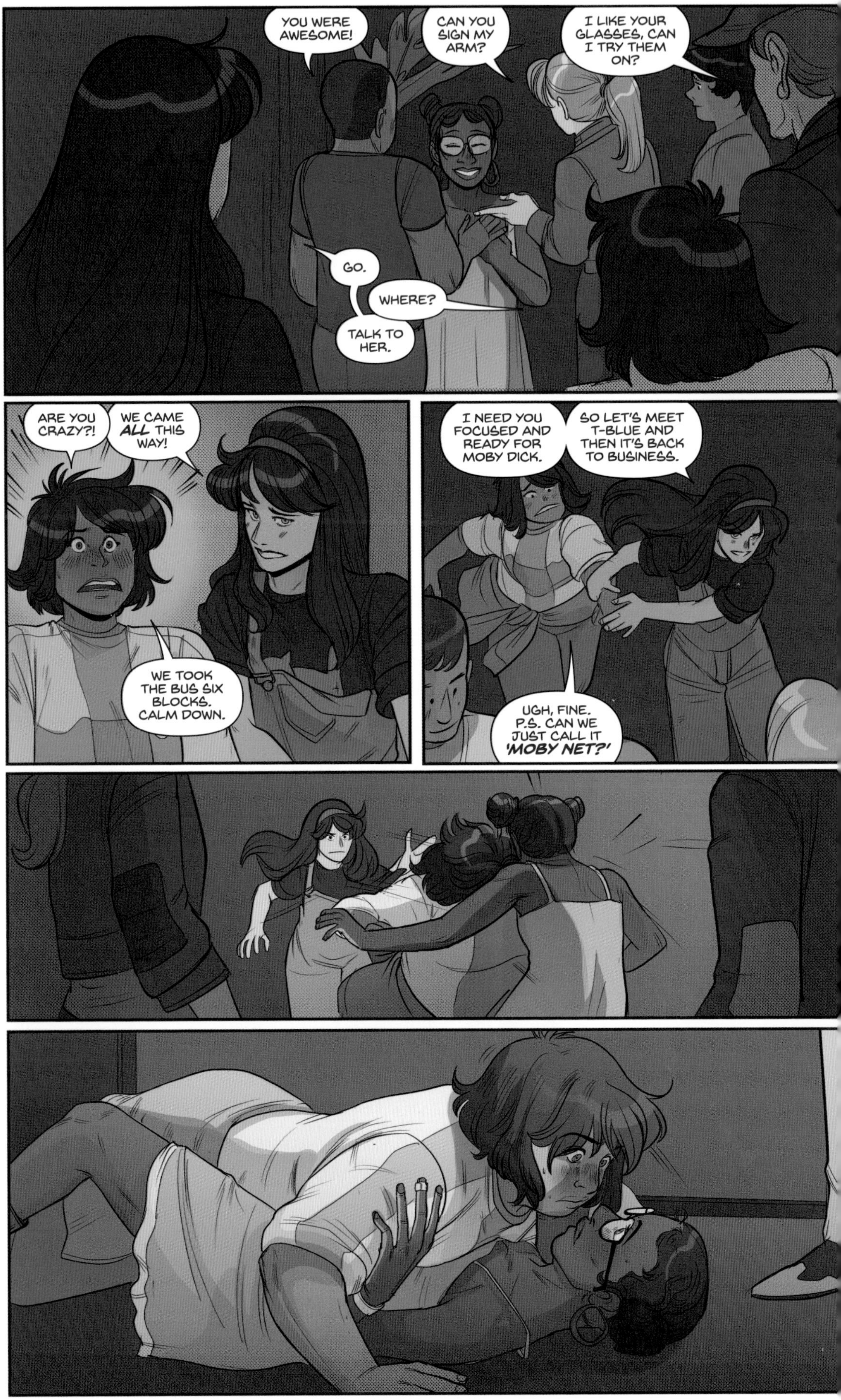
YOU WERE AWESOME!
CAN YOU SIGN MY ARM?
I LIKE YOUR GLASSES, CAN I TRY THEM ON?
GO.
WHERE?
TALK TO HER.
ARE YOU CRAZY?!
WE CAME ALL THIS WAY!
WE TOOK THE BUS SIX BLOCKS. CALM DOWN.
I NEED YOU FOCUSED AND READY FOR MOBY DICK.
SO LET'S MEET T-BLUE AND THEN IT'S BACK TO BUSINESS.
UGH, FINE. P.S. CAN WE JUST CALL IT 'MOBY NET?'

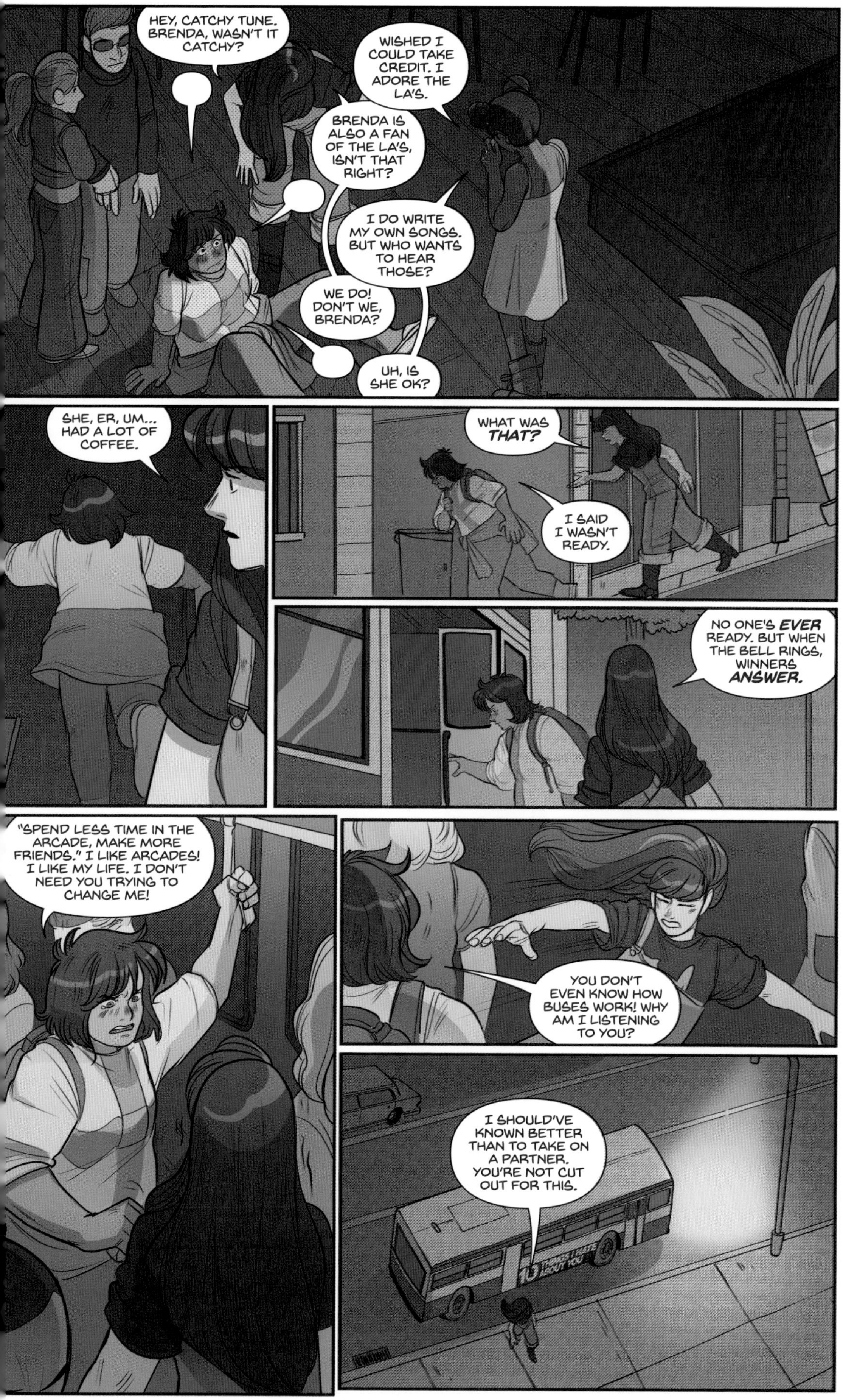
HEY, CATCHY TUNE. BRENDA, WASN'T IT CATCHY?
WISHED I COULD TAKE CREDIT. I ADORE THE LA'S.
BRENDA IS ALSO A FAN OF THE LA'S, ISN'T THAT RIGHT?
I DO WRITE MY OWN SONGS. BUT WHO WANTS TO HEAR THOSE?
WE DO! DON'T WE, BRENDA?
UH, IS SHE OK?
SHE, ER, UM... HAD A LOT OF COFFEE.
WHAT WAS *THAT?*
I SAID I WASN'T READY.
NO ONE'S ***EVER*** READY. BUT WHEN THE BELL RINGS, WINNERS ***ANSWER.***
"SPEND LESS TIME IN THE ARCADE, MAKE MORE FRIENDS." I LIKE ARCADES! I LIKE MY LIFE. I DON'T NEED YOU TRYING TO CHANGE ME!
YOU DON'T EVEN KNOW HOW BUSES WORK! WHY AM I LISTENING TO YOU?
I SHOULD'VE KNOWN BETTER THAN TO TAKE ON A PARTNER. YOU'RE NOT CUT OUT FOR THIS.

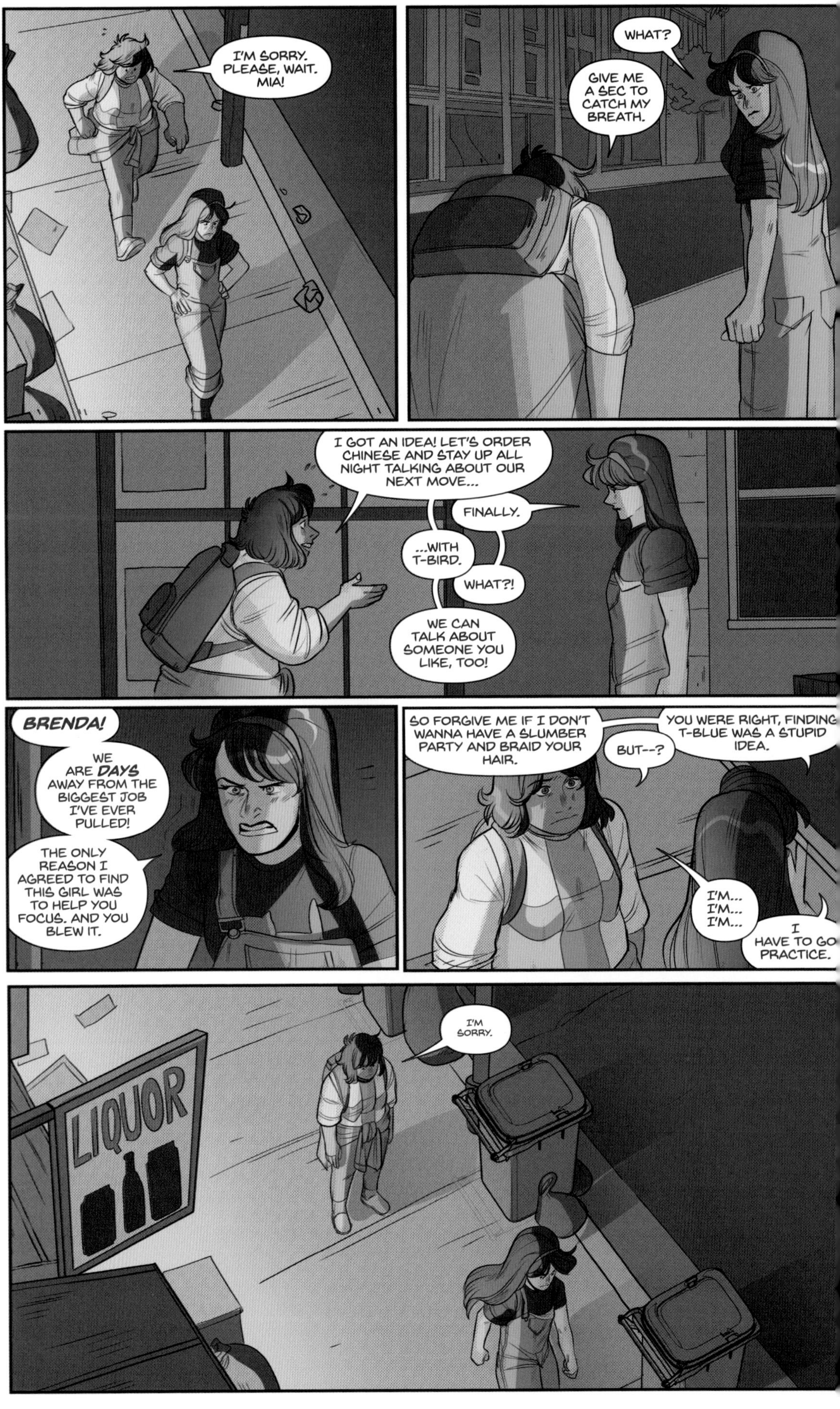
I'M SORRY. PLEASE, WAIT. MIA!
WHAT?
GIVE ME A SEC TO CATCH MY BREATH.
I GOT AN IDEA! LET'S ORDER CHINESE AND STAY UP ALL NIGHT TALKING ABOUT OUR NEXT MOVE...
FINALLY.
...WITH T-BIRD.
WHAT?!
WE CAN TALK ABOUT SOMEONE YOU LIKE, TOO!
BRENDA!
WE ARE DAYS AWAY FROM THE BIGGEST JOB I'VE EVER PULLED!
THE ONLY REASON I AGREED TO FIND THIS GIRL WAS TO HELP YOU FOCUS. AND YOU BLEW IT.
SO FORGIVE ME IF I DON'T WANNA HAVE A SLUMBER PARTY AND BRAID YOUR HAIR.
BUT--?
YOU WERE RIGHT, FINDING T-BLUE WAS A STUPID IDEA.
I'M... I'M... I'M...
I HAVE TO GO PRACTICE.
I'M SORRY.
LIQUOR

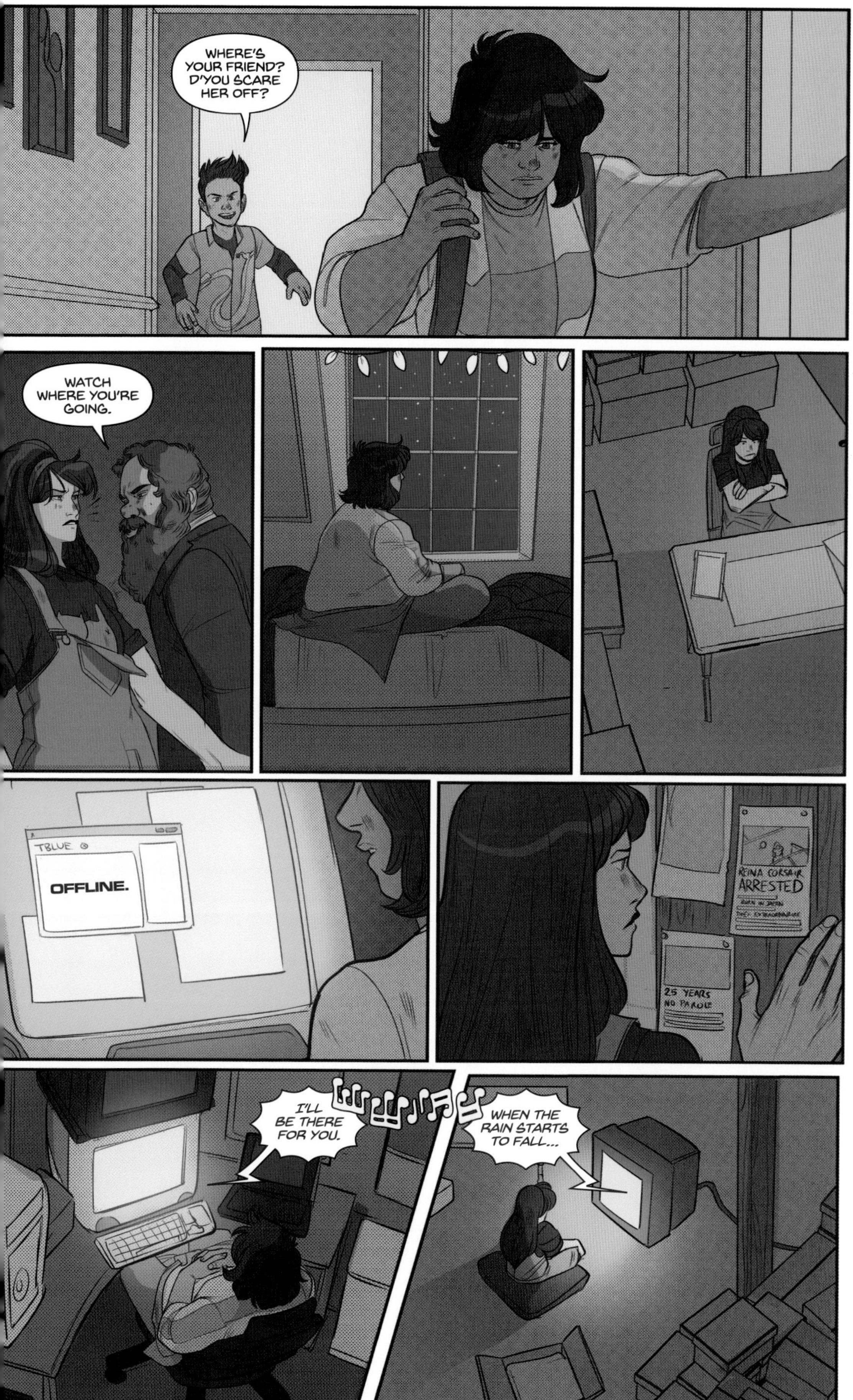
WHERE'S YOUR FRIEND? D'YOU SCARE HER OFF?
WATCH WHERE YOU'RE GOING.
TBLUE
OFFLINE.
REINA CORSAIR
ARRESTED
25 YEARS
NO PAROLE
I'LL BE THERE FOR YOU.
WHEN THE RAIN STARTS TO FALL...

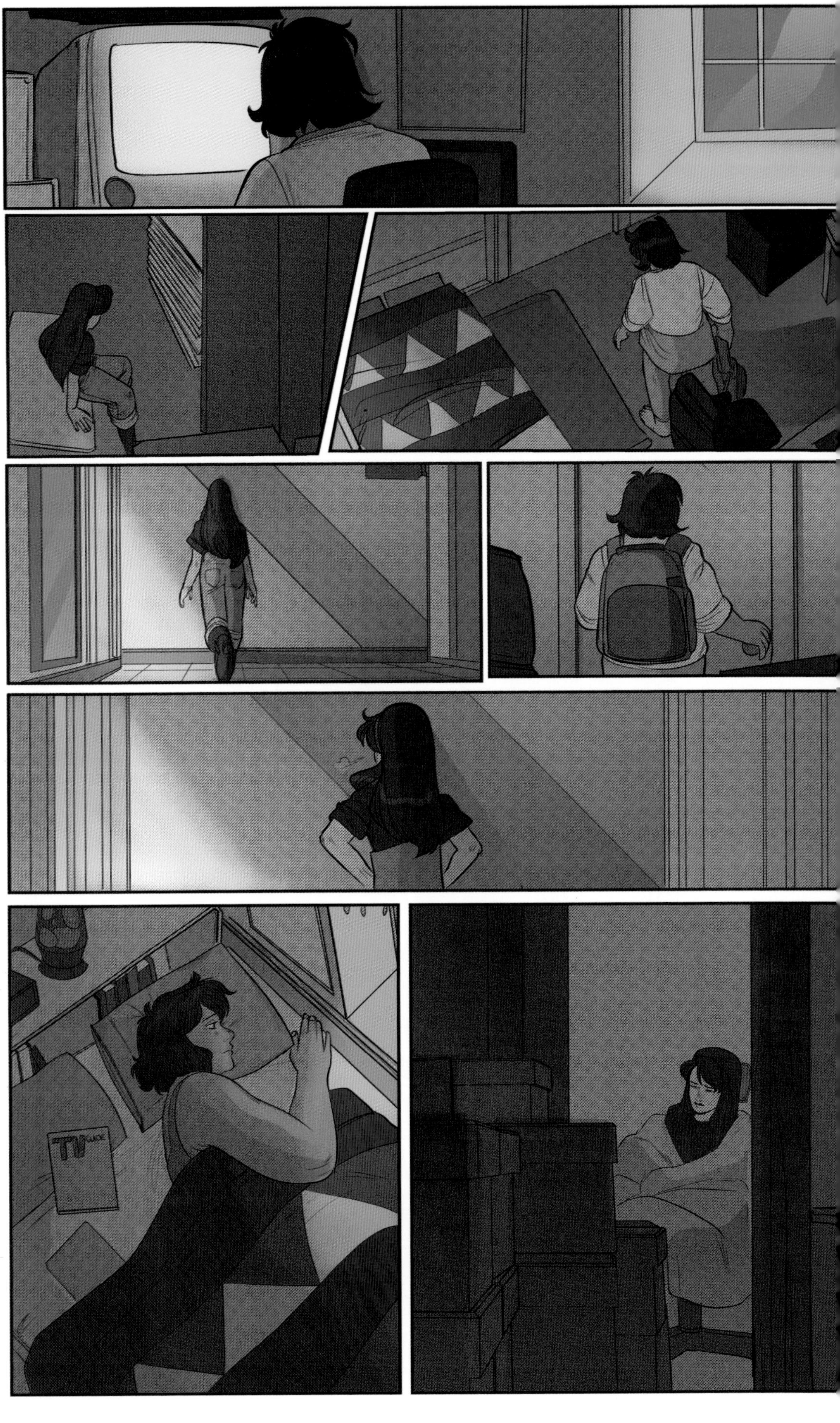
TV GUIDE

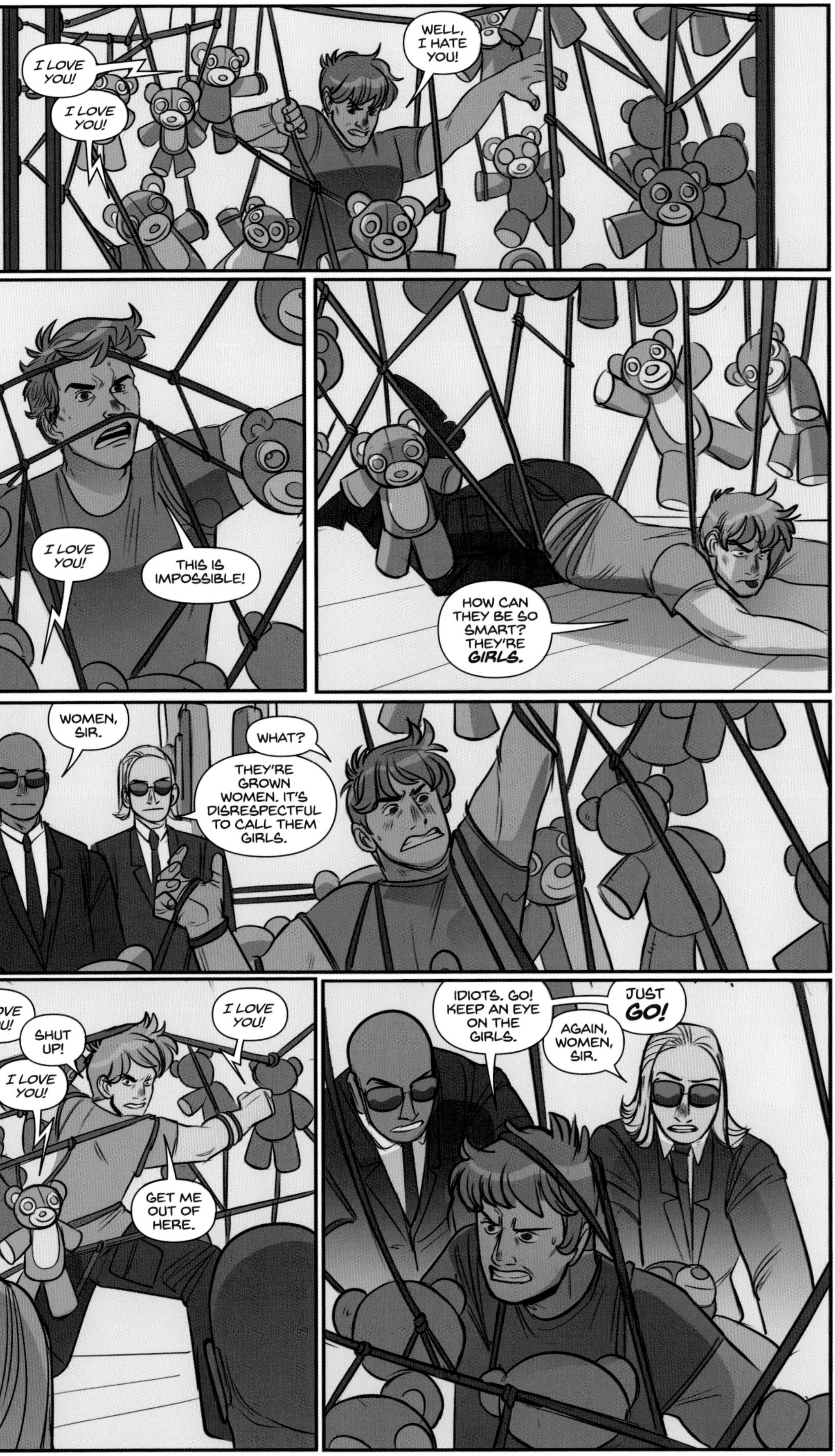
I LOVE YOU!
I LOVE YOU!
WELL, I HATE YOU!
I LOVE YOU!
THIS IS IMPOSSIBLE!
HOW CAN THEY BE SO SMART? THEY'RE GIRLS.
WOMEN, SIR.
WHAT?
THEY'RE GROWN WOMEN. IT'S DISRESPECTFUL TO CALL THEM GIRLS.
I LOVE YOU!
SHUT UP!
I LOVE YOU!
I LOVE YOU!
GET ME OUT OF HERE.
IDIOTS. GO! KEEP AN EYE ON THE GIRLS.
AGAIN, WOMEN, SIR.
JUST GO!

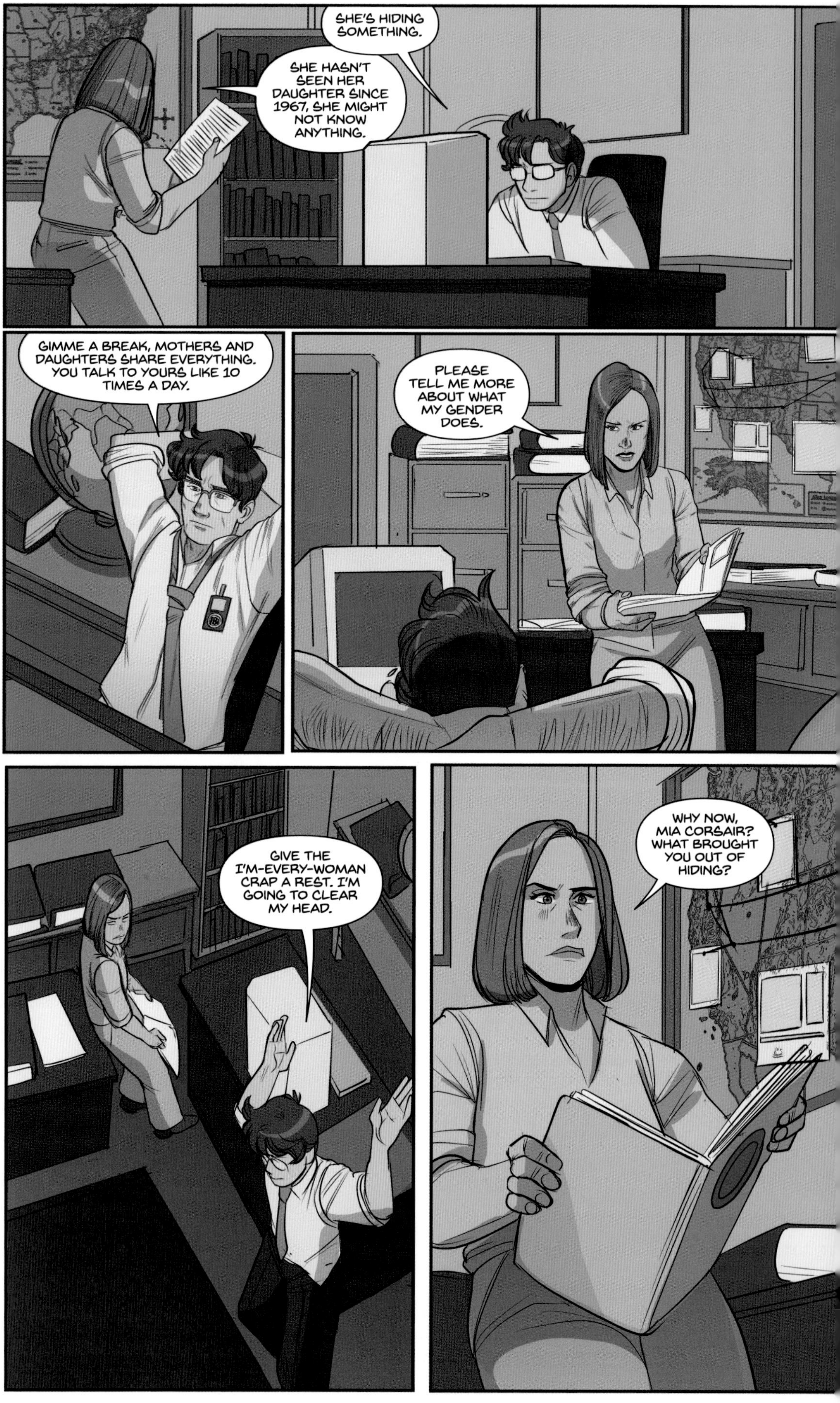
SHE HASN'T SEEN HER DAUGHTER SINCE 1967, SHE MIGHT NOT KNOW ANYTHING.
SHE'S HIDING SOMETHING.
GIMME A BREAK, MOTHERS AND DAUGHTERS SHARE EVERYTHING. YOU TALK TO YOURS LIKE 10 TIMES A DAY.
PLEASE TELL ME MORE ABOUT WHAT MY GENDER DOES.
GIVE THE I'M-EVERY-WOMAN CRAP A REST. I'M GOING TO CLEAR MY HEAD.
WHY NOW, MIA CORSAIR? WHAT BROUGHT YOU OUT OF HIDING?

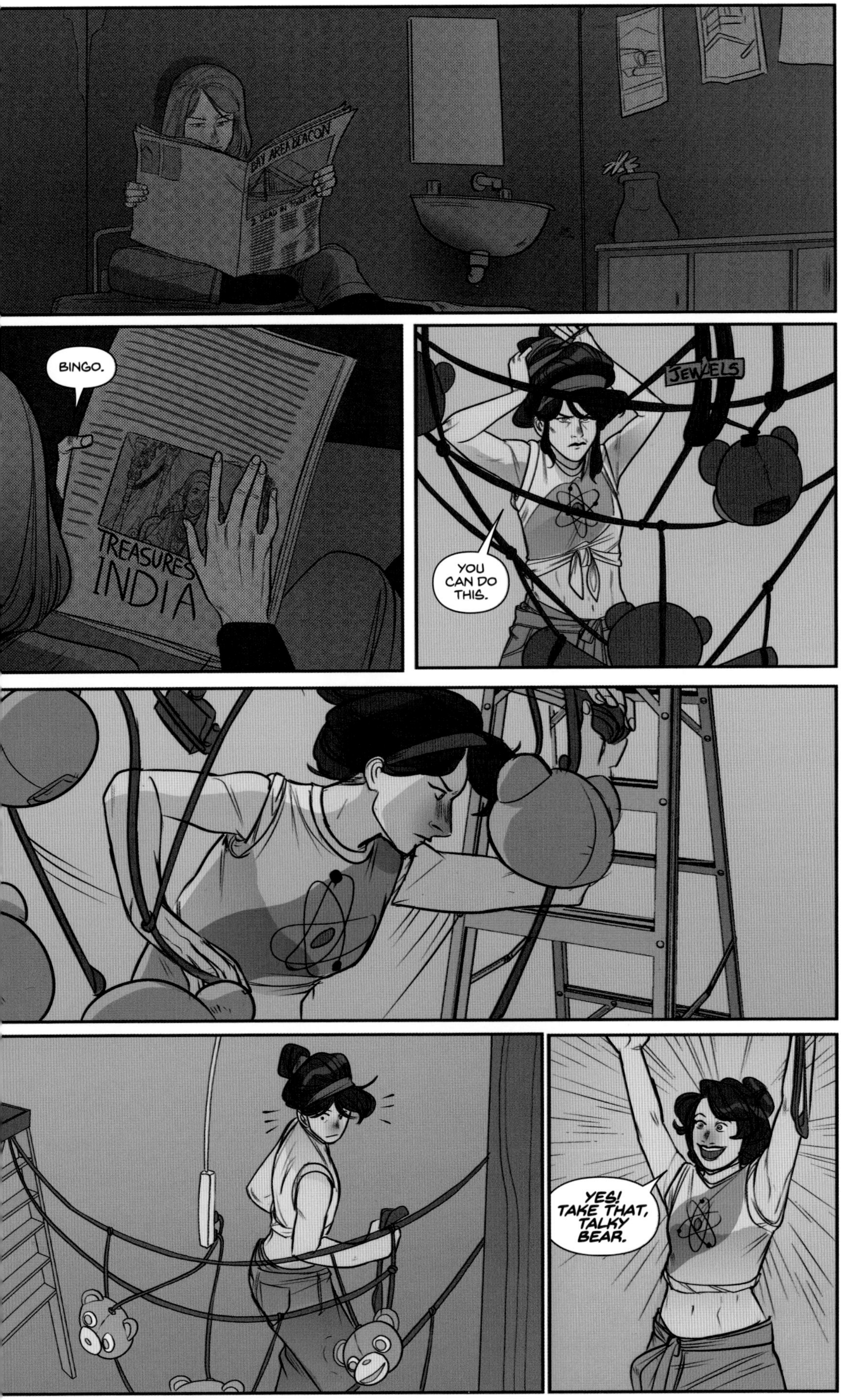
BAY AREA BEACON
BINGO.
TREASURES
INDIA
JEWELS
YOU CAN DO THIS.
YES! TAKE THAT, TALKY BEAR.

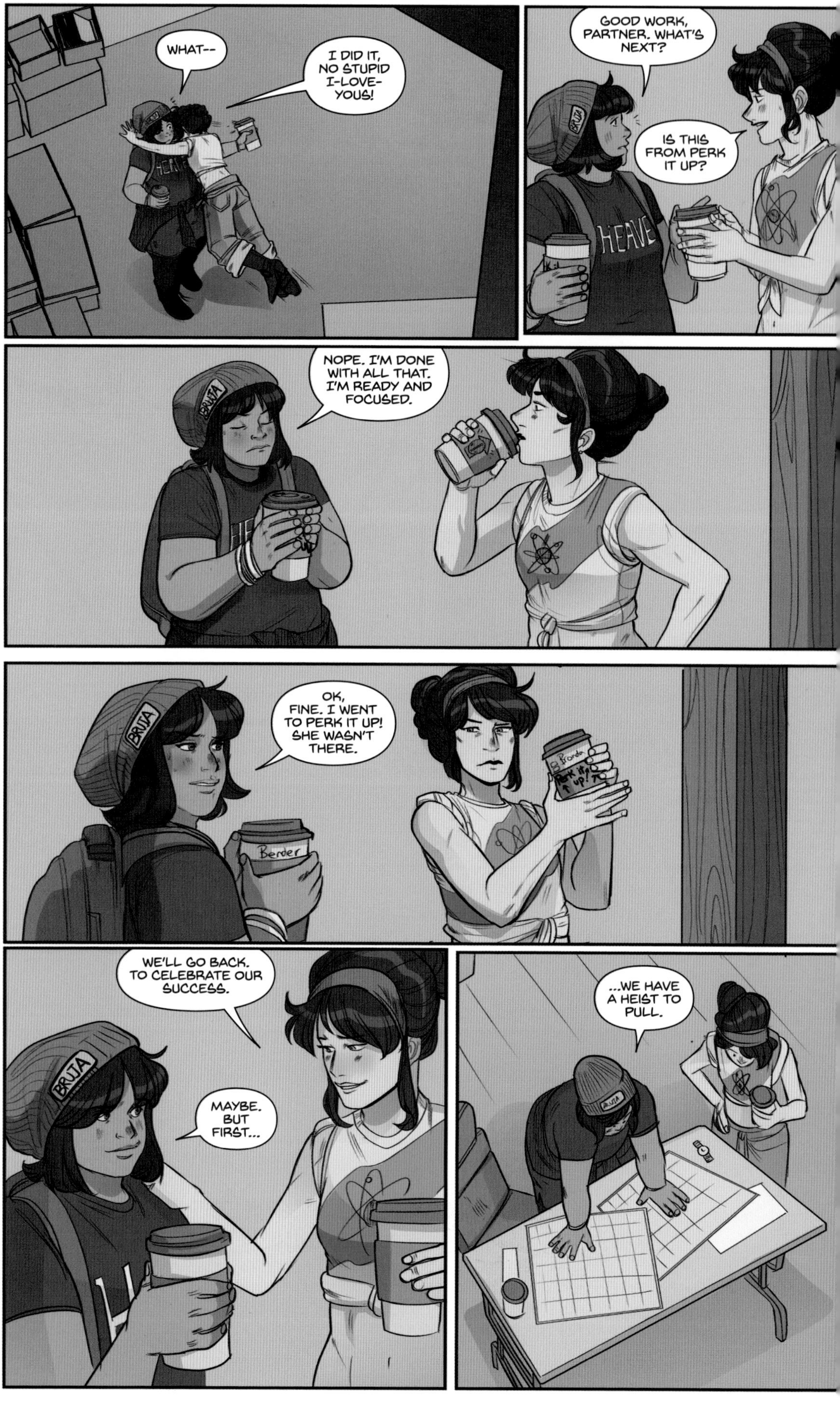
WHAT--
I DID IT, NO STUPID I-LOVE-YOUS!
GOOD WORK, PARTNER. WHAT'S NEXT?
IS THIS FROM PERK IT UP?
NOPE. I'M DONE WITH ALL THAT. I'M READY AND FOCUSED.
OK, FINE. I WENT TO PERK IT UP! SHE WASN'T THERE.
Berder
Perk it up!
WE'LL GO BACK. TO CELEBRATE OUR SUCCESS.
MAYBE. BUT FIRST...
...WE HAVE A HEIST TO PULL.

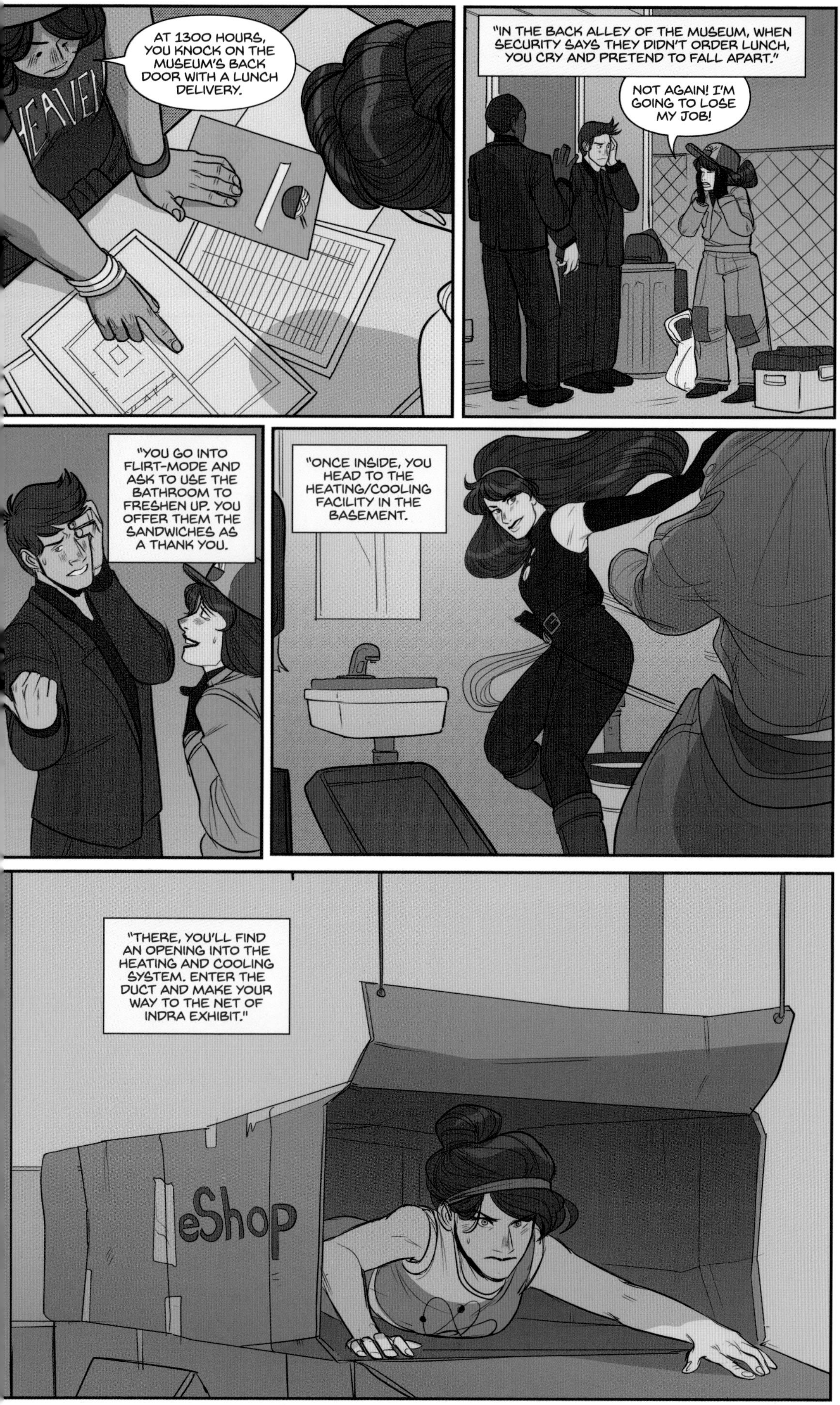
AT 1300 HOURS, YOU KNOCK ON THE MUSEUM'S BACK DOOR WITH A LUNCH DELIVERY.
HEAVEN
"IN THE BACK ALLEY OF THE MUSEUM, WHEN SECURITY SAYS THEY DIDN'T ORDER LUNCH, YOU CRY AND PRETEND TO FALL APART."
NOT AGAIN! I'M GOING TO LOSE MY JOB!
"YOU GO INTO FLIRT-MODE AND ASK TO USE THE BATHROOM TO FRESHEN UP. YOU OFFER THEM THE SANDWICHES AS A THANK YOU.
"ONCE INSIDE, YOU HEAD TO THE HEATING/COOLING FACILITY IN THE BASEMENT.
"THERE, YOU'LL FIND AN OPENING INTO THE HEATING AND COOLING SYSTEM. ENTER THE DUCT AND MAKE YOUR WAY TO THE NET OF INDRA EXHIBIT."
eShop

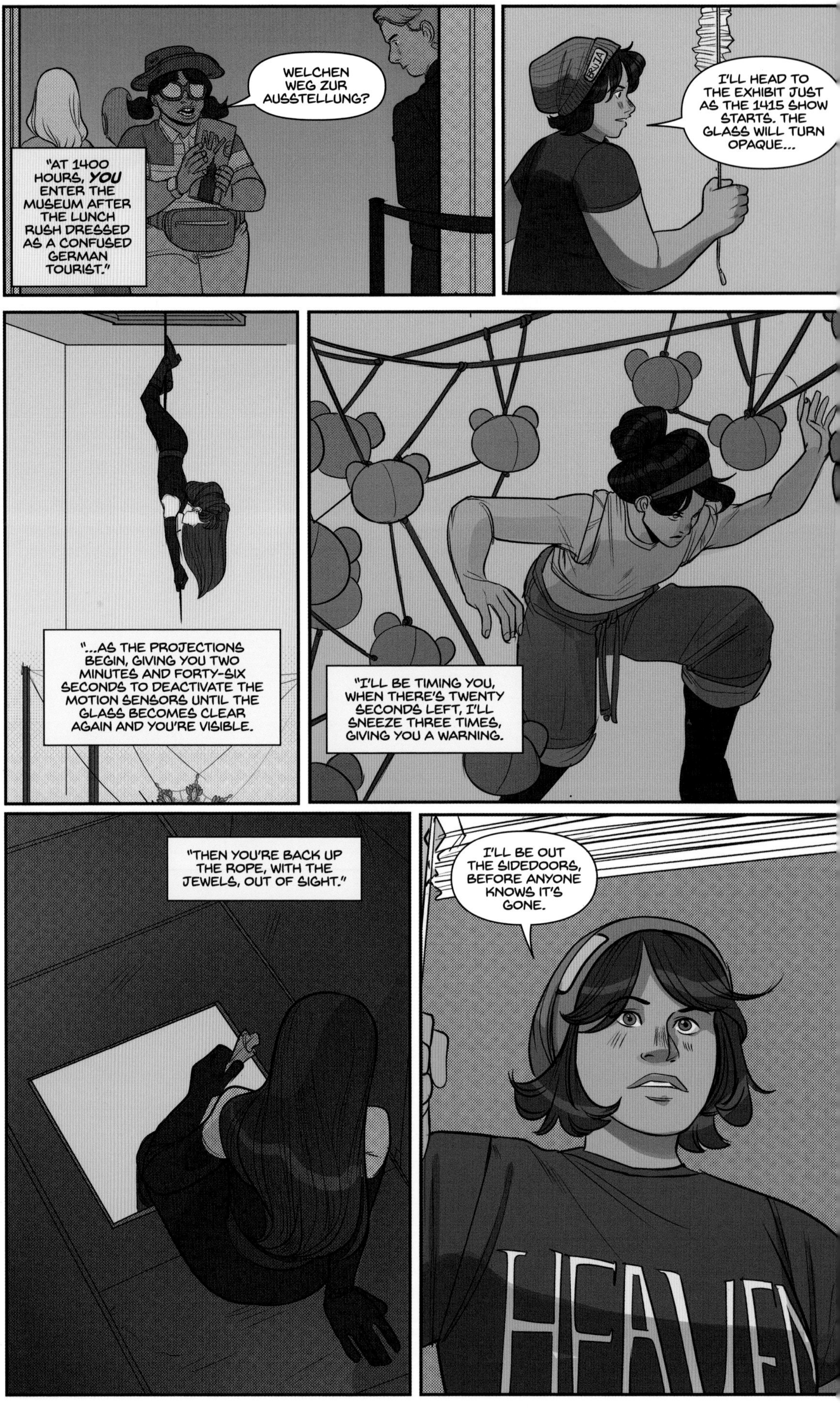
WELCHEN WEG ZUR AUSSTELLUNG?
"AT 1400 HOURS, *YOU* ENTER THE MUSEUM AFTER THE LUNCH RUSH DRESSED AS A CONFUSED GERMAN TOURIST."
BRUJA
I'LL HEAD TO THE EXHIBIT JUST AS THE 1415 SHOW STARTS. THE GLASS WILL TURN OPAQUE...
"...AS THE PROJECTIONS BEGIN, GIVING YOU TWO MINUTES AND FORTY-SIX SECONDS TO DEACTIVATE THE MOTION SENSORS UNTIL THE GLASS BECOMES CLEAR AGAIN AND YOU'RE VISIBLE.
"I'LL BE TIMING YOU, WHEN THERE'S TWENTY SECONDS LEFT, I'LL SNEEZE THREE TIMES, GIVING YOU A WARNING.
"THEN YOU'RE BACK UP THE ROPE, WITH THE JEWELS, OUT OF SIGHT."
I'LL BE OUT THE SIDEDOORS, BEFORE ANYONE KNOWS IT'S GONE.
HEAVEN

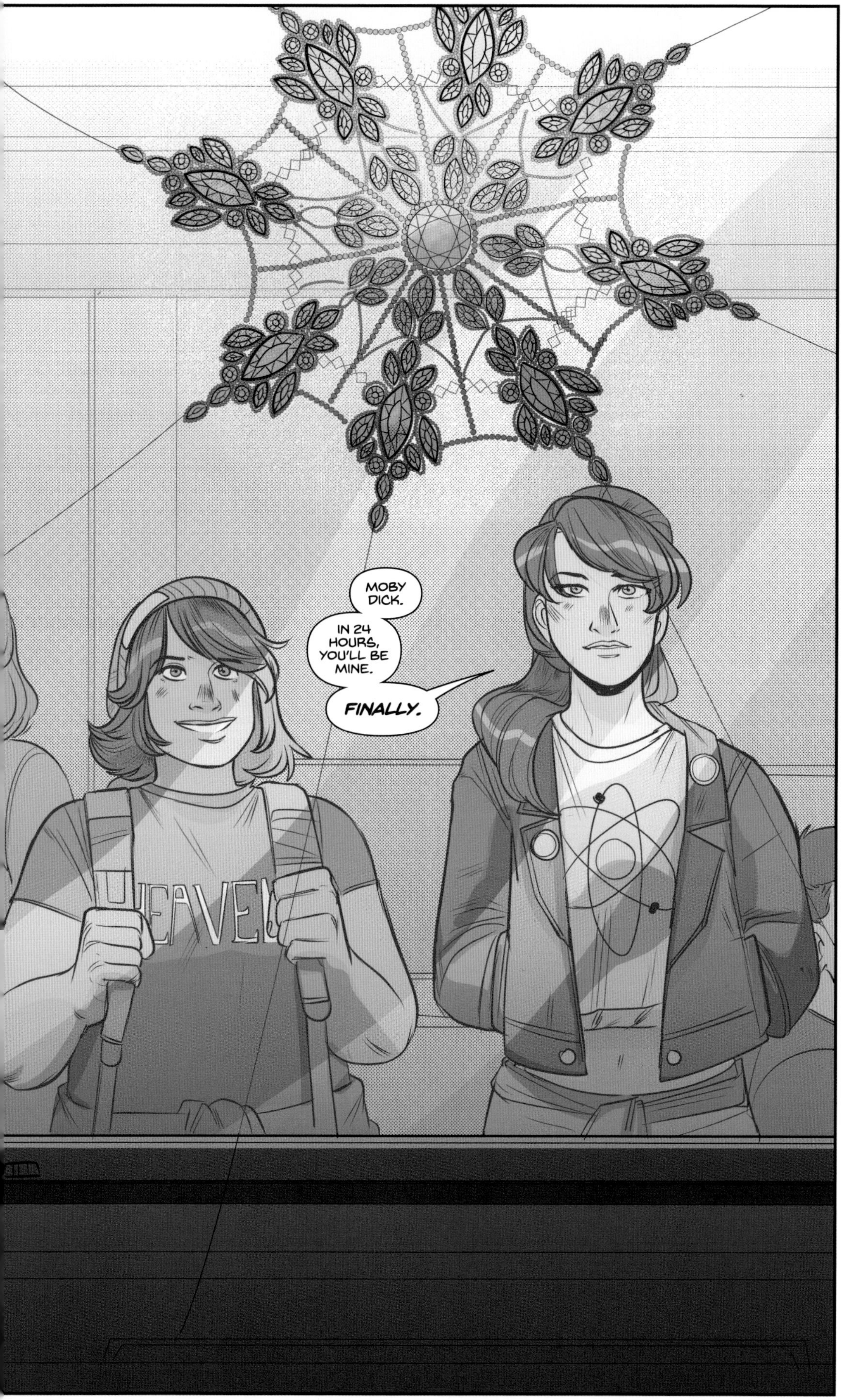

MOBY DICK.
IN 24 HOURS, YOU'LL BE MINE.
FINALLY.
HEAVEN

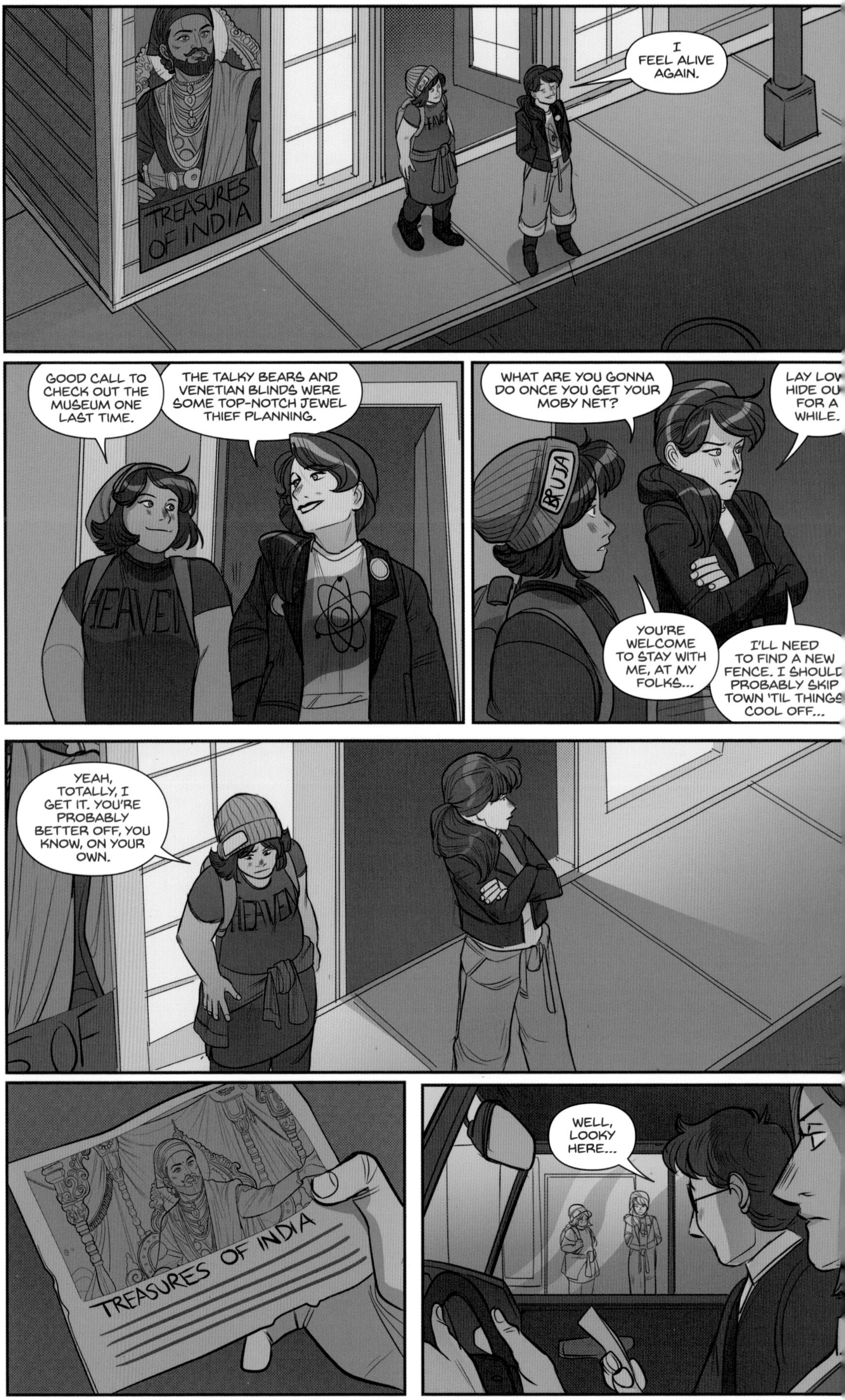
TREASURES OF INDIA
I FEEL ALIVE AGAIN.
GOOD CALL TO CHECK OUT THE MUSEUM ONE LAST TIME.
THE TALKY BEARS AND VENETIAN BLINDS WERE SOME TOP-NOTCH JEWEL THIEF PLANNING.
HEAVEN
WHAT ARE YOU GONNA DO ONCE YOU GET YOUR MOBY NET?
LAY LOW HIDE OU FOR A WHILE.
BRUJA
YOU'RE WELCOME TO STAY WITH ME, AT MY FOLKS...
I'LL NEED TO FIND A NEW FENCE. I SHOULD PROBABLY SKIP TOWN 'TIL THINGS COOL OFF...
YEAH, TOTALLY, I GET IT. YOU'RE PROBABLY BETTER OFF, YOU KNOW, ON YOUR OWN.
TREASURES OF INDIA
WELL, LOOKY HERE...

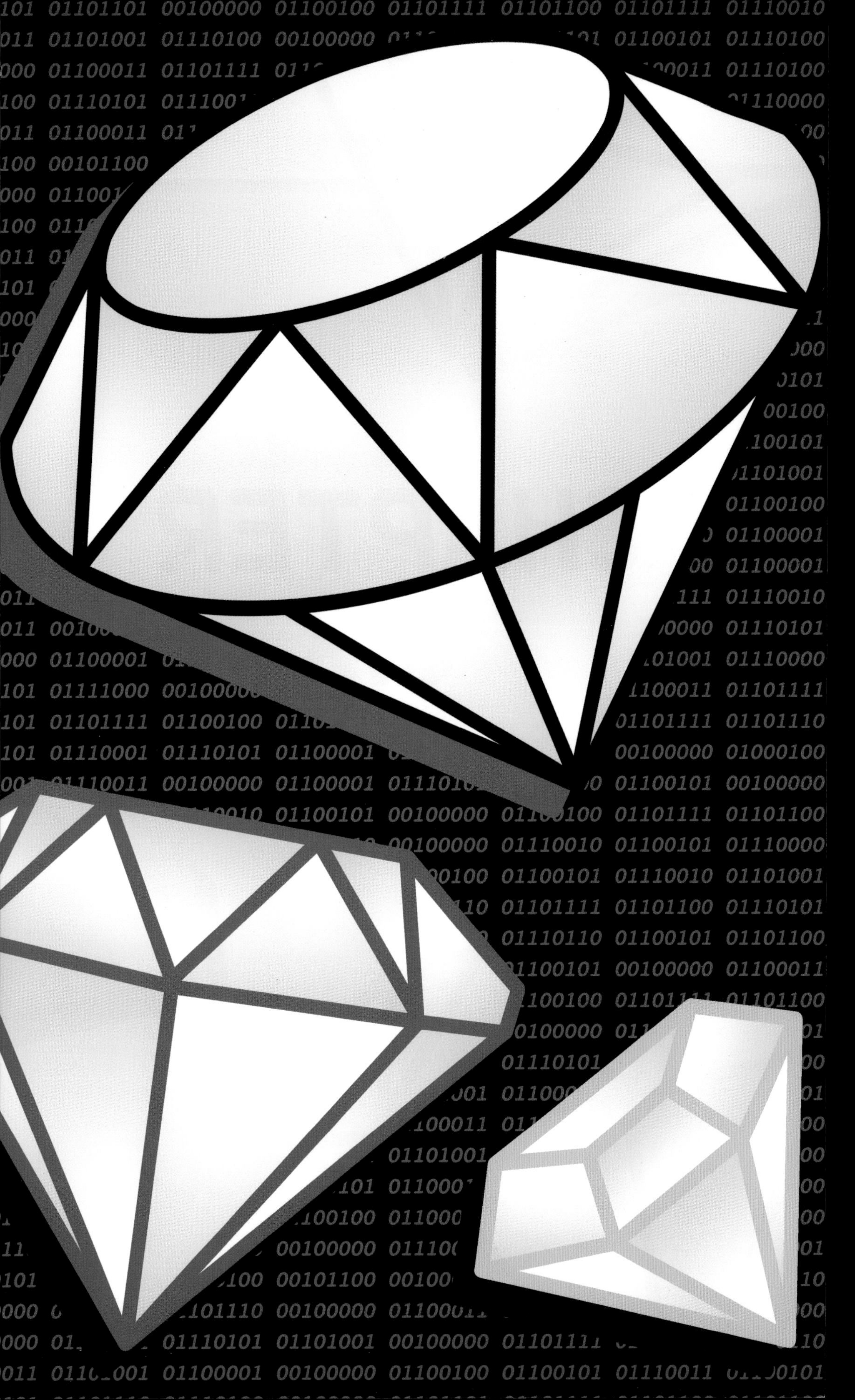

CHAPTER SIX

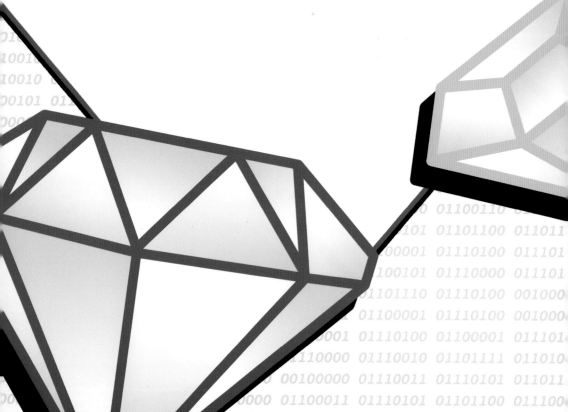

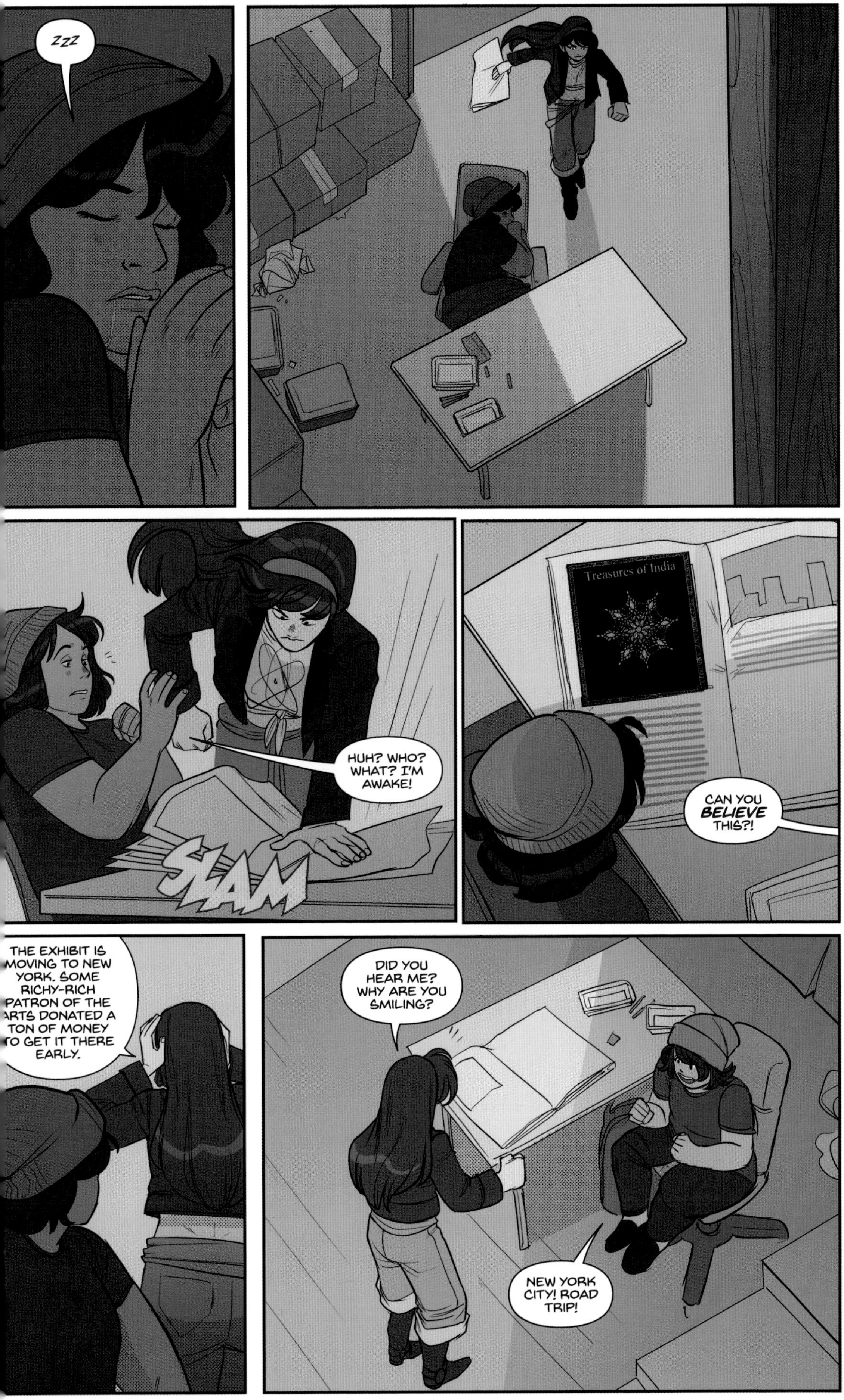
ZZZ
HUH? WHO? WHAT? I'M AWAKE!
SLAM
Treasures of India
CAN YOU BELIEVE THIS?!
THE EXHIBIT IS MOVING TO NEW YORK. SOME RICHY-RICH PATRON OF THE ARTS DONATED A TON OF MONEY TO GET IT THERE EARLY.
DID YOU HEAR ME? WHY ARE YOU SMILING?
NEW YORK CITY! ROAD TRIP!

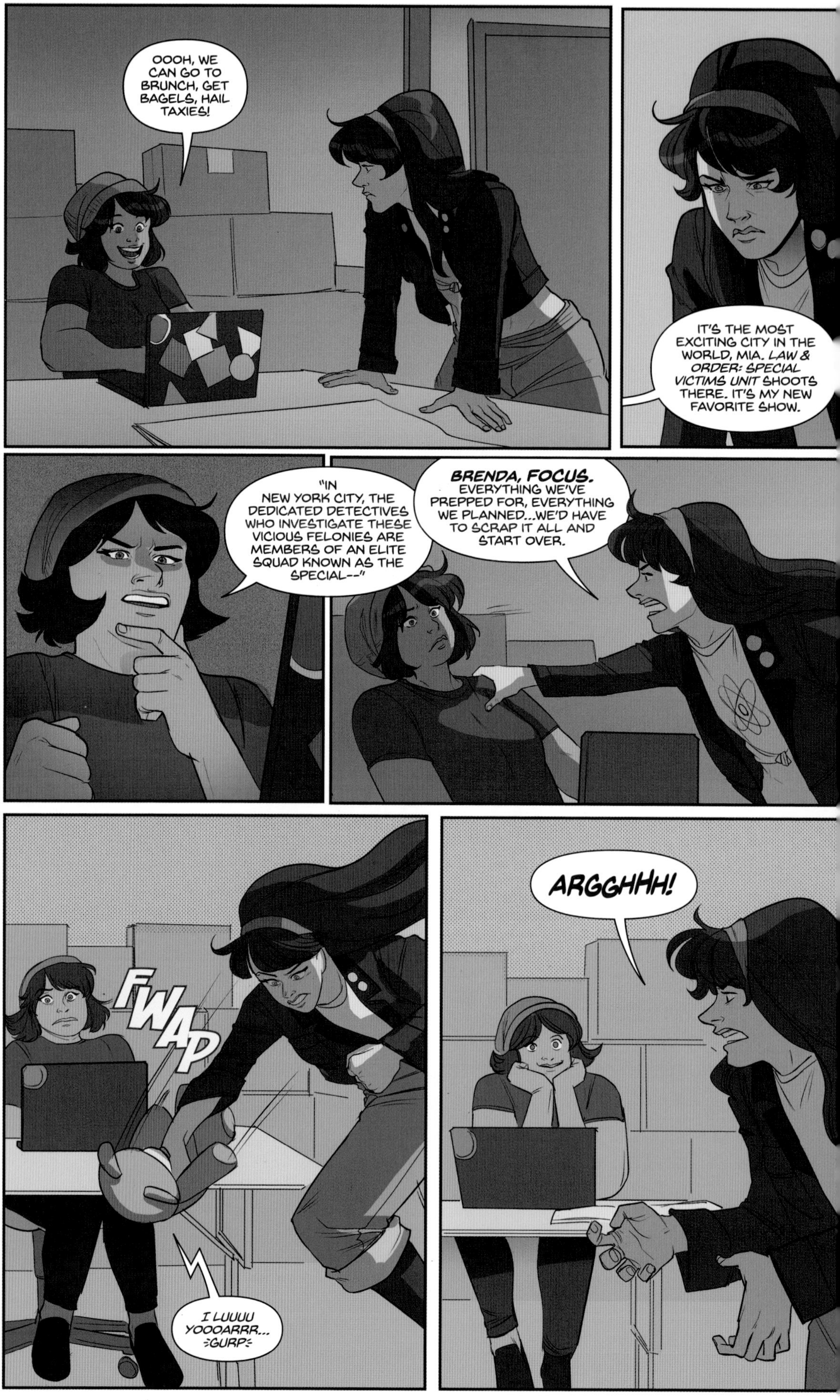
OOOH, WE CAN GO TO BRUNCH, GET BAGELS, HAIL TAXIES!
IT'S THE MOST EXCITING CITY IN THE WORLD, MIA. *LAW & ORDER: SPECIAL VICTIMS UNIT* SHOOTS THERE. IT'S MY NEW FAVORITE SHOW.
"IN NEW YORK CITY, THE DEDICATED DETECTIVES WHO INVESTIGATE THESE VICIOUS FELONIES ARE MEMBERS OF AN ELITE SQUAD KNOWN AS THE SPECIAL--"
BRENDA, FOCUS. EVERYTHING WE'VE PREPPED FOR, EVERYTHING WE PLANNED...WE'D HAVE TO SCRAP IT ALL AND START OVER.
FWAP
I LUUUU YOOOARRR... =GURP=
ARGGHHH!

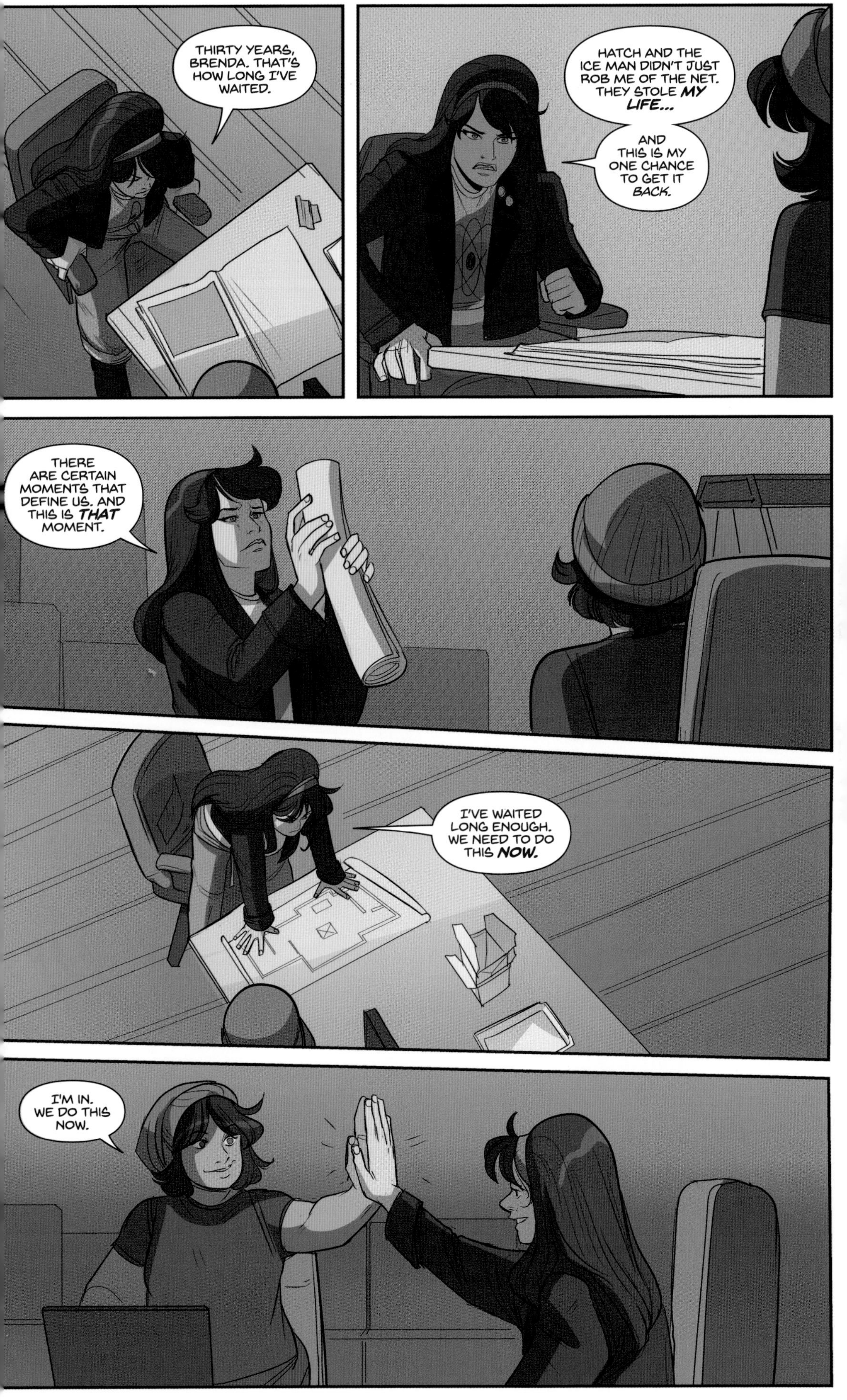
THIRTY YEARS, BRENDA. THAT'S HOW LONG I'VE WAITED.
HATCH AND THE ICE MAN DIDN'T JUST ROB ME OF THE NET. THEY STOLE MY LIFE...
AND THIS IS MY ONE CHANCE TO GET IT BACK.
THERE ARE CERTAIN MOMENTS THAT DEFINE US. AND THIS IS THAT MOMENT.
I'VE WAITED LONG ENOUGH. WE NEED TO DO THIS NOW.
I'M IN. WE DO THIS NOW.

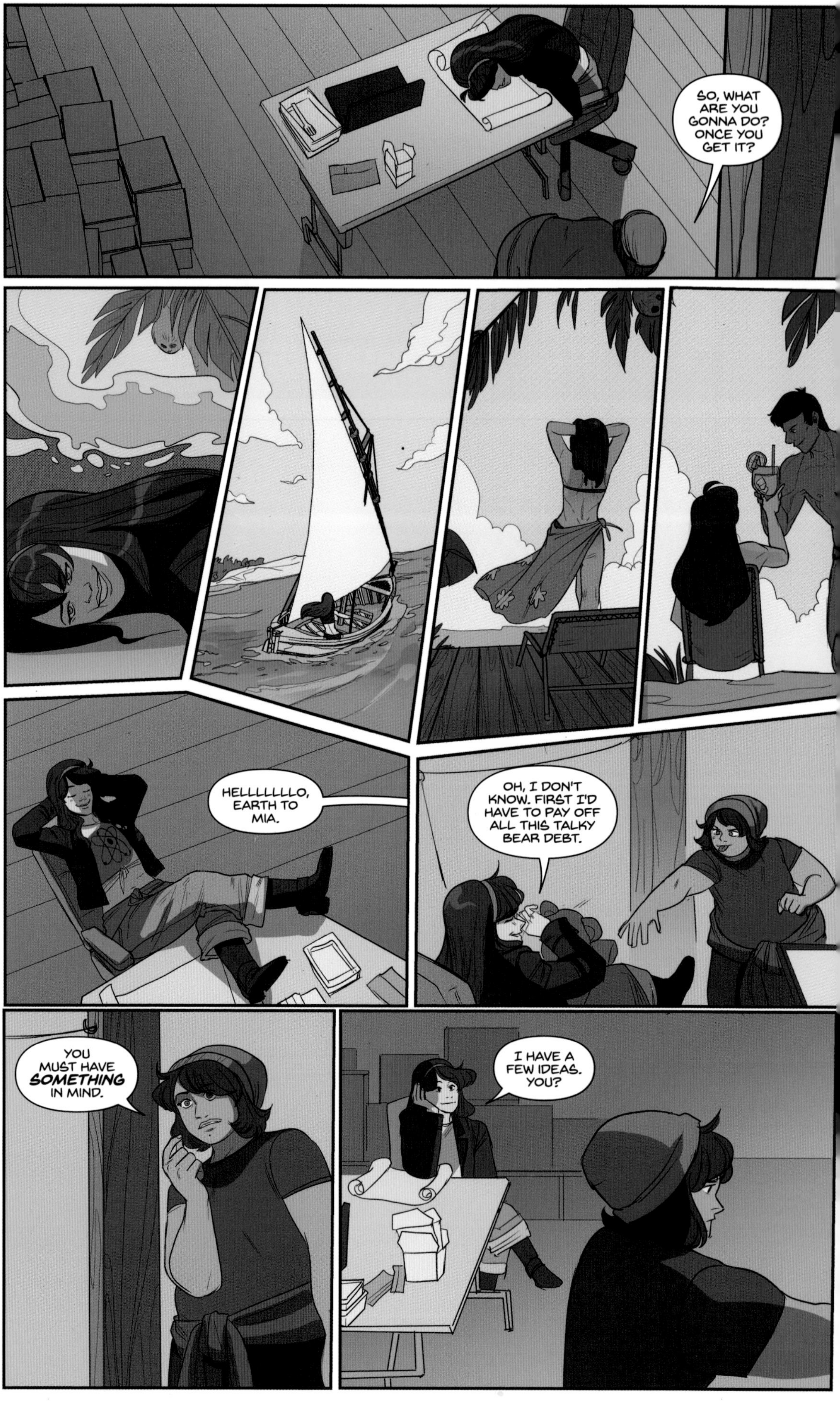
SO, WHAT ARE YOU GONNA DO? ONCE YOU GET IT?
HELLLLLLLO, EARTH TO MIA.
OH, I DON'T KNOW. FIRST I'D HAVE TO PAY OFF ALL THIS TALKY BEAR DEBT.
YOU MUST HAVE **SOMETHING** IN MIND.
I HAVE A FEW IDEAS. YOU?

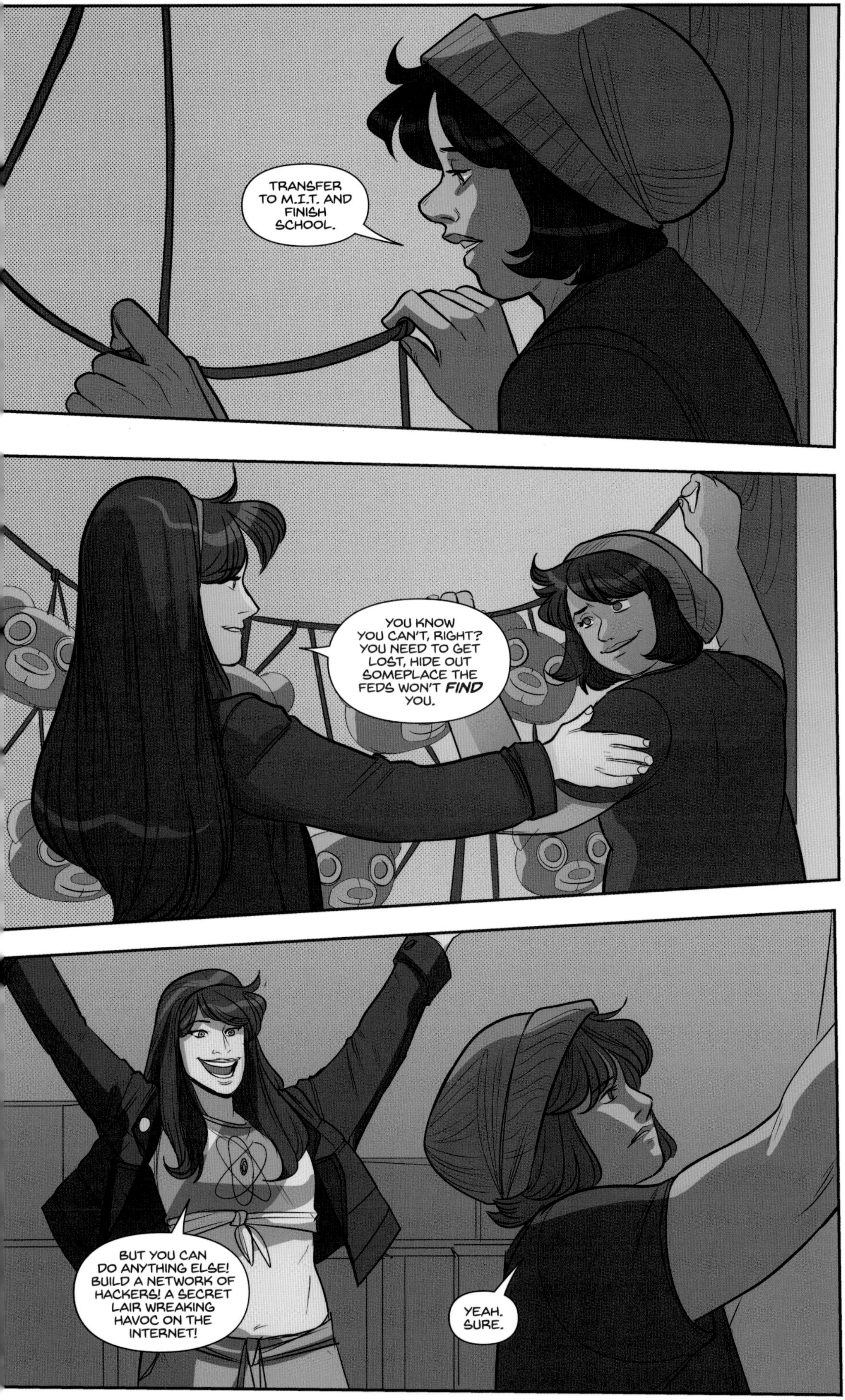
TRANSFER TO M.I.T. AND FINISH SCHOOL.
YOU KNOW YOU CAN'T, RIGHT? YOU NEED TO GET LOST, HIDE OUT SOMEPLACE THE FEDS WON'T *FIND* YOU.
BUT YOU CAN DO ANYTHING ELSE! BUILD A NETWORK OF HACKERS! A SECRET LAIR WREAKING HAVOC ON THE INTERNET!
YEAH. SURE.

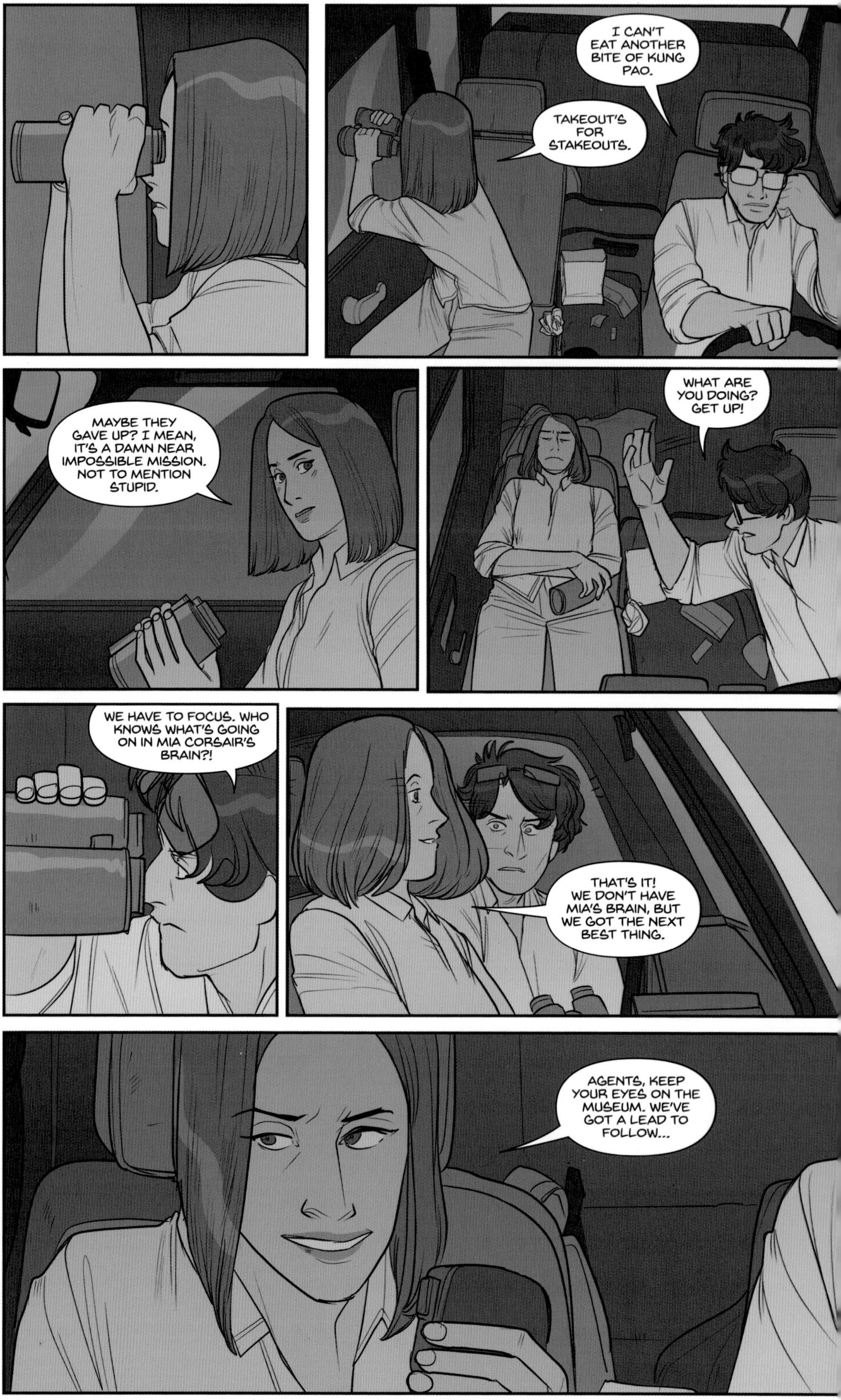
I CAN'T EAT ANOTHER BITE OF KUNG PAO.
TAKEOUT'S FOR STAKEOUTS.
MAYBE THEY GAVE UP? I MEAN, IT'S A DAMN NEAR IMPOSSIBLE MISSION. NOT TO MENTION STUPID.
WHAT ARE YOU DOING? GET UP!
WE HAVE TO FOCUS. WHO KNOWS WHAT'S GOING ON IN MIA CORSAIR'S BRAIN?!
THAT'S IT! WE DON'T HAVE MIA'S BRAIN, BUT WE GOT THE NEXT BEST THING.
AGENTS, KEEP YOUR EYES ON THE MUSEUM. WE'VE GOT A LEAD TO FOLLOW...

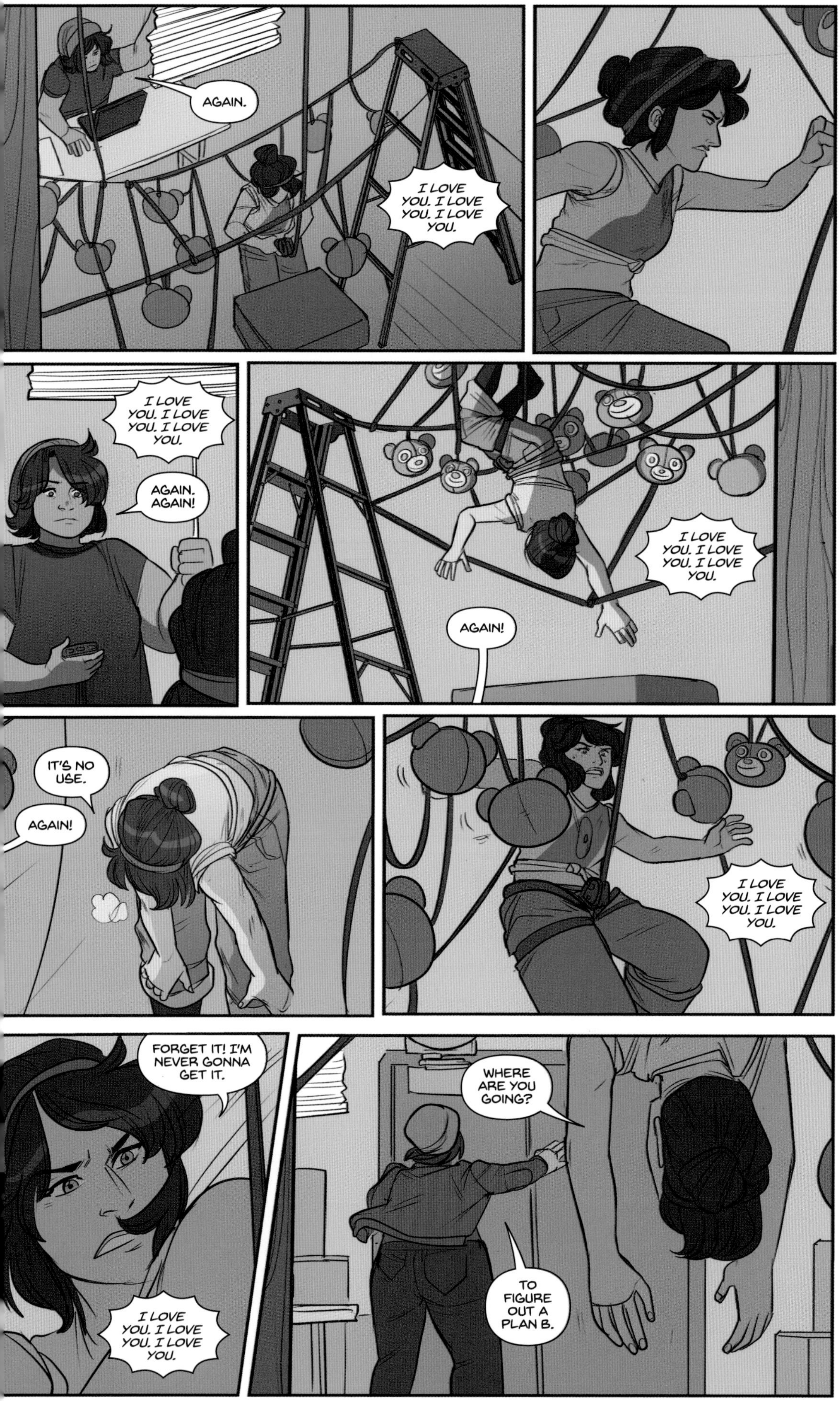
AGAIN.
I LOVE YOU. I LOVE YOU. I LOVE YOU.
I LOVE YOU. I LOVE YOU. I LOVE YOU.
AGAIN. AGAIN!
I LOVE YOU. I LOVE YOU. I LOVE YOU.
AGAIN!
IT'S NO USE.
AGAIN!
I LOVE YOU. I LOVE YOU. I LOVE YOU.
FORGET IT! I'M NEVER GONNA GET IT.
I LOVE YOU. I LOVE YOU. I LOVE YOU.
WHERE ARE YOU GOING?
TO FIGURE OUT A PLAN B.

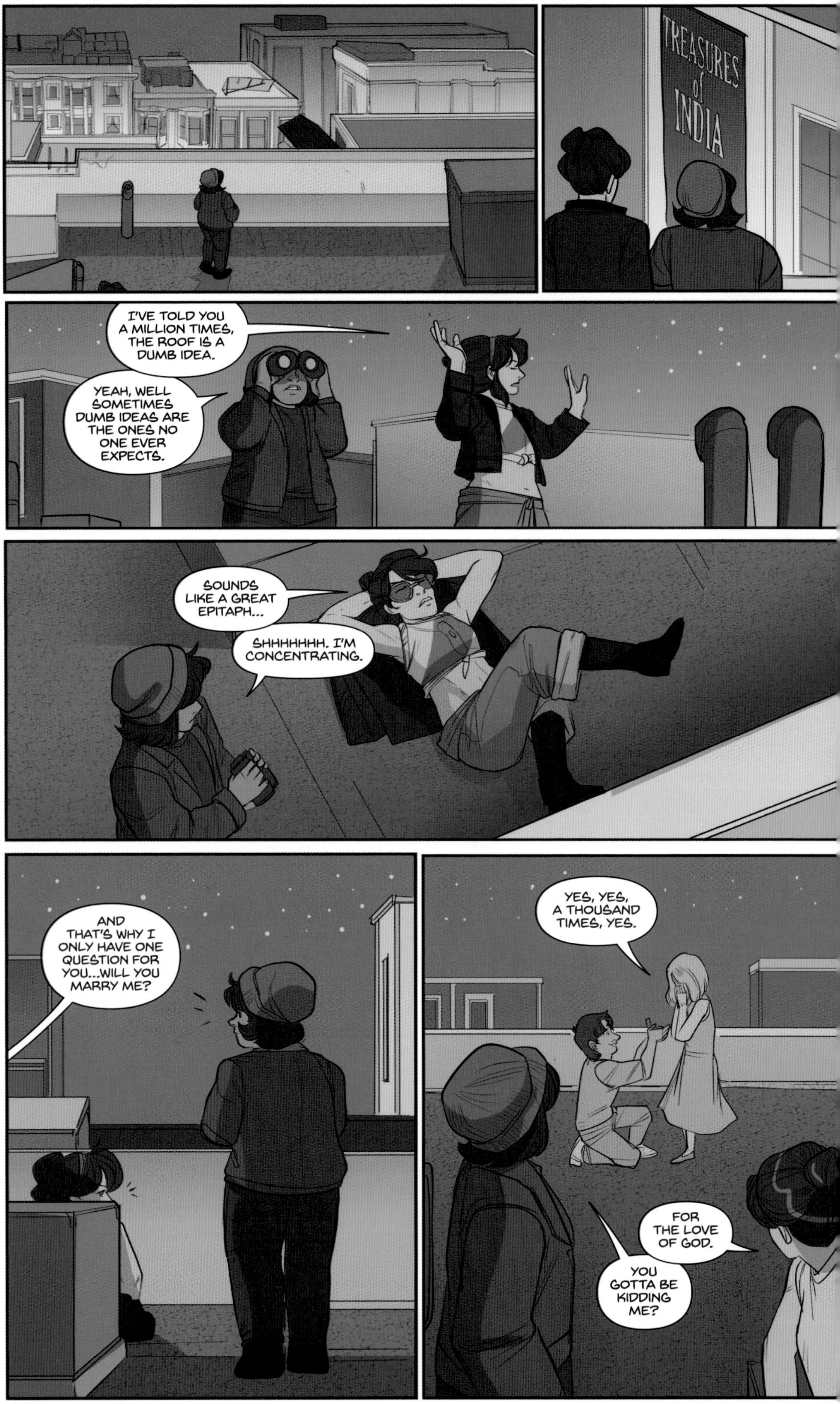
TREASURES of INDIA
I'VE TOLD YOU A MILLION TIMES, THE ROOF IS A DUMB IDEA.
YEAH, WELL SOMETIMES DUMB IDEAS ARE THE ONES NO ONE EVER EXPECTS.
SOUNDS LIKE A GREAT EPITAPH...
SHHHHHHH. I'M CONCENTRATING.
AND THAT'S WHY I ONLY HAVE ONE QUESTION FOR YOU...WILL YOU MARRY ME?
YES, YES, A THOUSAND TIMES, YES.
FOR THE LOVE OF GOD.
YOU GOTTA BE KIDDING ME?

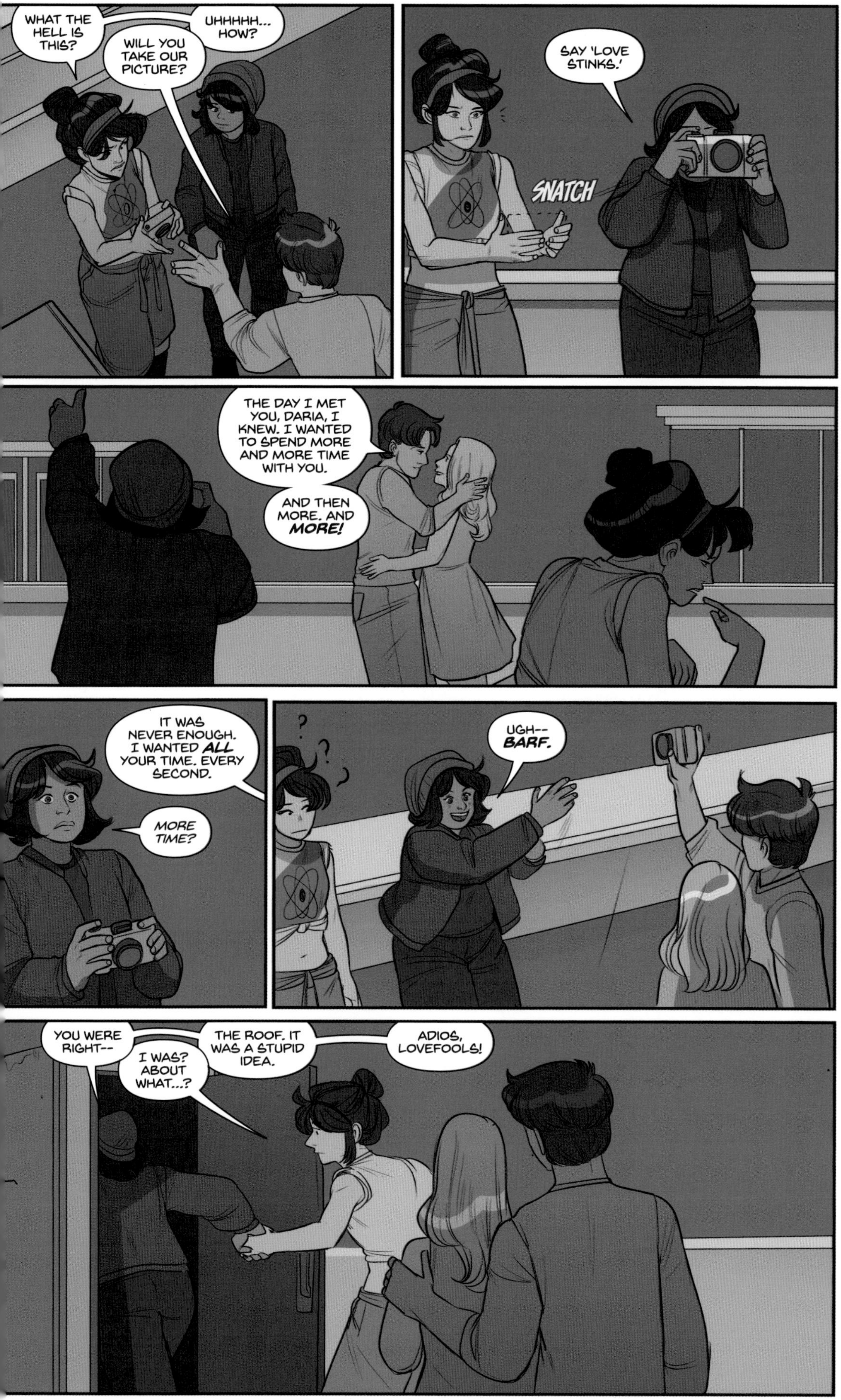
WHAT THE HELL IS THIS?
UHHHHH... HOW?
WILL YOU TAKE OUR PICTURE?
SAY 'LOVE STINKS.'
SNATCH
THE DAY I MET YOU, DARIA, I KNEW. I WANTED TO SPEND MORE AND MORE TIME WITH YOU.
AND THEN MORE. AND *MORE!*
IT WAS NEVER ENOUGH. I WANTED *ALL* YOUR TIME. EVERY SECOND.
MORE TIME?
?
?
UGH-- *BARF.*
YOU WERE RIGHT--
I WAS? ABOUT WHAT...?
THE ROOF. IT WAS A STUPID IDEA.
ADIOS, LOVEFOOLS!

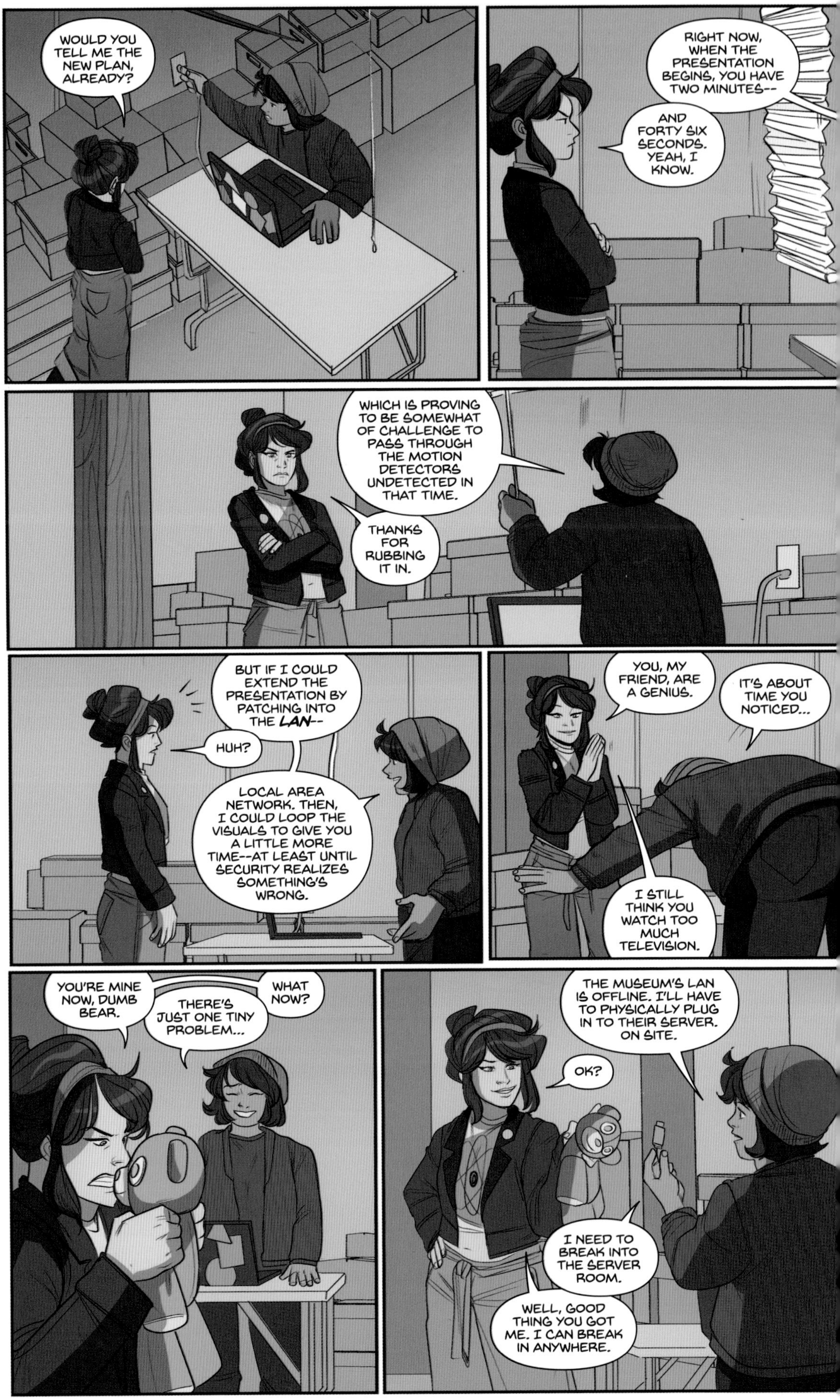
WOULD YOU TELL ME THE NEW PLAN, ALREADY?
RIGHT NOW, WHEN THE PRESENTATION BEGINS, YOU HAVE TWO MINUTES--
AND FORTY SIX SECONDS. YEAH, I KNOW.
WHICH IS PROVING TO BE SOMEWHAT OF CHALLENGE TO PASS THROUGH THE MOTION DETECTORS UNDETECTED IN THAT TIME.
THANKS FOR RUBBING IT IN.
BUT IF I COULD EXTEND THE PRESENTATION BY PATCHING INTO THE LAN--
HUH?
LOCAL AREA NETWORK. THEN, I COULD LOOP THE VISUALS TO GIVE YOU A LITTLE MORE TIME--AT LEAST UNTIL SECURITY REALIZES SOMETHING'S WRONG.
YOU, MY FRIEND, ARE A GENIUS.
IT'S ABOUT TIME YOU NOTICED...
I STILL THINK YOU WATCH TOO MUCH TELEVISION.
YOU'RE MINE NOW, DUMB BEAR.
THERE'S JUST ONE TINY PROBLEM...
WHAT NOW?
THE MUSEUM'S LAN IS OFFLINE. I'LL HAVE TO PHYSICALLY PLUG IN TO THEIR SERVER. ON SITE.
OK?
I NEED TO BREAK INTO THE SERVER ROOM.
WELL, GOOD THING YOU GOT ME. I CAN BREAK IN ANYWHERE.

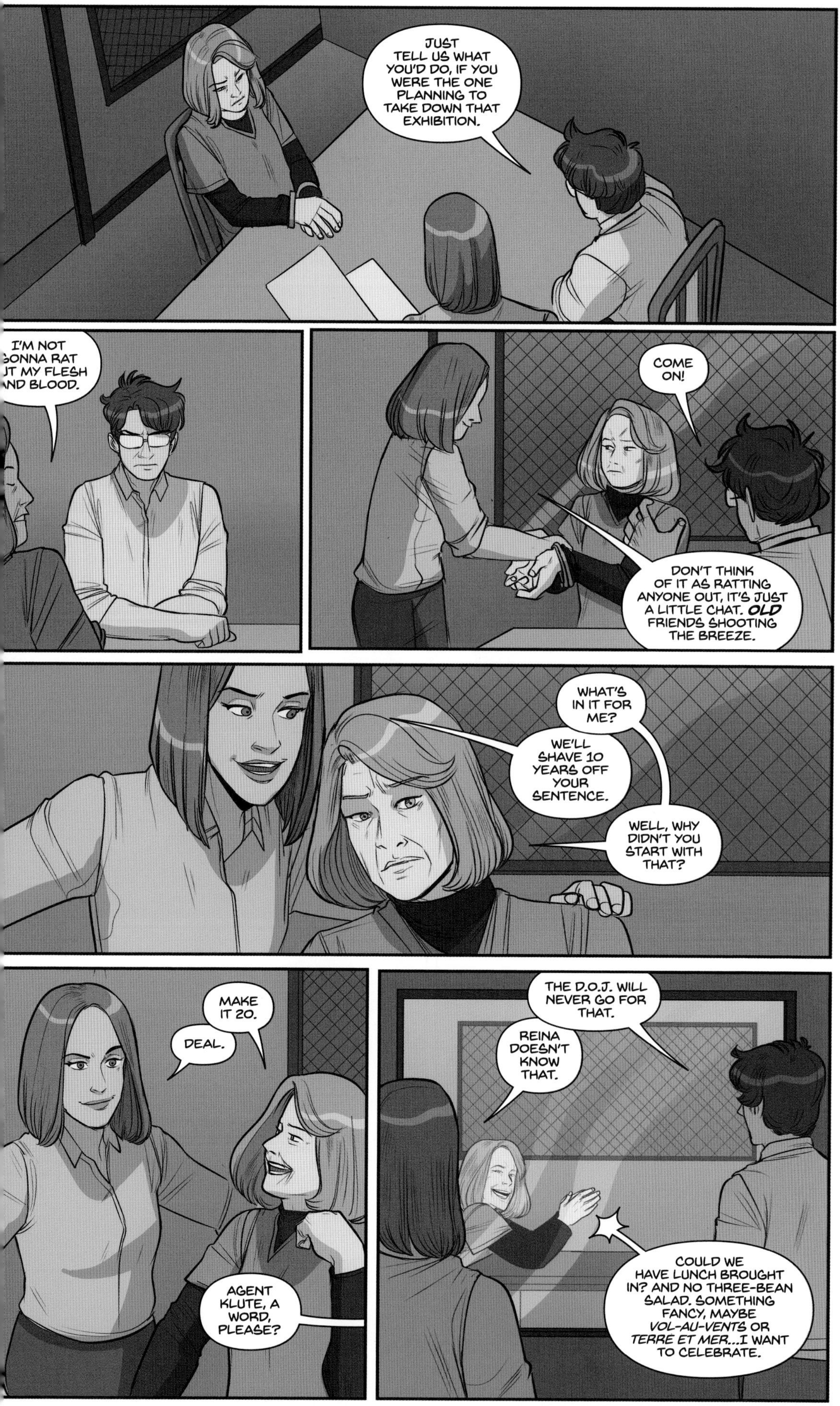
JUST TELL US WHAT YOU'D DO, IF YOU WERE THE ONE PLANNING TO TAKE DOWN THAT EXHIBITION.
I'M NOT GONNA RAT UT MY FLESH AND BLOOD.
COME ON!
DON'T THINK OF IT AS RATTING ANYONE OUT, IT'S JUST A LITTLE CHAT. ***OLD*** FRIENDS SHOOTING THE BREEZE.
WHAT'S IN IT FOR ME?
WE'LL SHAVE 10 YEARS OFF YOUR SENTENCE.
WELL, WHY DIDN'T YOU START WITH THAT?
MAKE IT 20.
DEAL.
AGENT KLUTE, A WORD, PLEASE?
THE D.O.J. WILL NEVER GO FOR THAT.
REINA DOESN'T KNOW THAT.
COULD WE HAVE LUNCH BROUGHT IN? AND NO THREE-BEAN SALAD. SOMETHING FANCY, MAYBE *VOL-AU-VENTS* OR *TERRE ET MER*...I WANT TO CELEBRATE.

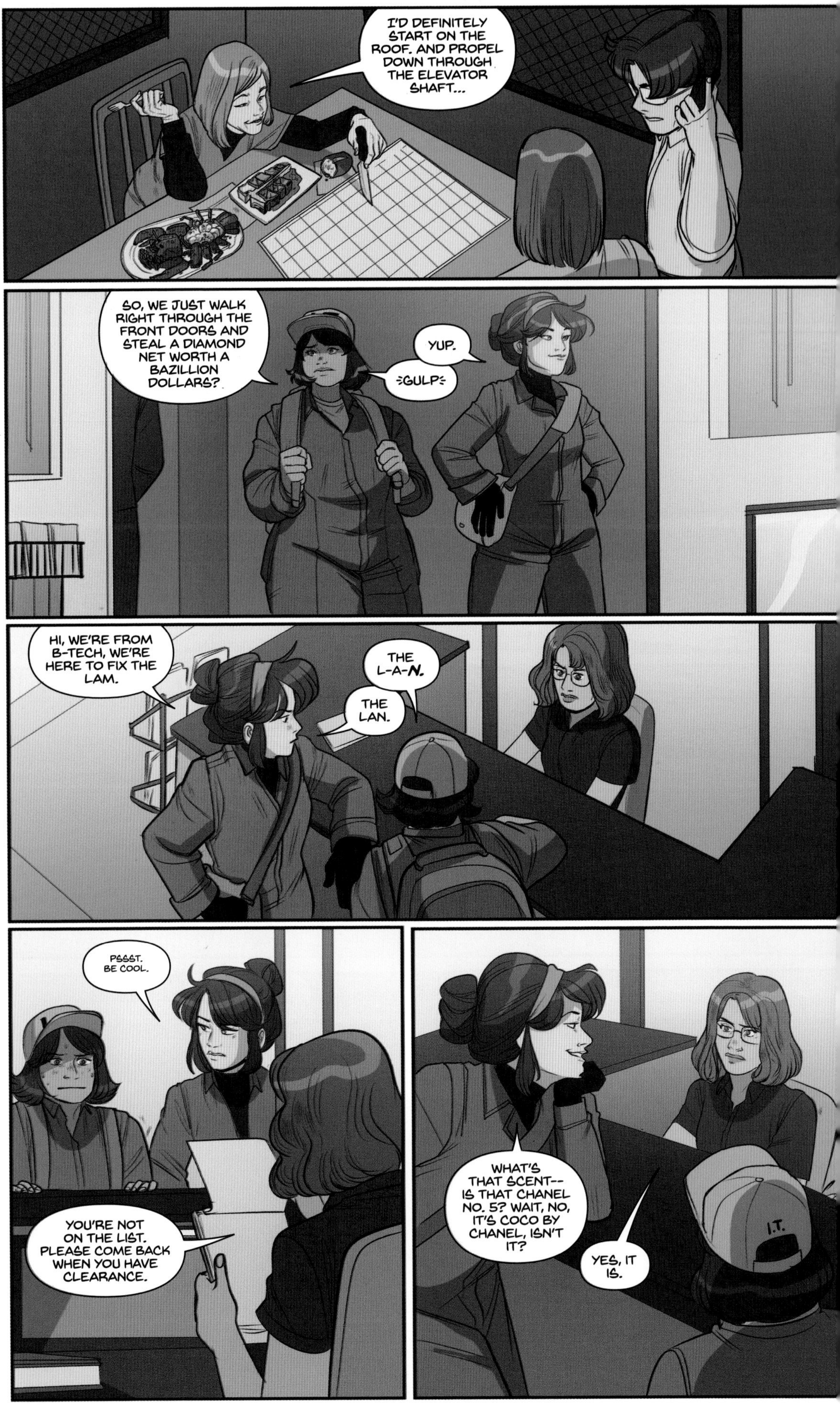
I'D DEFINITELY START ON THE ROOF. AND PROPEL DOWN THROUGH THE ELEVATOR SHAFT...
SO, WE JUST WALK RIGHT THROUGH THE FRONT DOORS AND STEAL A DIAMOND NET WORTH A BAZILLION DOLLARS?
YUP.
GULP
HI, WE'RE FROM B-TECH, WE'RE HERE TO FIX THE LAM.
THE L-A-N.
THE LAN.
PSSST. BE COOL.
YOU'RE NOT ON THE LIST. PLEASE COME BACK WHEN YOU HAVE CLEARANCE.
WHAT'S THAT SCENT-- IS THAT CHANEL NO. 5? WAIT, NO, IT'S COCO BY CHANEL, ISN'T IT?
YES, IT IS.
I.T.

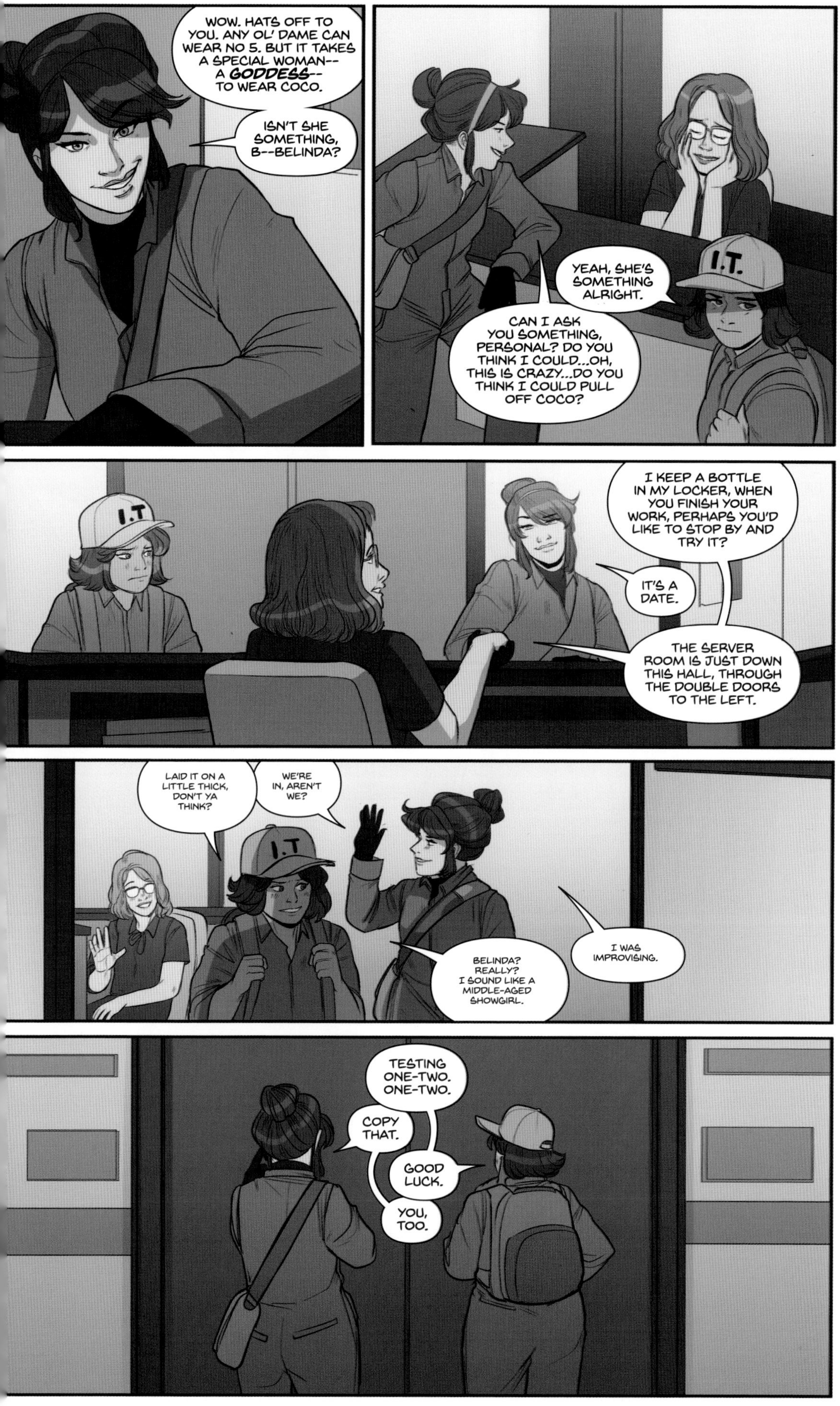
WOW. HATS OFF TO YOU. ANY OL' DAME CAN WEAR NO 5. BUT IT TAKES A SPECIAL WOMAN-- A GODDESS-- TO WEAR COCO.
ISN'T SHE SOMETHING, B--BELINDA?
YEAH, SHE'S SOMETHING ALRIGHT.
CAN I ASK YOU SOMETHING, PERSONAL? DO YOU THINK I COULD...OH, THIS IS CRAZY...DO YOU THINK I COULD PULL OFF COCO?
I KEEP A BOTTLE IN MY LOCKER, WHEN YOU FINISH YOUR WORK, PERHAPS YOU'D LIKE TO STOP BY AND TRY IT?
IT'S A DATE.
THE SERVER ROOM IS JUST DOWN THIS HALL, THROUGH THE DOUBLE DOORS TO THE LEFT.
LAID IT ON A LITTLE THICK, DON'T YA THINK?
WE'RE IN, AREN'T WE?
BELINDA? REALLY? I SOUND LIKE A MIDDLE-AGED SHOWGIRL.
I WAS IMPROVISING.
TESTING ONE-TWO. ONE-TWO.
COPY THAT.
GOOD LUCK.
YOU, TOO.

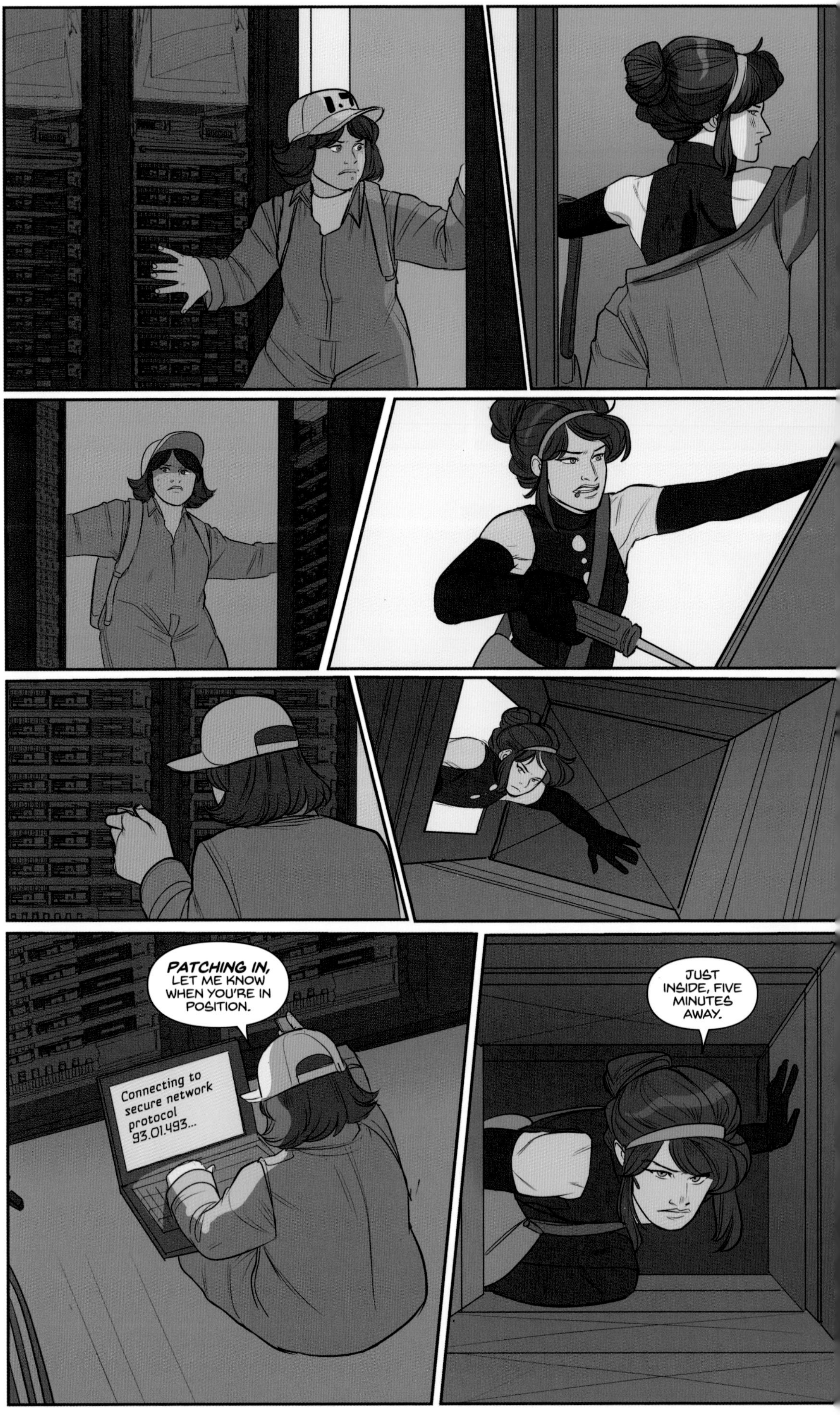
PATCHING IN, LET ME KNOW WHEN YOU'RE IN POSITION.
Connecting to secure network protocol 93.01.493...
JUST INSIDE, FIVE MINUTES AWAY.

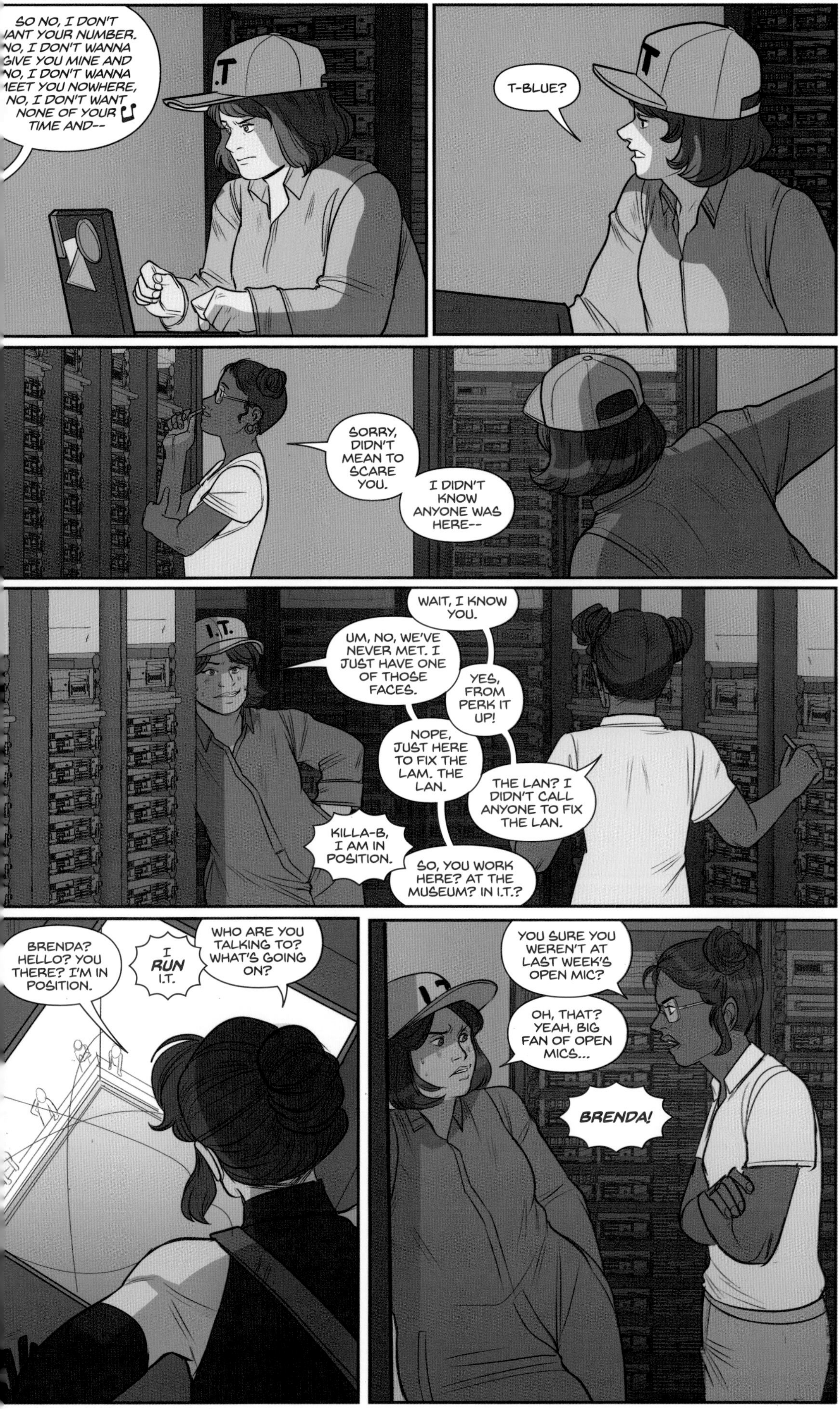
SO NO, I DON'T WANT YOUR NUMBER. NO, I DON'T WANNA GIVE YOU MINE AND NO, I DON'T WANNA MEET YOU NOWHERE, NO, I DON'T WANT NONE OF YOUR TIME AND--
I.T
T-BLUE?
SORRY, DIDN'T MEAN TO SCARE YOU.
I DIDN'T KNOW ANYONE WAS HERE--
WAIT, I KNOW YOU.
I.T.
UM, NO, WE'VE NEVER MET. I JUST HAVE ONE OF THOSE FACES.
YES, FROM PERK IT UP!
NOPE, JUST HERE TO FIX THE LAM. THE LAN.
THE LAN? I DIDN'T CALL ANYONE TO FIX THE LAN.
KILLA-B, I AM IN POSITION.
SO, YOU WORK HERE? AT THE MUSEUM? IN I.T.?
BRENDA? HELLO? YOU THERE? I'M IN POSITION.
I RUN I.T.
WHO ARE YOU TALKING TO? WHAT'S GOING ON?
YOU SURE YOU WEREN'T AT LAST WEEK'S OPEN MIC?
OH, THAT? YEAH, BIG FAN OF OPEN MICS...
BRENDA!

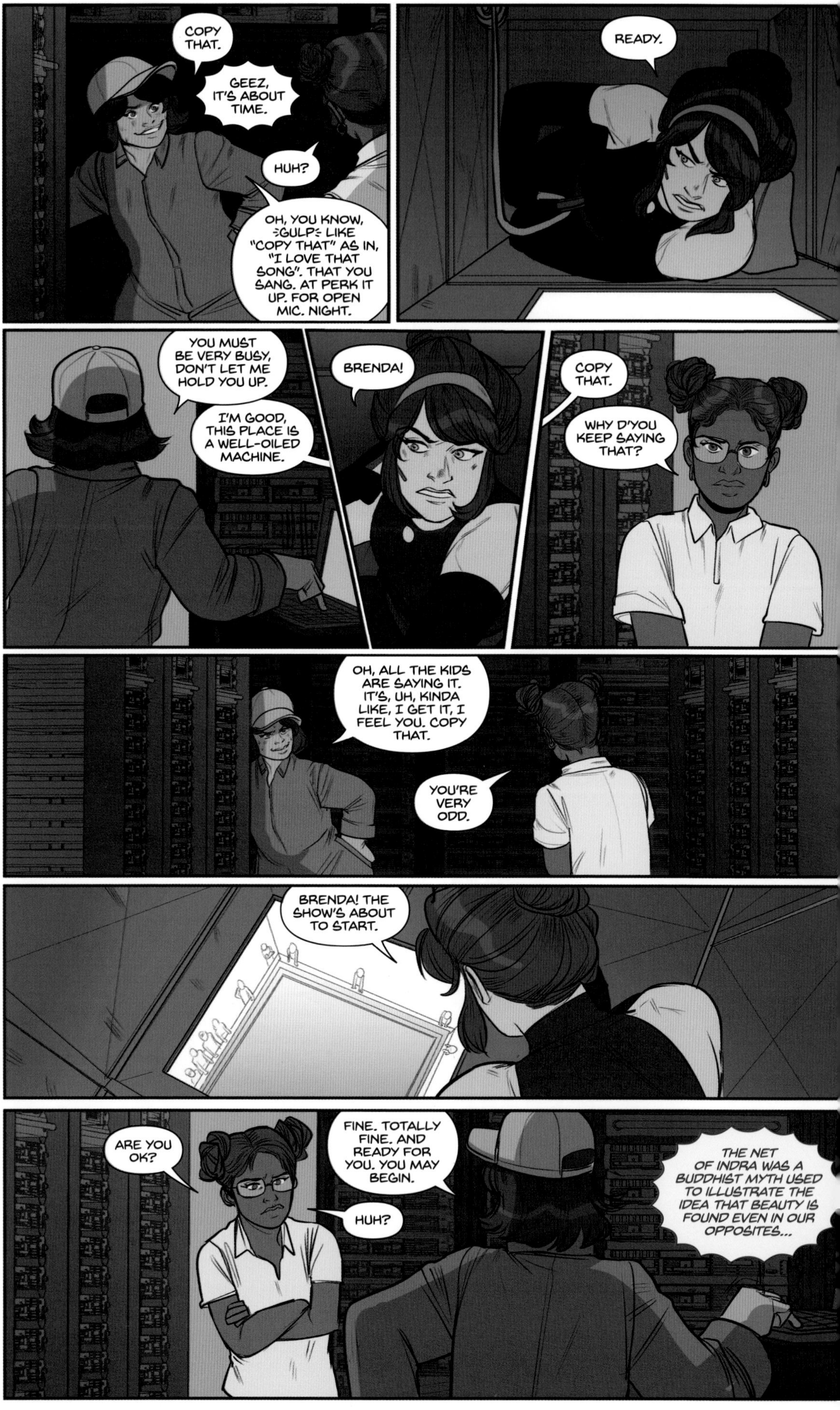
COPY THAT.
GEEZ, IT'S ABOUT TIME.
HUH?
OH, YOU KNOW, =GULP= LIKE "COPY THAT" AS IN, "I LOVE THAT SONG". THAT YOU SANG. AT PERK IT UP. FOR OPEN MIC. NIGHT.
READY.
YOU MUST BE VERY BUSY, DON'T LET ME HOLD YOU UP.
I'M GOOD, THIS PLACE IS A WELL-OILED MACHINE.
BRENDA!
COPY THAT.
WHY D'YOU KEEP SAYING THAT?
OH, ALL THE KIDS ARE SAYING IT. IT'S, UH, KINDA LIKE, I GET IT, I FEEL YOU. COPY THAT.
YOU'RE VERY ODD.
BRENDA! THE SHOW'S ABOUT TO START.
ARE YOU OK?
FINE. TOTALLY FINE. AND READY FOR YOU. YOU MAY BEGIN.
HUH?
THE NET OF INDRA WAS A BUDDHIST MYTH USED TO ILLUSTRATE THE IDEA THAT BEAUTY IS FOUND EVEN IN OUR OPPOSITES...

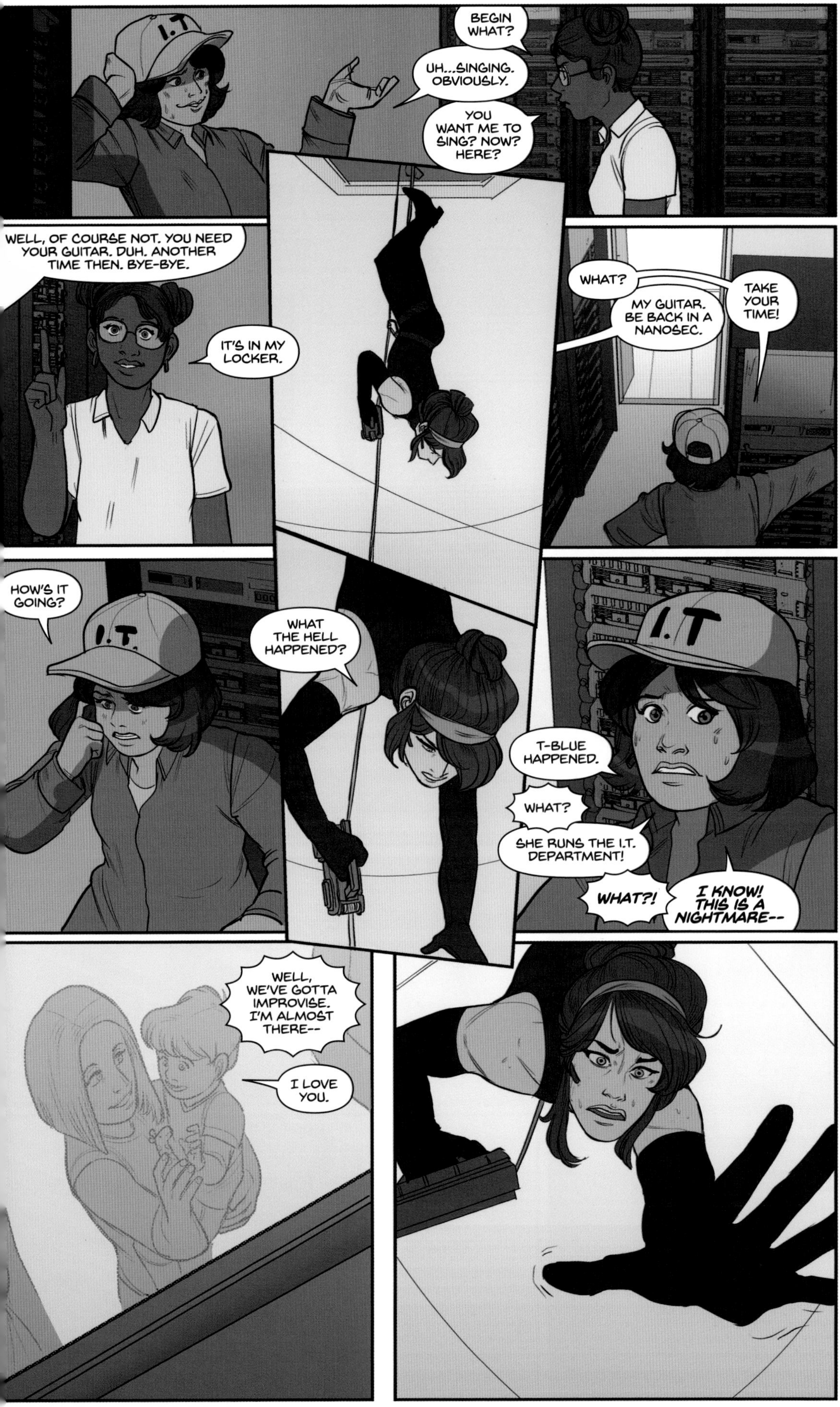
BEGIN WHAT?
UH...SINGING. OBVIOUSLY.
YOU WANT ME TO SING? NOW? HERE?
WELL, OF COURSE NOT. YOU NEED YOUR GUITAR. DUH. ANOTHER TIME THEN. BYE-BYE.
IT'S IN MY LOCKER.
WHAT?
MY GUITAR. BE BACK IN A NANOSEC.
TAKE YOUR TIME!
HOW'S IT GOING?
WHAT THE HELL HAPPENED?
T-BLUE HAPPENED.
WHAT?
SHE RUNS THE I.T. DEPARTMENT!
WHAT?!
I KNOW! THIS IS A NIGHTMARE--
WELL, WE'VE GOTTA IMPROVISE. I'M ALMOST THERE--
I LOVE YOU.

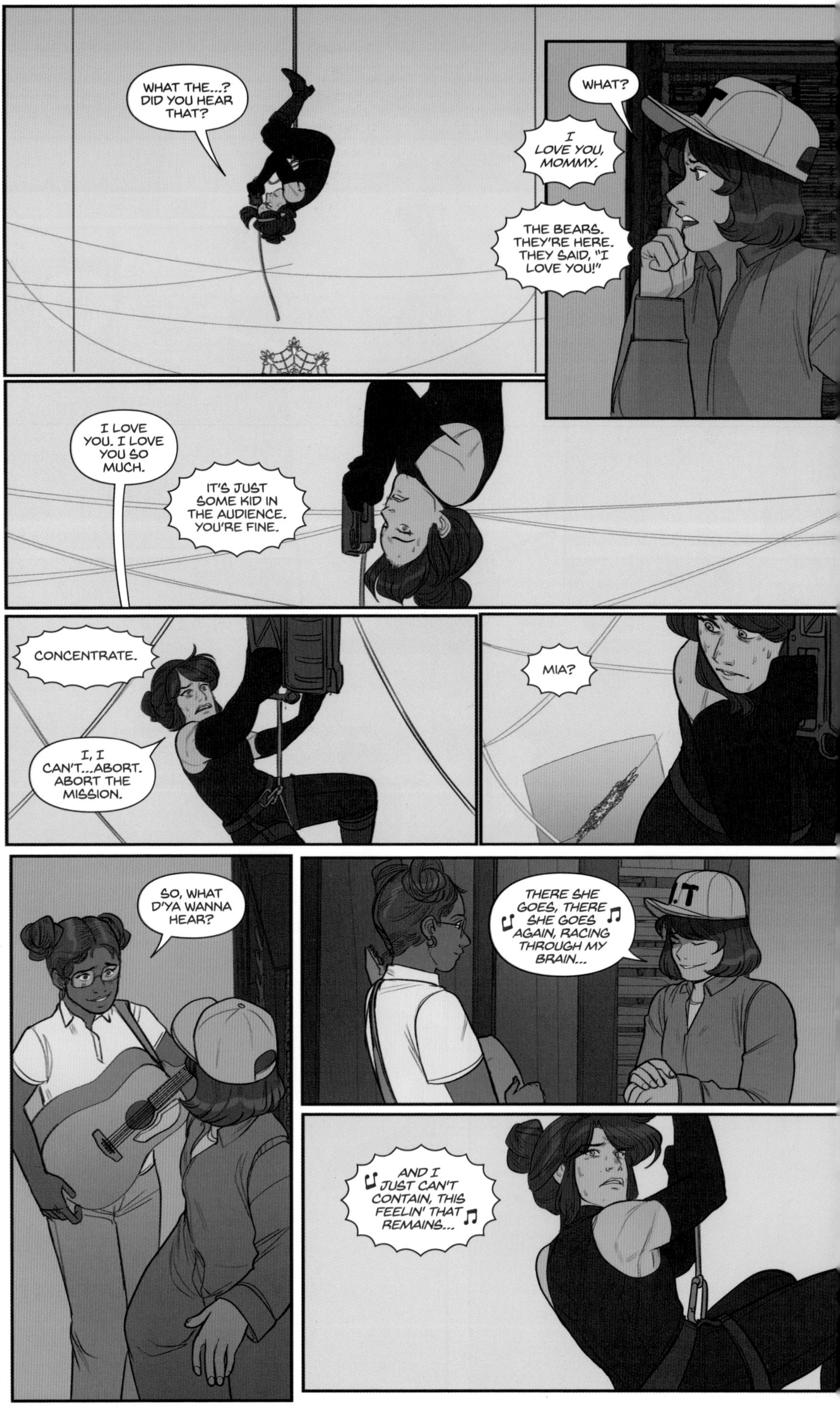
WHAT THE...? DID YOU HEAR THAT?
WHAT?
I LOVE YOU, MOMMY.
THE BEARS. THEY'RE HERE. THEY SAID, "I LOVE YOU!"
I LOVE YOU. I LOVE YOU SO MUCH.
IT'S JUST SOME KID IN THE AUDIENCE. YOU'RE FINE.
CONCENTRATE.
I, I CAN'T...ABORT. ABORT THE MISSION.
MIA?
SO, WHAT D'YA WANNA HEAR?
THERE SHE GOES, THERE SHE GOES AGAIN, RACING THROUGH MY BRAIN...
AND I JUST CAN'T CONTAIN, THIS FEELIN' THAT REMAINS...

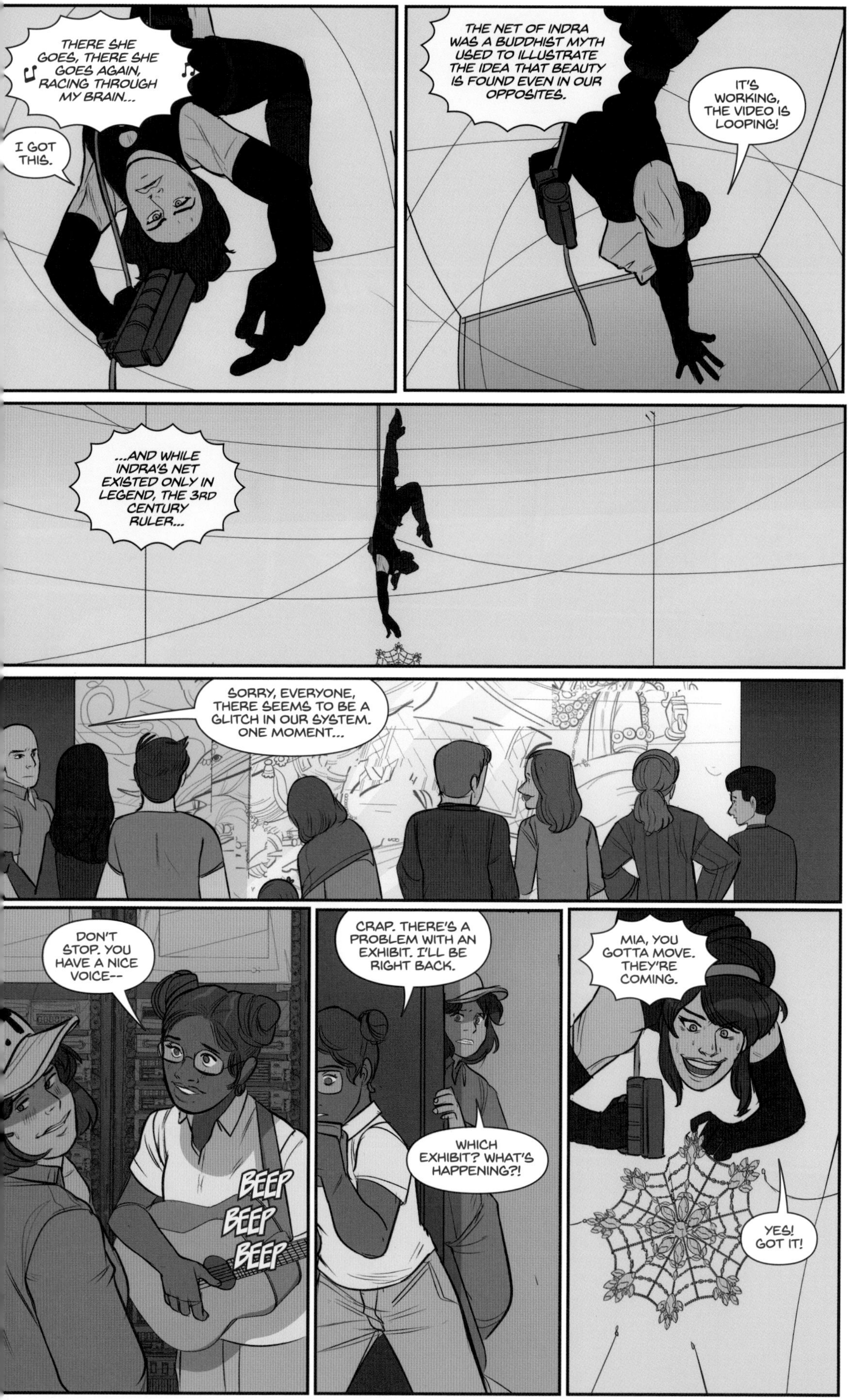
THERE SHE GOES, THERE SHE GOES AGAIN, RACING THROUGH MY BRAIN...
I GOT THIS.
THE NET OF INDRA WAS A BUDDHIST MYTH USED TO ILLUSTRATE THE IDEA THAT BEAUTY IS FOUND EVEN IN OUR OPPOSITES.
IT'S WORKING, THE VIDEO IS LOOPING!
...AND WHILE INDRA'S NET EXISTED ONLY IN LEGEND, THE 3RD CENTURY RULER...
SORRY, EVERYONE, THERE SEEMS TO BE A GLITCH IN OUR SYSTEM. ONE MOMENT...
DON'T STOP. YOU HAVE A NICE VOICE--
BEEP BEEP BEEP
CRAP. THERE'S A PROBLEM WITH AN EXHIBIT. I'LL BE RIGHT BACK.
WHICH EXHIBIT? WHAT'S HAPPENING?!
MIA, YOU GOTTA MOVE. THEY'RE COMING.
YES! GOT IT!

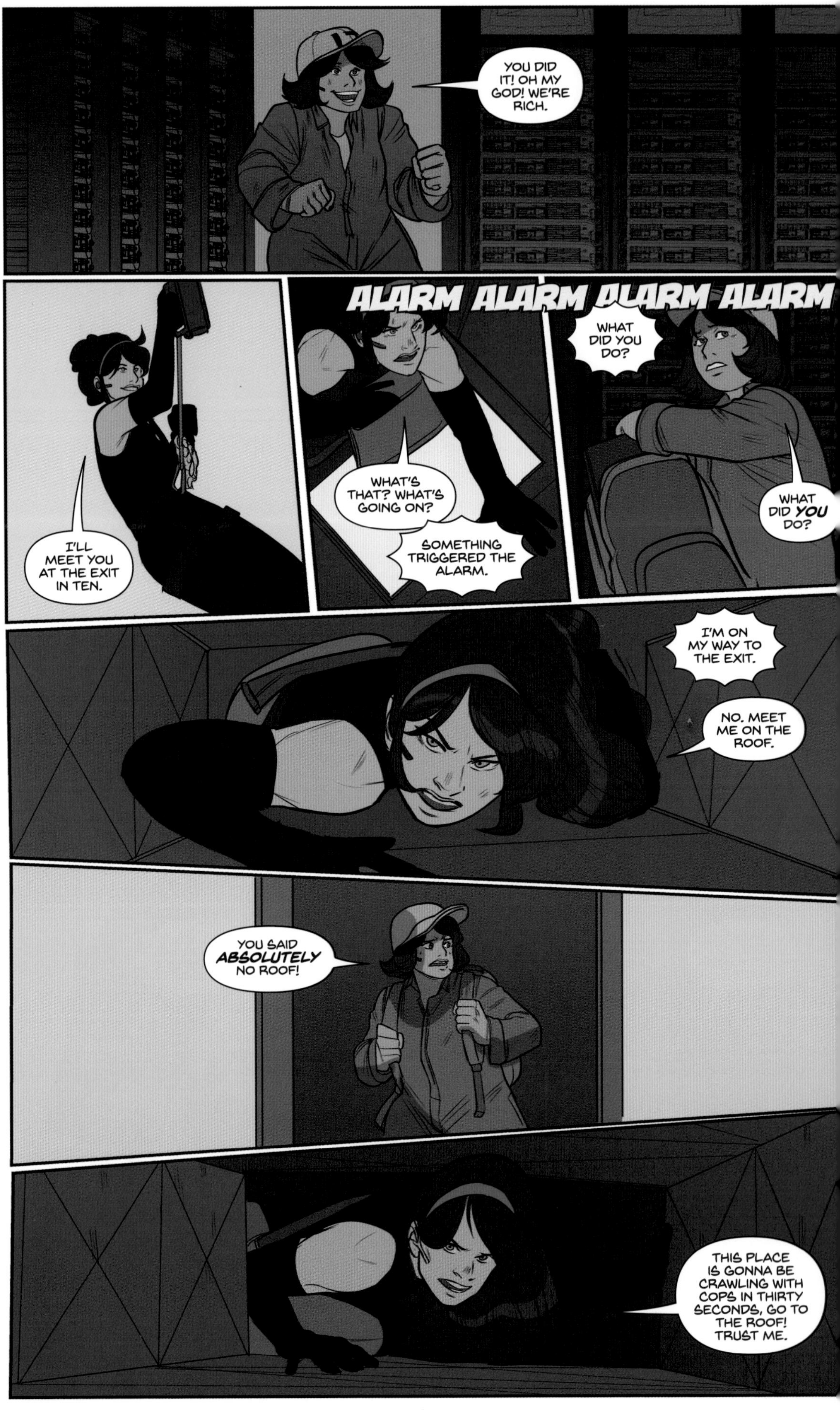
YOU DID IT! OH MY GOD! WE'RE RICH.
ALARM ALARM ALARM ALARM
I'LL MEET YOU AT THE EXIT IN TEN.
WHAT'S THAT? WHAT'S GOING ON?
SOMETHING TRIGGERED THE ALARM.
WHAT DID YOU DO?
WHAT DID *YOU* DO?
I'M ON MY WAY TO THE EXIT.
NO. MEET ME ON THE ROOF.
YOU SAID ***ABSOLUTELY*** NO ROOF!
THIS PLACE IS GONNA BE CRAWLING WITH COPS IN THIRTY SECONDS, GO TO THE ROOF! TRUST ME.

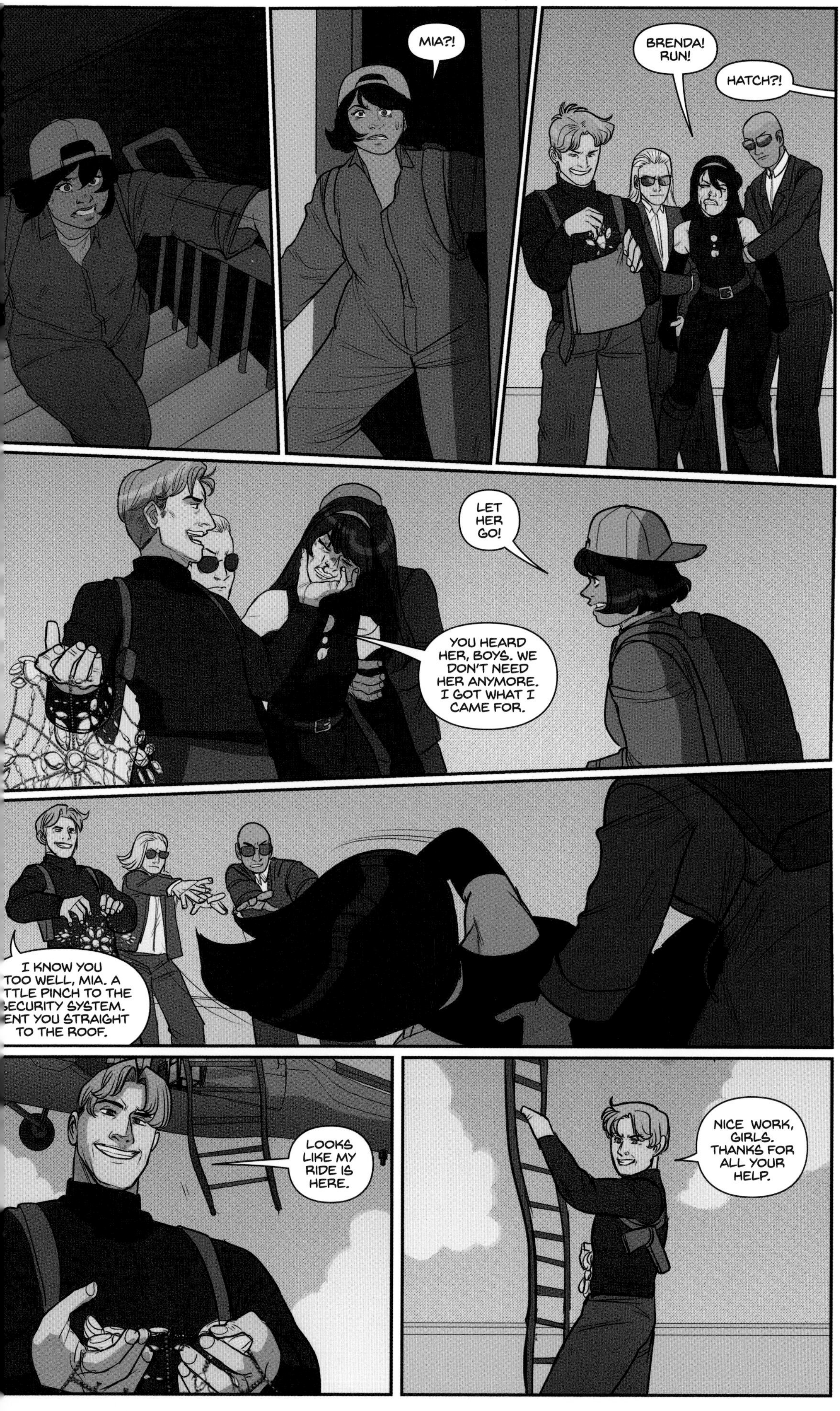
MIA?!
BRENDA! RUN!
HATCH?!
LET HER GO!
YOU HEARD HER, BOYS. WE DON'T NEED HER ANYMORE. I GOT WHAT I CAME FOR.
I KNOW YOU TOO WELL, MIA. A TTLE PINCH TO THE SECURITY SYSTEM. ENT YOU STRAIGHT TO THE ROOF.
LOOKS LIKE MY RIDE IS HERE.
NICE WORK, GIRLS. THANKS FOR ALL YOUR HELP.

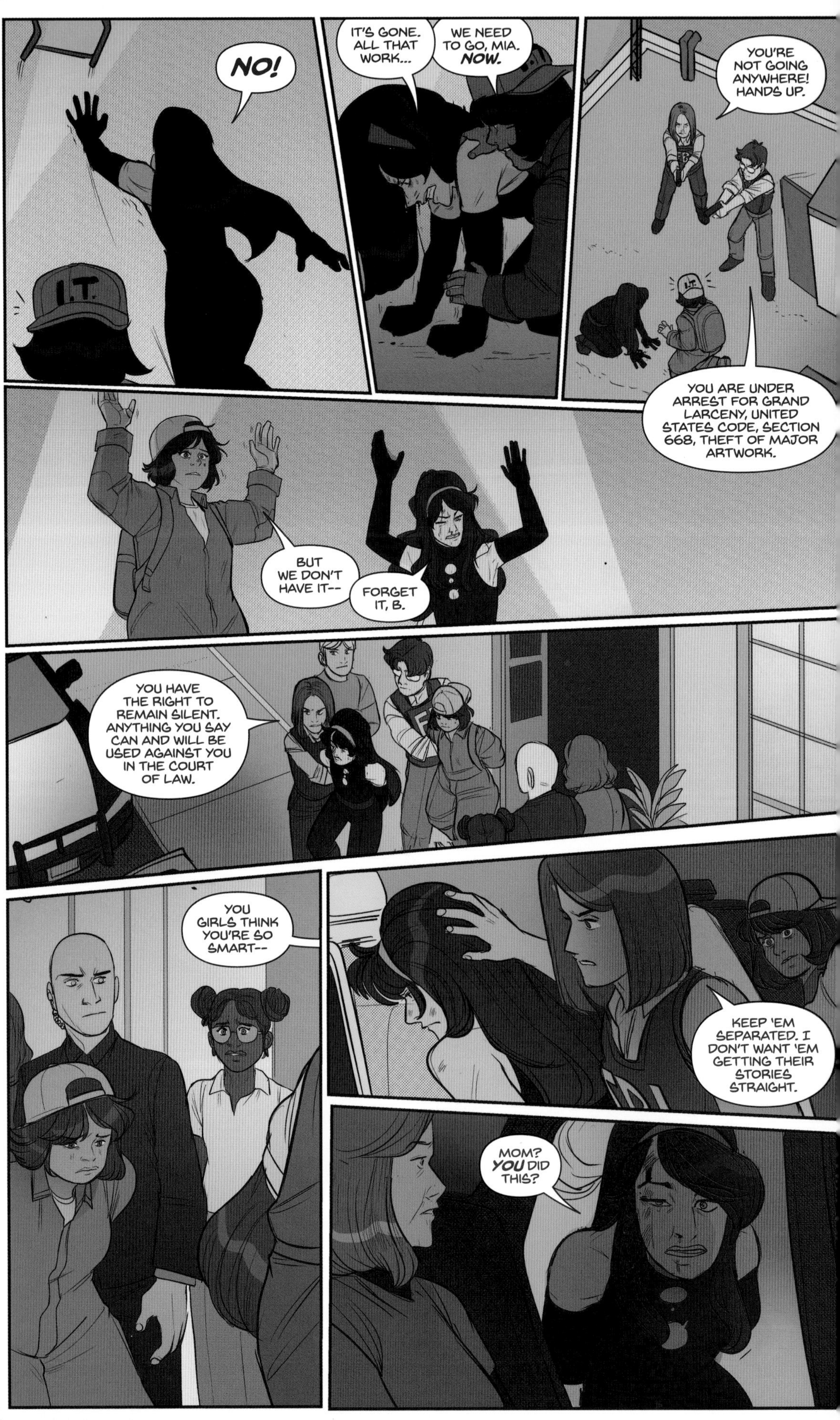
NO!
IT'S GONE. ALL THAT WORK...
WE NEED TO GO, MIA. NOW.
YOU'RE NOT GOING ANYWHERE! HANDS UP.
I.T.
YOU ARE UNDER ARREST FOR GRAND LARCENY, UNITED STATES CODE, SECTION 668, THEFT OF MAJOR ARTWORK.
BUT WE DON'T HAVE IT--
FORGET IT, B.
YOU HAVE THE RIGHT TO REMAIN SILENT. ANYTHING YOU SAY CAN AND WILL BE USED AGAINST YOU IN THE COURT OF LAW.
YOU GIRLS THINK YOU'RE SO SMART--
KEEP 'EM SEPARATED. I DON'T WANT 'EM GETTING THEIR STORIES STRAIGHT.
MOM? YOU DID THIS?

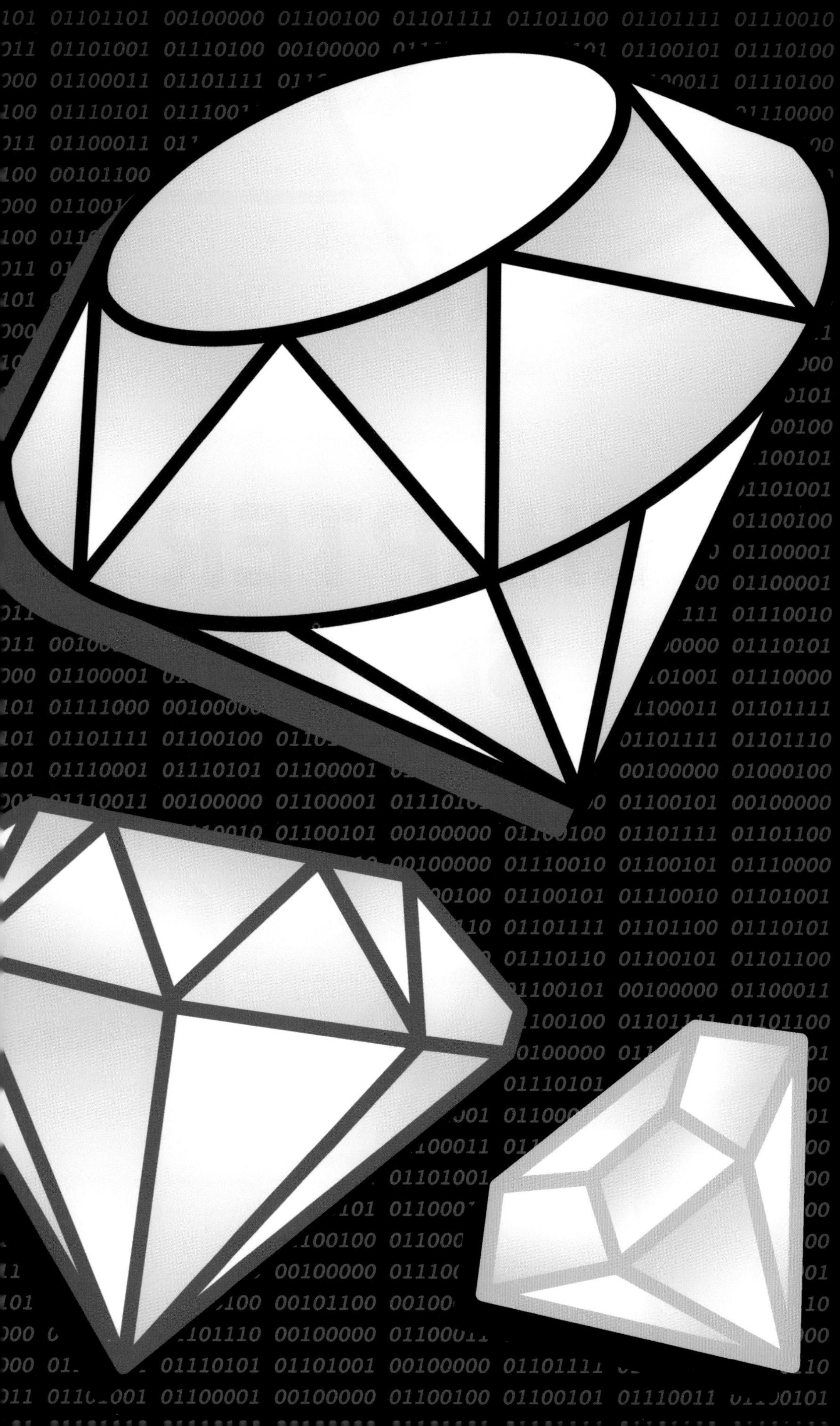

CHAPTER SEVEN

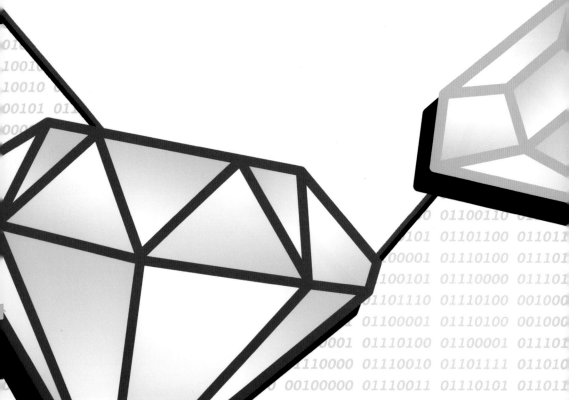

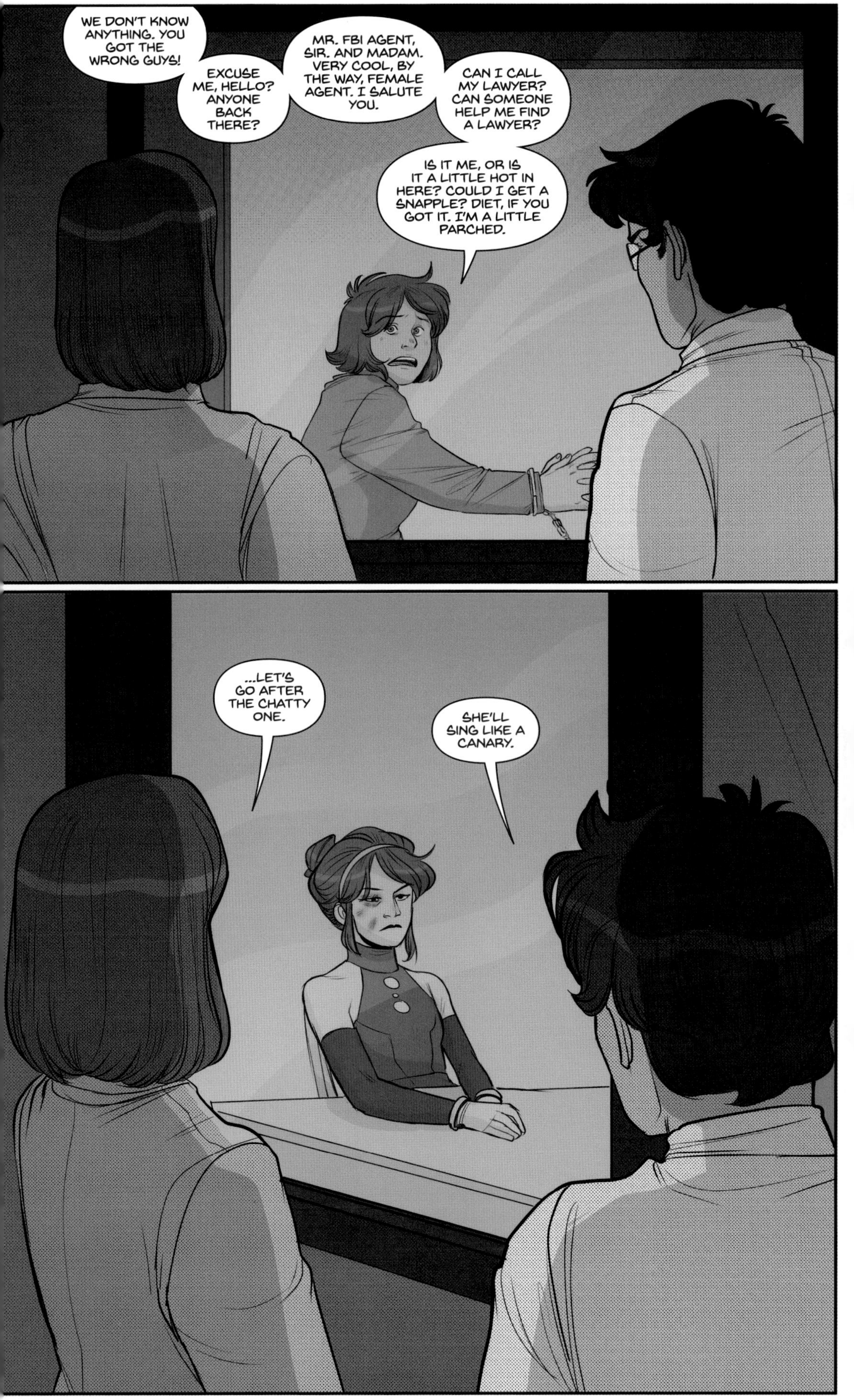
WE DON'T KNOW ANYTHING. YOU GOT THE WRONG GUYS!
EXCUSE ME, HELLO? ANYONE BACK THERE?
MR. FBI AGENT, SIR. AND MADAM. VERY COOL, BY THE WAY, FEMALE AGENT. I SALUTE YOU.
CAN I CALL MY LAWYER? CAN SOMEONE HELP ME FIND A LAWYER?
IS IT ME, OR IS IT A LITTLE HOT IN HERE? COULD I GET A SNAPPLE? DIET, IF YOU GOT IT. I'M A LITTLE PARCHED.
...LET'S GO AFTER THE CHATTY ONE.
SHE'LL SING LIKE A CANARY.

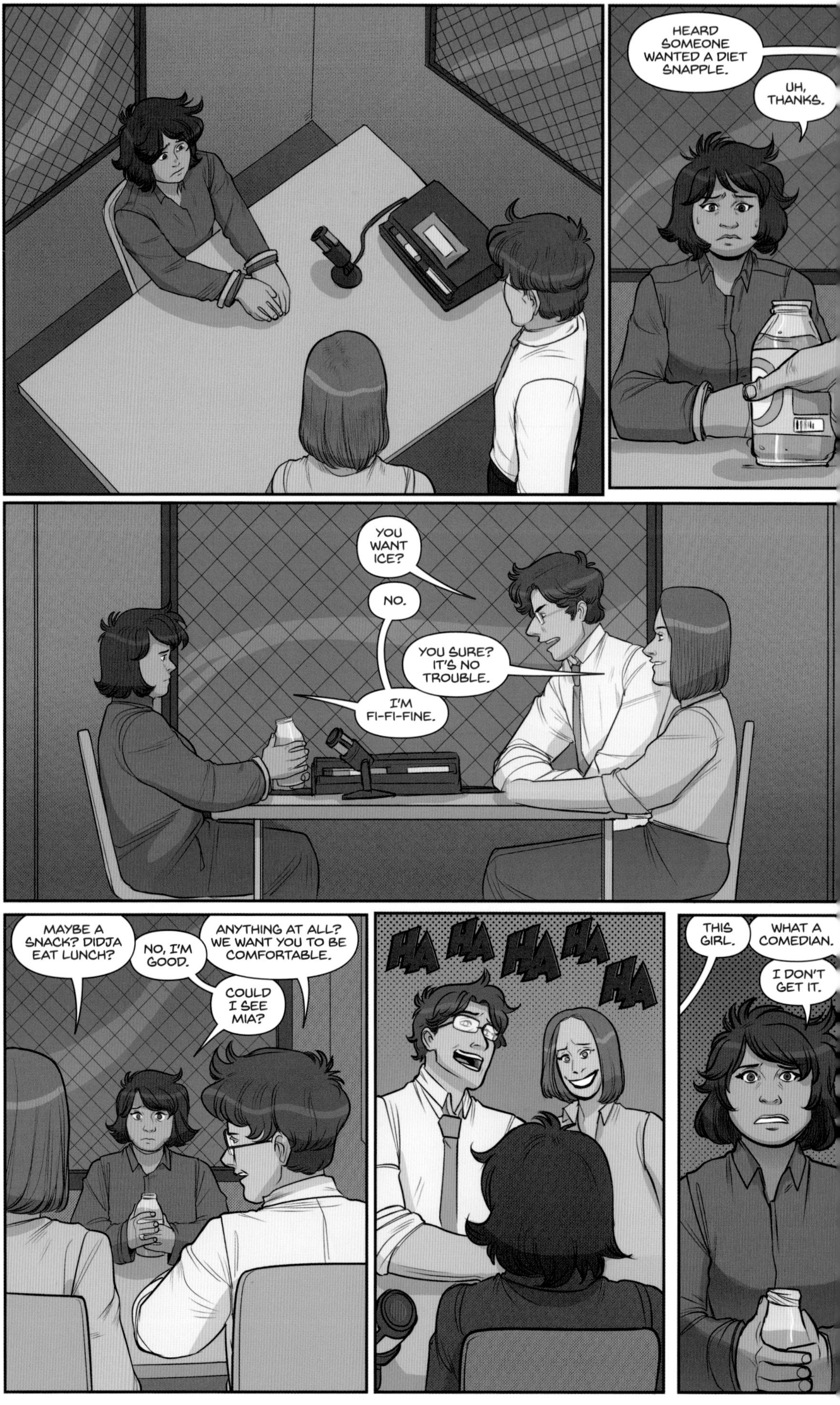
HEARD SOMEONE WANTED A DIET SNAPPLE.
UH, THANKS.
YOU WANT ICE?
NO.
YOU SURE? IT'S NO TROUBLE.
I'M FI-FI-FINE.
MAYBE A SNACK? DIDJA EAT LUNCH?
NO, I'M GOOD.
ANYTHING AT ALL? WE WANT YOU TO BE COMFORTABLE.
COULD I SEE MIA?
HA HA HA HA HA
THIS GIRL.
WHAT A COMEDIAN.
I DON'T GET IT.

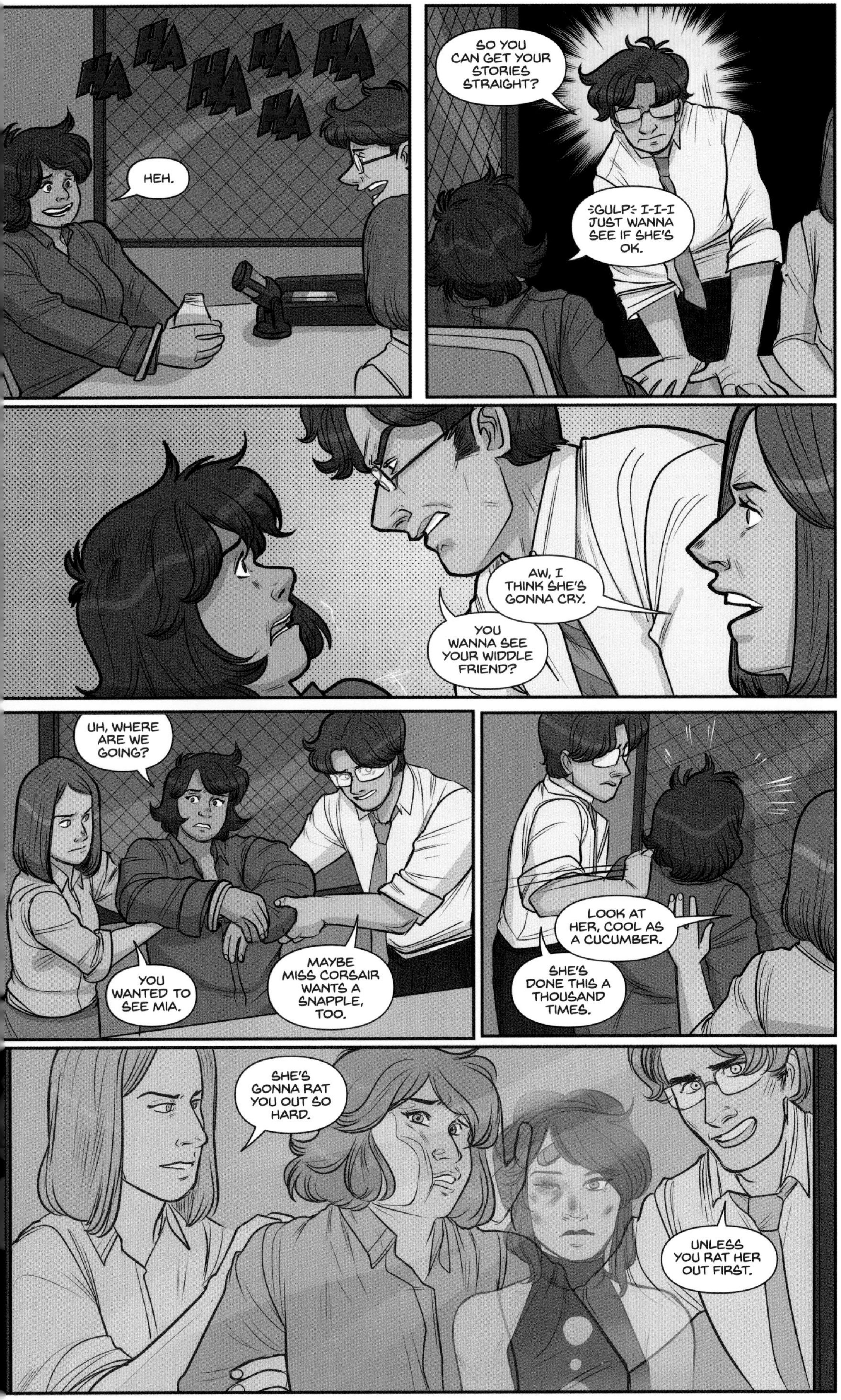
HA HA HA HA HA HA HA
HEH.
SO YOU CAN GET YOUR STORIES STRAIGHT?
⸗GULP⸗ I-I-I JUST WANNA SEE IF SHE'S OK.
YOU WANNA SEE YOUR WIDDLE FRIEND?
AW, I THINK SHE'S GONNA CRY.
UH, WHERE ARE WE GOING?
YOU WANTED TO SEE MIA.
MAYBE MISS CORSAIR WANTS A SNAPPLE, TOO.
LOOK AT HER, COOL AS A CUCUMBER.
SHE'S DONE THIS A THOUSAND TIMES.
SHE'S GONNA RAT YOU OUT SO HARD.
UNLESS YOU RAT HER OUT FIRST.

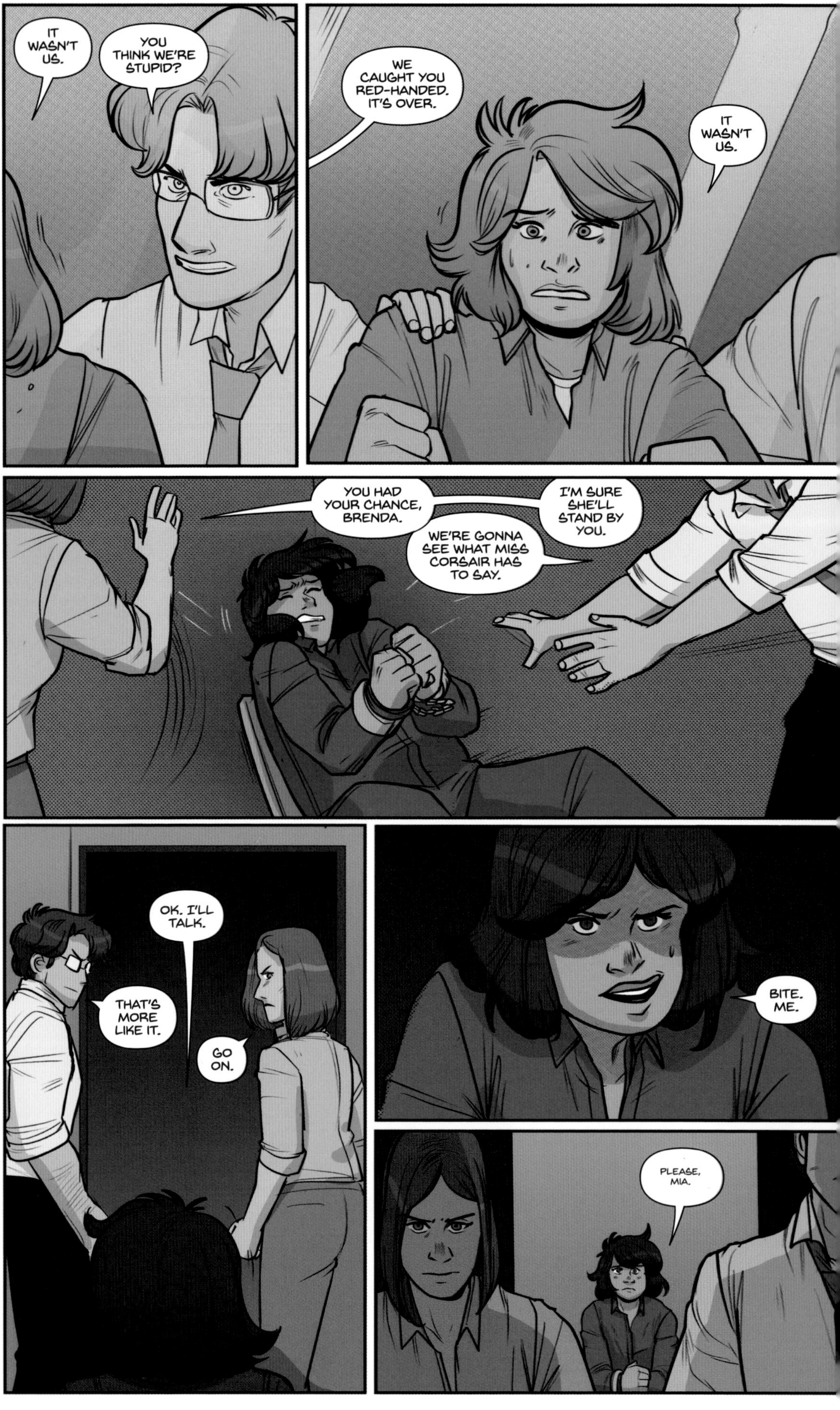
IT WASN'T US.
YOU THINK WE'RE STUPID?
WE CAUGHT YOU RED-HANDED. IT'S OVER.
IT WASN'T US.
YOU HAD YOUR CHANCE, BRENDA.
I'M SURE SHE'LL STAND BY YOU.
WE'RE GONNA SEE WHAT MISS CORSAIR HAS TO SAY.
OK. I'LL TALK.
THAT'S MORE LIKE IT.
GO ON.
BITE. ME.
PLEASE, MIA.

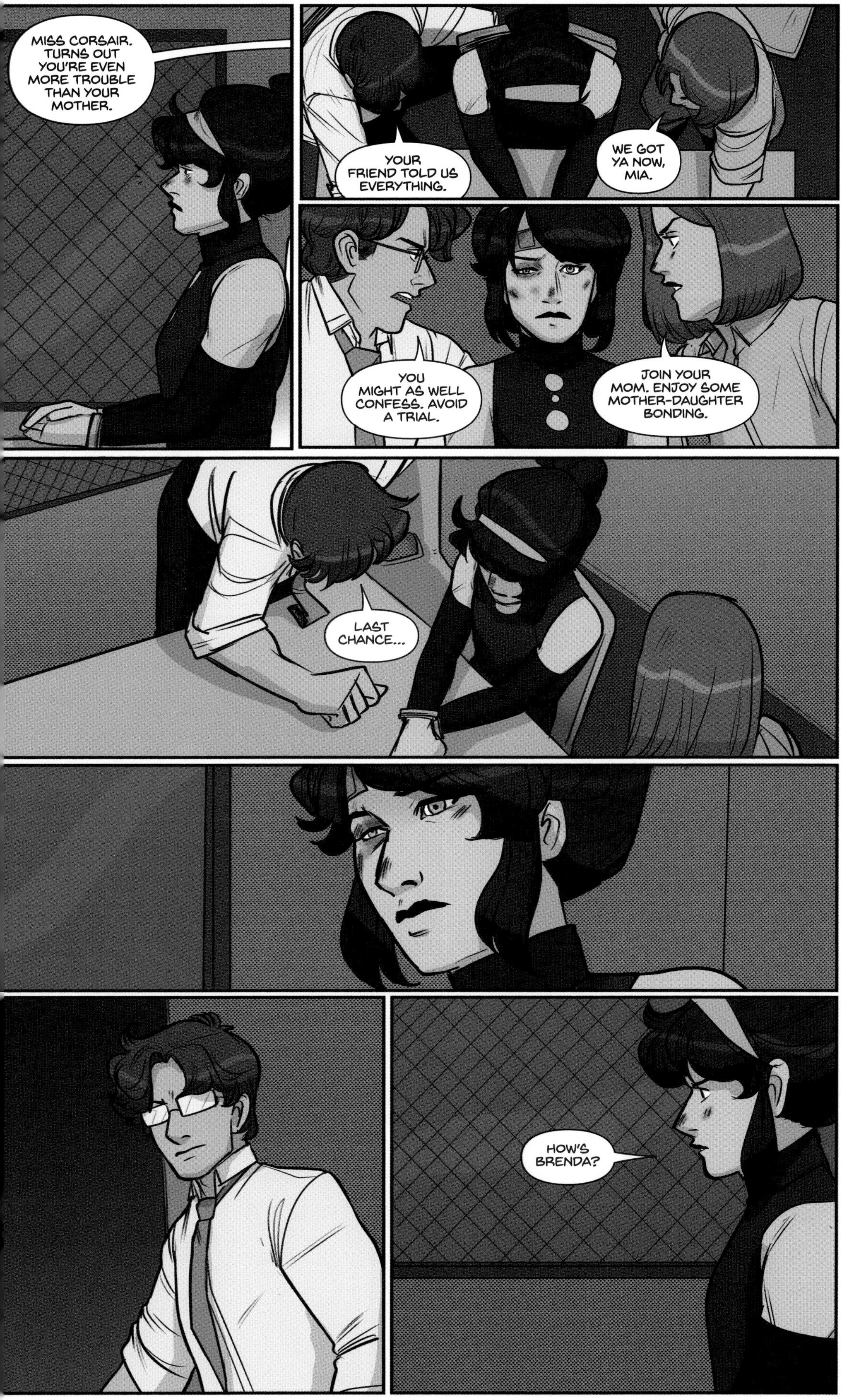
MISS CORSAIR. TURNS OUT YOU'RE EVEN MORE TROUBLE THAN YOUR MOTHER.
YOUR FRIEND TOLD US EVERYTHING.
WE GOT YA NOW, MIA.
YOU MIGHT AS WELL CONFESS. AVOID A TRIAL.
JOIN YOUR MOM. ENJOY SOME MOTHER-DAUGHTER BONDING.
LAST CHANCE...
HOW'S BRENDA?

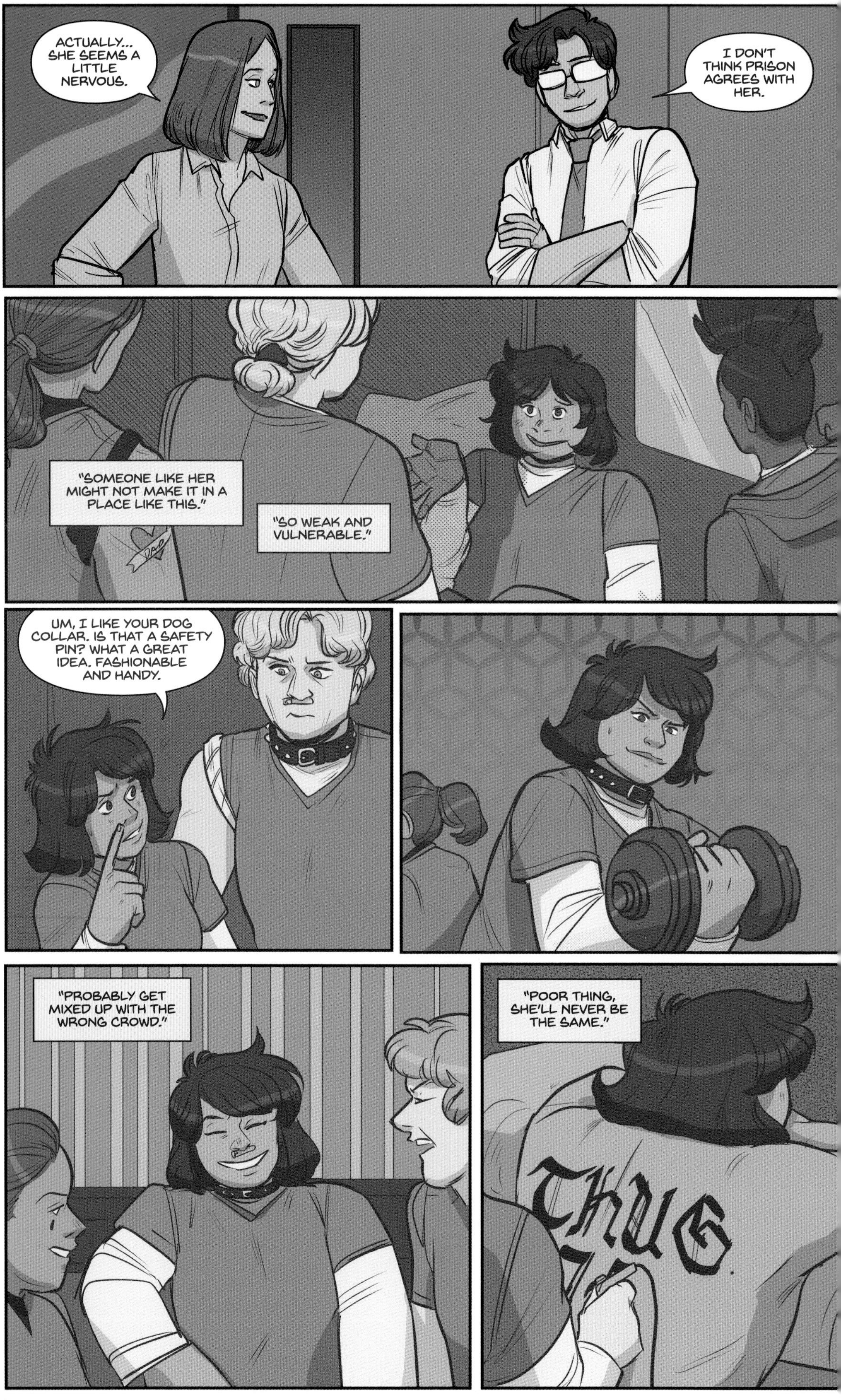
ACTUALLY... SHE SEEMS A LITTLE NERVOUS.
I DON'T THINK PRISON AGREES WITH HER.
"SOMEONE LIKE HER MIGHT NOT MAKE IT IN A PLACE LIKE THIS."
"SO WEAK AND VULNERABLE."
UM, I LIKE YOUR DOG COLLAR. IS THAT A SAFETY PIN? WHAT A GREAT IDEA. FASHIONABLE AND HANDY.
"PROBABLY GET MIXED UP WITH THE WRONG CROWD."
"POOR THING, SHE'LL NEVER BE THE SAME."
THUG

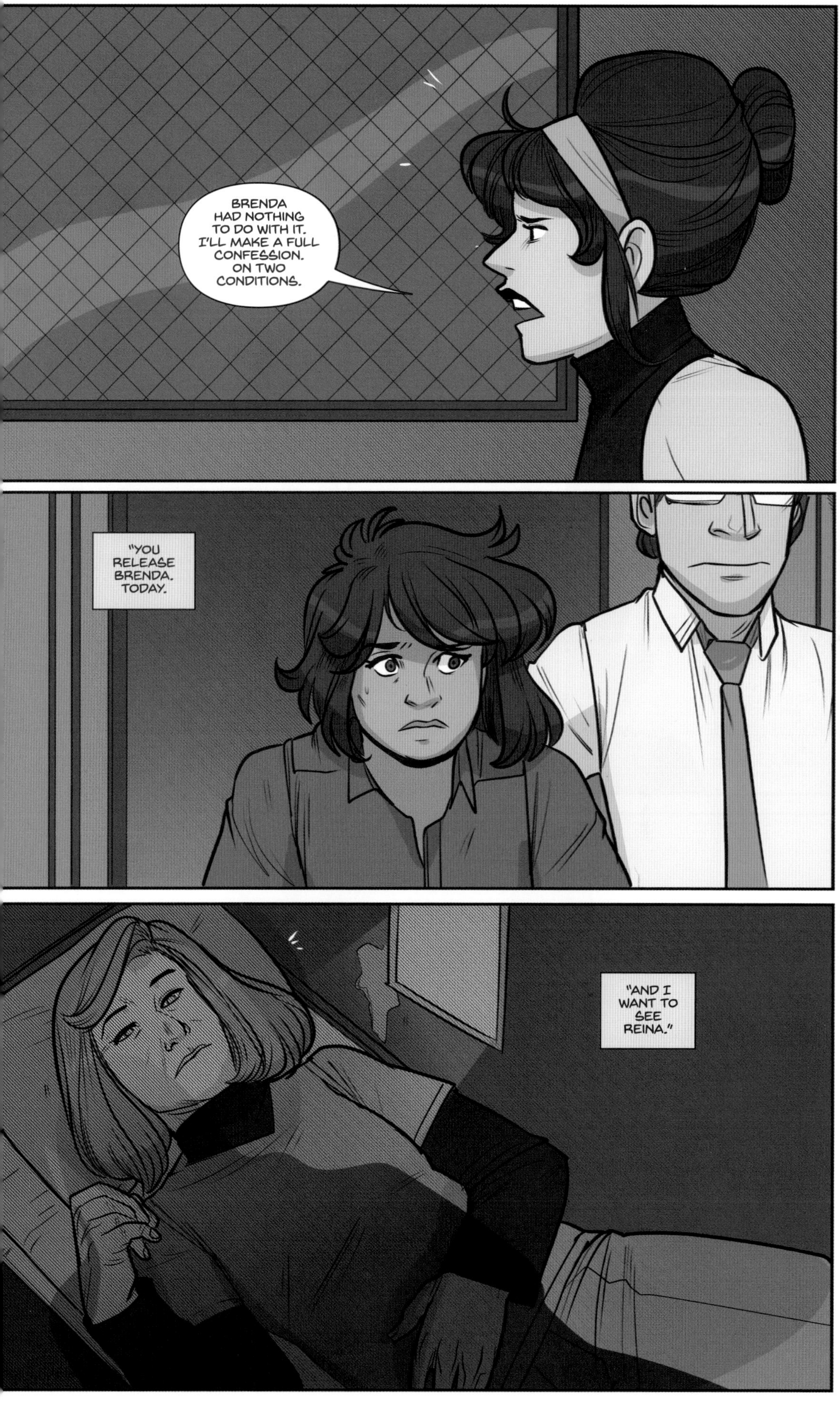
BRENDA HAD NOTHING TO DO WITH IT. I'LL MAKE A FULL CONFESSION. ON TWO CONDITIONS.
"YOU RELEASE BRENDA. TODAY.
"AND I WANT TO SEE REINA."

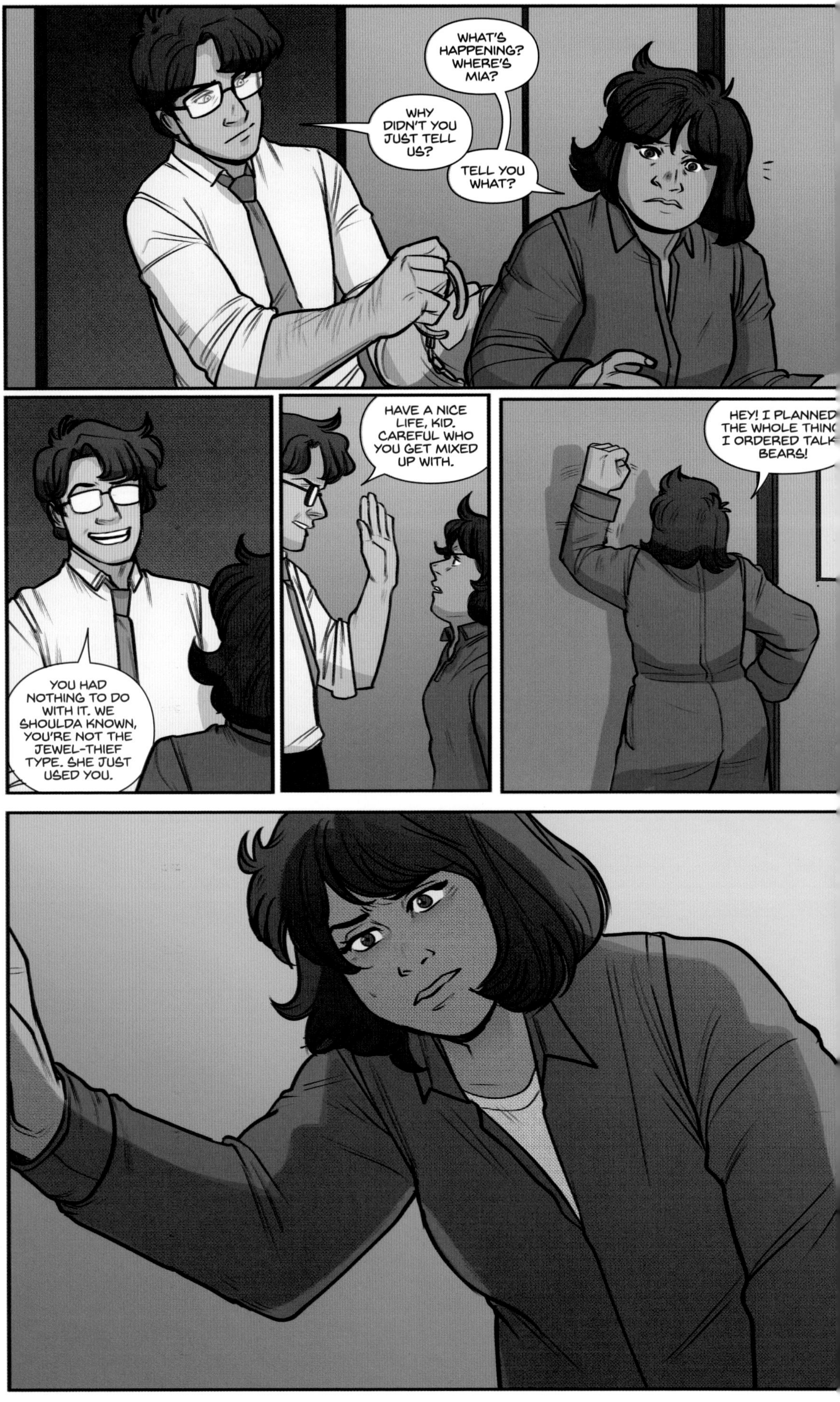
WHY DIDN'T YOU JUST TELL US?
WHAT'S HAPPENING? WHERE'S MIA?
TELL YOU WHAT?
YOU HAD NOTHING TO DO WITH IT. WE SHOULDA KNOWN, YOU'RE NOT THE JEWEL-THIEF TYPE. SHE JUST USED YOU.
HAVE A NICE LIFE, KID. CAREFUL WHO YOU GET MIXED UP WITH.
HEY! I PLANNED THE WHOLE THIN
I ORDERED TALK BEARS!

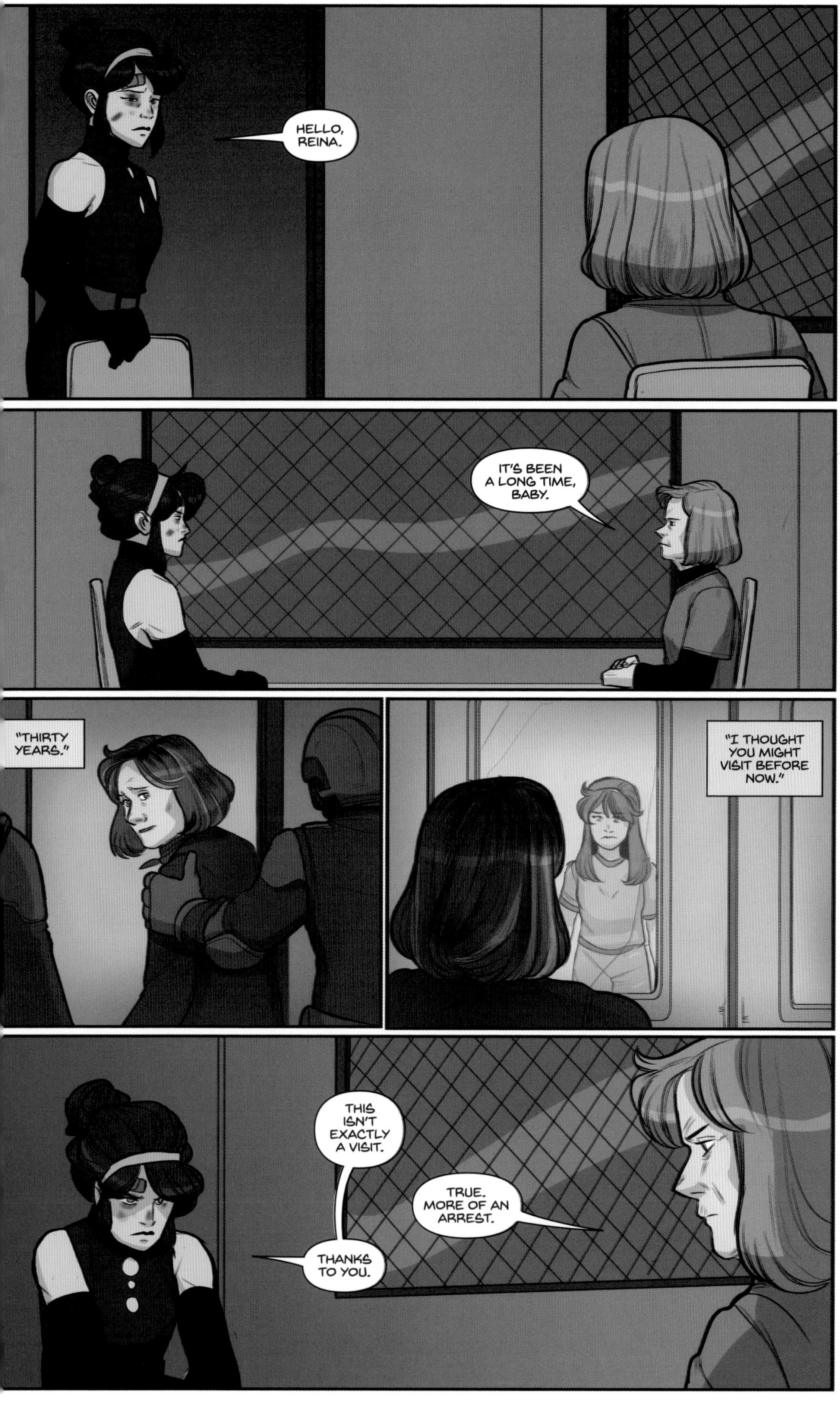
HELLO, REINA.
IT'S BEEN A LONG TIME, BABY.
"THIRTY YEARS."
"I THOUGHT YOU MIGHT VISIT BEFORE NOW."
THIS ISN'T EXACTLY A VISIT.
THANKS TO YOU.
TRUE. MORE OF AN ARREST.

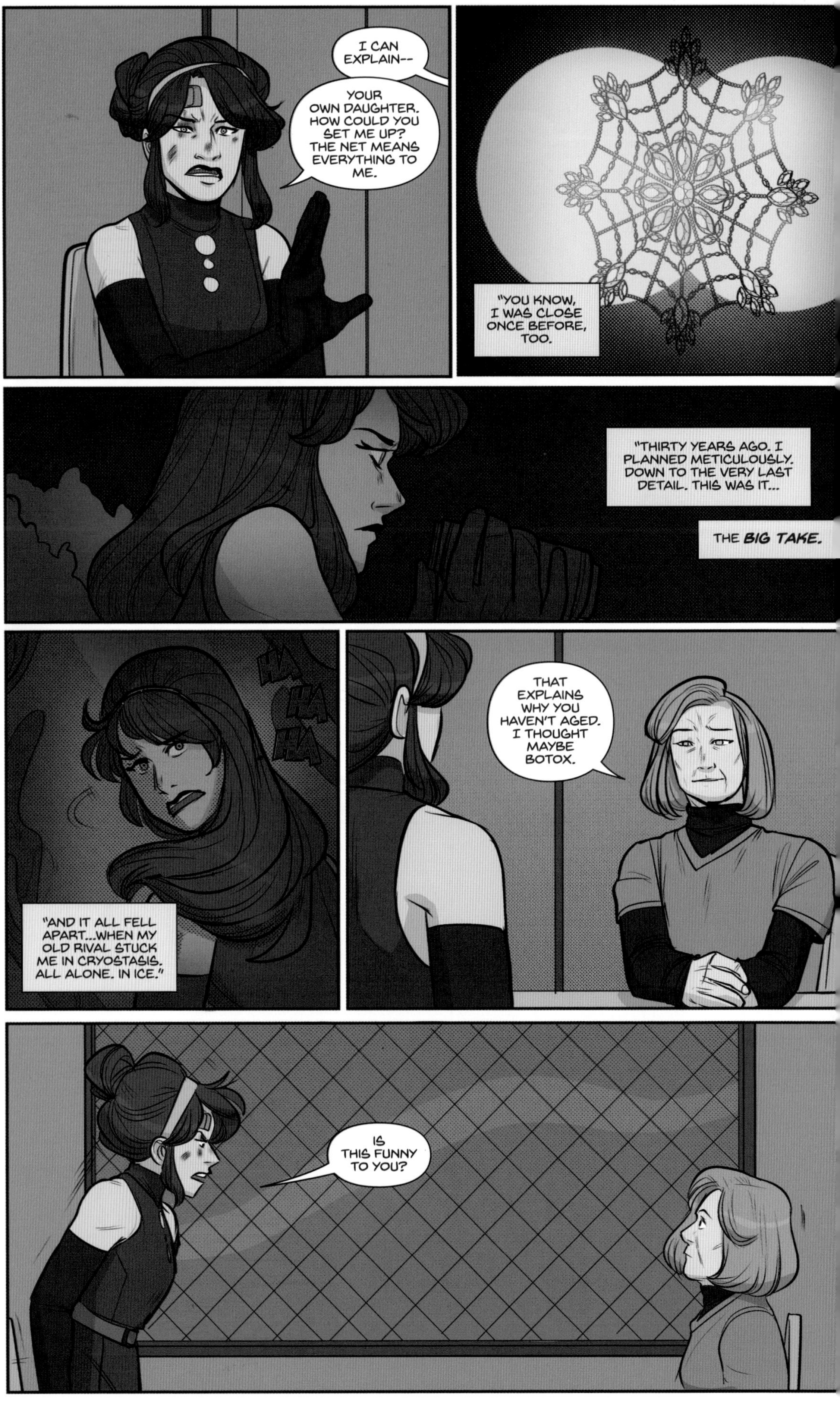
I CAN EXPLAIN--
YOUR OWN DAUGHTER. HOW COULD YOU SET ME UP? THE NET MEANS EVERYTHING TO ME.
"YOU KNOW, I WAS CLOSE ONCE BEFORE, TOO.
"THIRTY YEARS AGO. I PLANNED METICULOUSLY. DOWN TO THE VERY LAST DETAIL. THIS WAS IT...
THE BIG TAKE.
HA HA HA HA
"AND IT ALL FELL APART...WHEN MY OLD RIVAL STUCK ME IN CRYOSTASIS. ALL ALONE. IN ICE."
THAT EXPLAINS WHY YOU HAVEN'T AGED. I THOUGHT MAYBE BOTOX.
IS THIS FUNNY TO YOU?

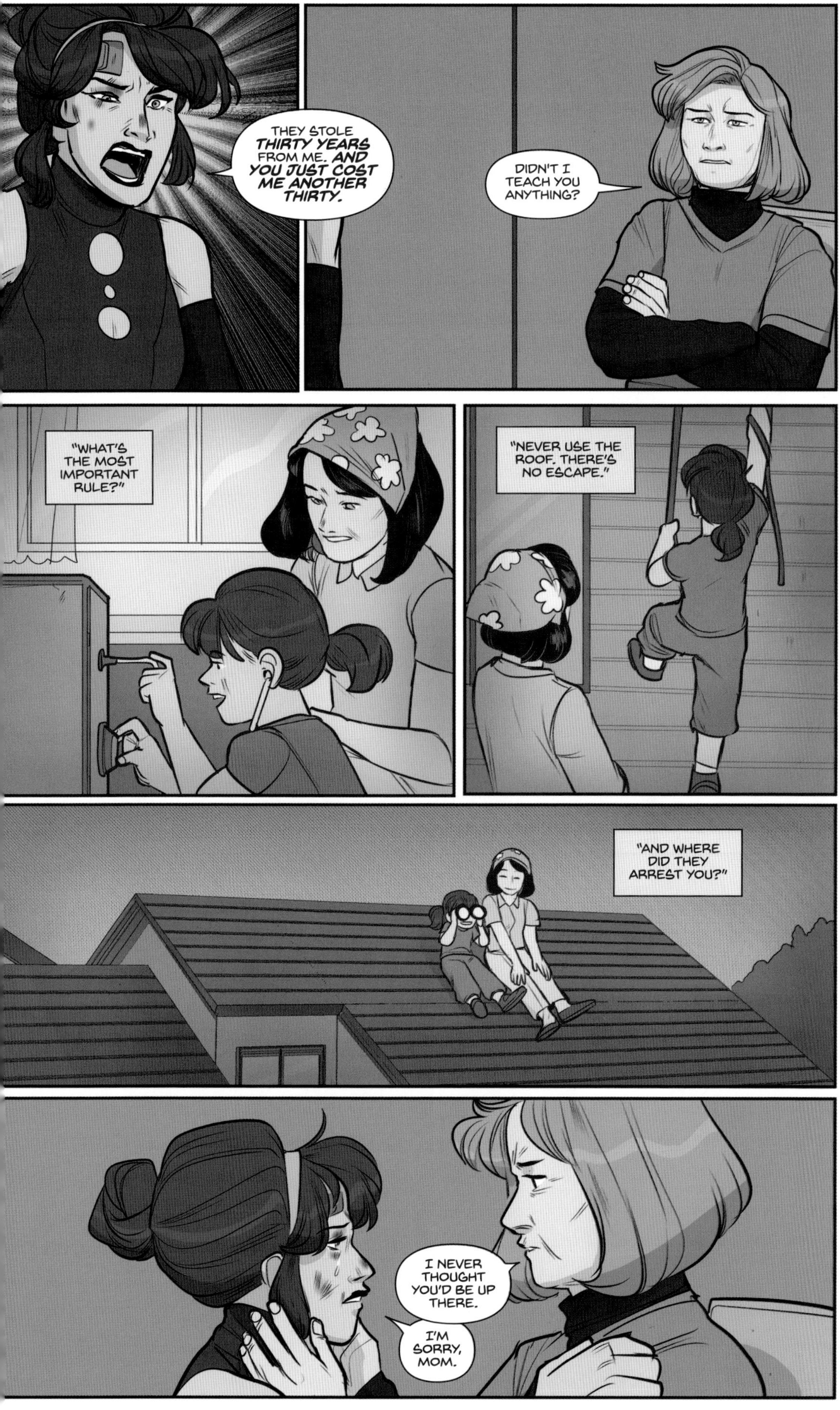
THEY STOLE THIRTY YEARS FROM ME. AND YOU JUST COST ME ANOTHER THIRTY.
DIDN'T I TEACH YOU ANYTHING?
"WHAT'S THE MOST IMPORTANT RULE?"
"NEVER USE THE ROOF. THERE'S NO ESCAPE."
"AND WHERE DID THEY ARREST YOU?"
I NEVER THOUGHT YOU'D BE UP THERE.
I'M SORRY, MOM.

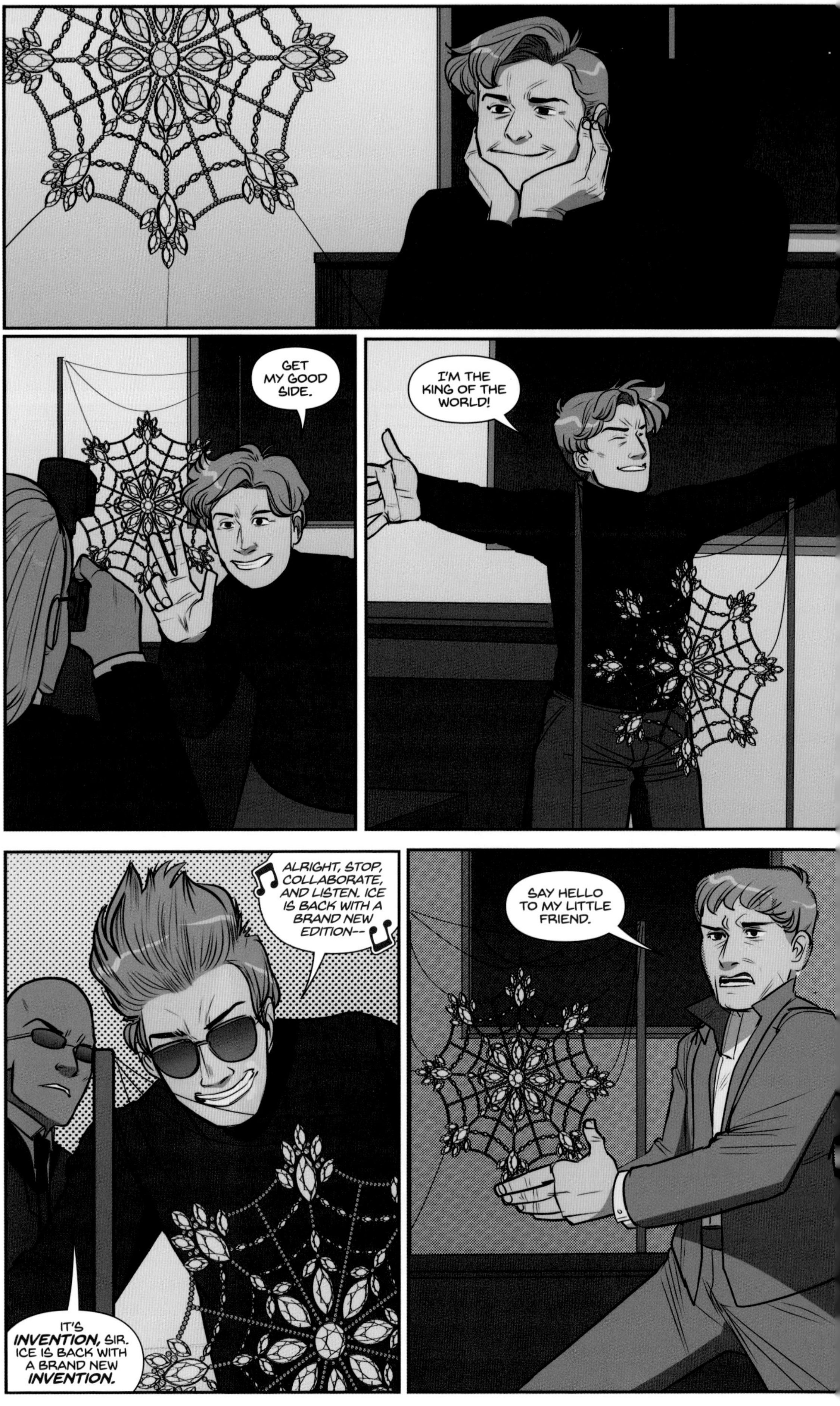
GET MY GOOD SIDE.
I'M THE KING OF THE WORLD!
ALRIGHT, STOP, COLLABORATE, AND LISTEN. ICE IS BACK WITH A BRAND NEW EDITION--
IT'S *INVENTION,* SIR. ICE IS BACK WITH A BRAND NEW *INVENTION.*
SAY HELLO TO MY LITTLE FRIEND.

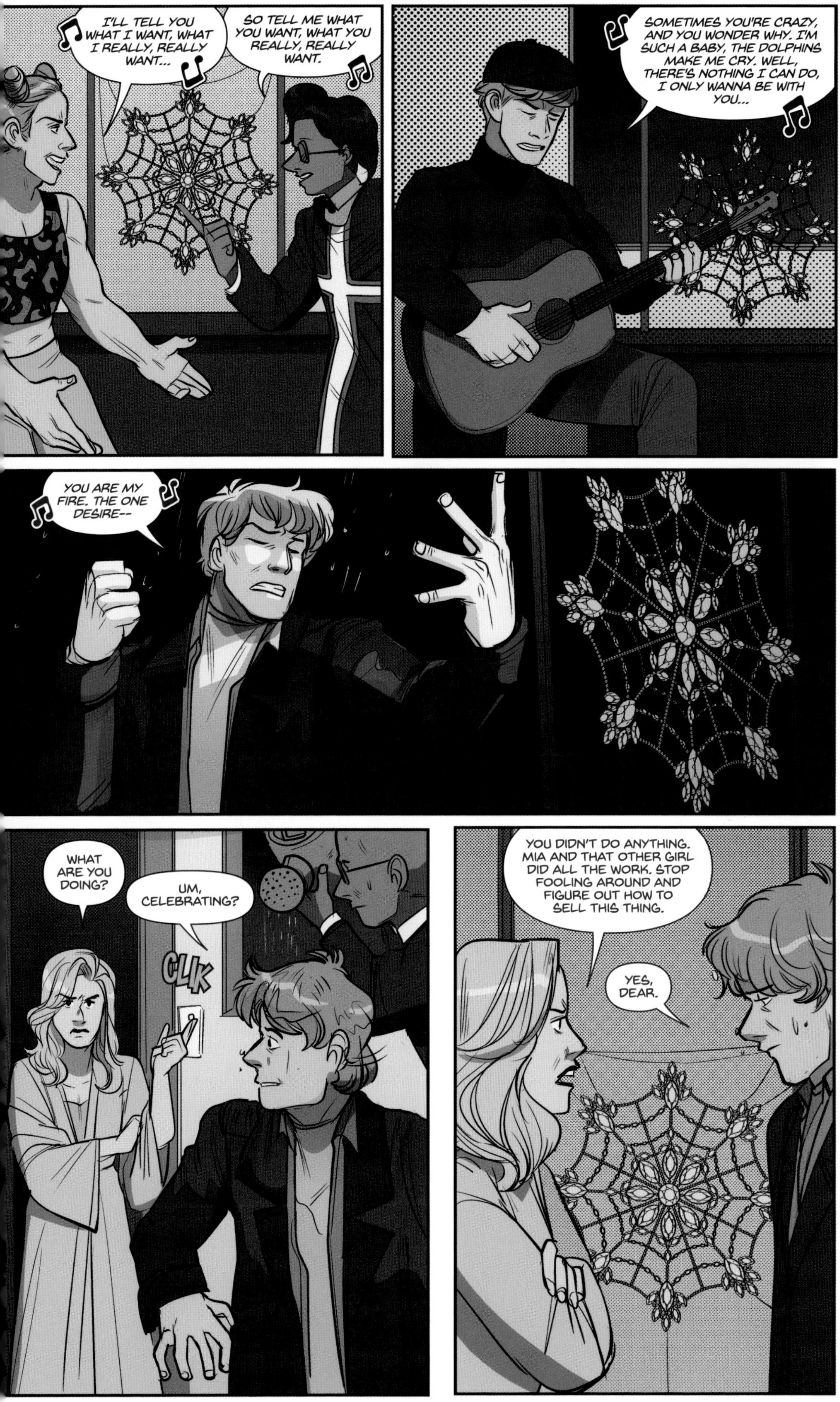
I'LL TELL YOU WHAT I WANT, WHAT I REALLY, REALLY WANT...
SO TELL ME WHAT YOU WANT, WHAT YOU REALLY, REALLY WANT.
SOMETIMES YOU'RE CRAZY, AND YOU WONDER WHY. I'M SUCH A BABY, THE DOLPHINS MAKE ME CRY. WELL, THERE'S NOTHING I CAN DO, I ONLY WANNA BE WITH YOU...
YOU ARE MY FIRE. THE ONE DESIRE--
WHAT ARE YOU DOING?
UM, CELEBRATING?
CLIK
YOU DIDN'T DO ANYTHING. MIA AND THAT OTHER GIRL DID ALL THE WORK. STOP FOOLING AROUND AND FIGURE OUT HOW TO SELL THIS THING.
YES, DEAR.

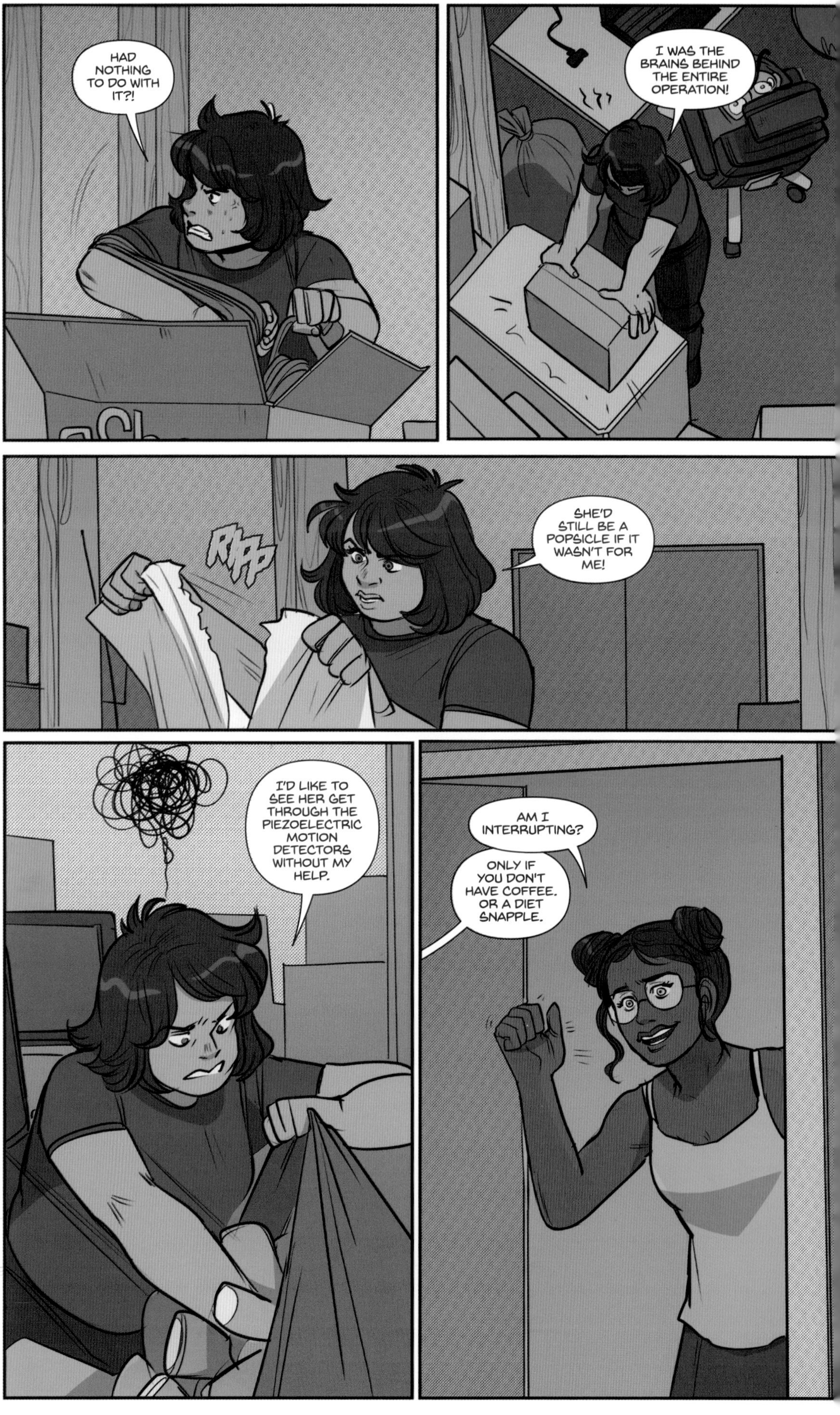
HAD NOTHING TO DO WITH IT?!
I WAS THE BRAINS BEHIND THE ENTIRE OPERATION!
RIPP
SHE'D STILL BE A POPSICLE IF IT WASN'T FOR ME!
I'D LIKE TO SEE HER GET THROUGH THE PIEZOELECTRIC MOTION DETECTORS WITHOUT MY HELP.
AM I INTERRUPTING?
ONLY IF YOU DON'T HAVE COFFEE. OR A DIET SNAPPLE.

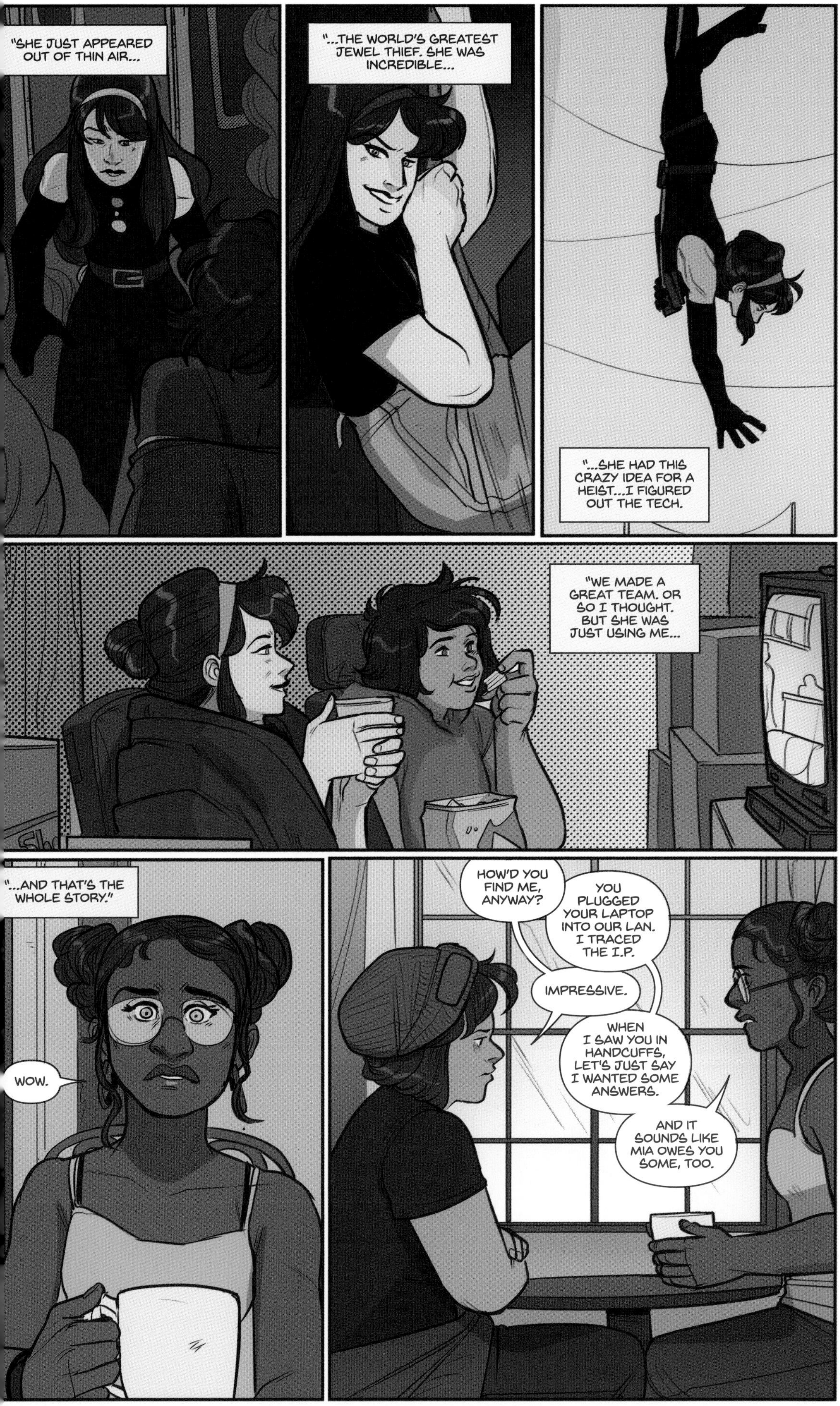
"SHE JUST APPEARED OUT OF THIN AIR...
"...THE WORLD'S GREATEST JEWEL THIEF. SHE WAS INCREDIBLE...
"...SHE HAD THIS CRAZY IDEA FOR A HEIST...I FIGURED OUT THE TECH.
"WE MADE A GREAT TEAM. OR SO I THOUGHT. BUT SHE WAS JUST USING ME...
"...AND THAT'S THE WHOLE STORY."
WOW.
HOW'D YOU FIND ME, ANYWAY?
YOU PLUGGED YOUR LAPTOP INTO OUR LAN. I TRACED THE I.P.
IMPRESSIVE.
WHEN I SAW YOU IN HANDCUFFS, LET'S JUST SAY I WANTED SOME ANSWERS.
AND IT SOUNDS LIKE MIA OWES YOU SOME, TOO.

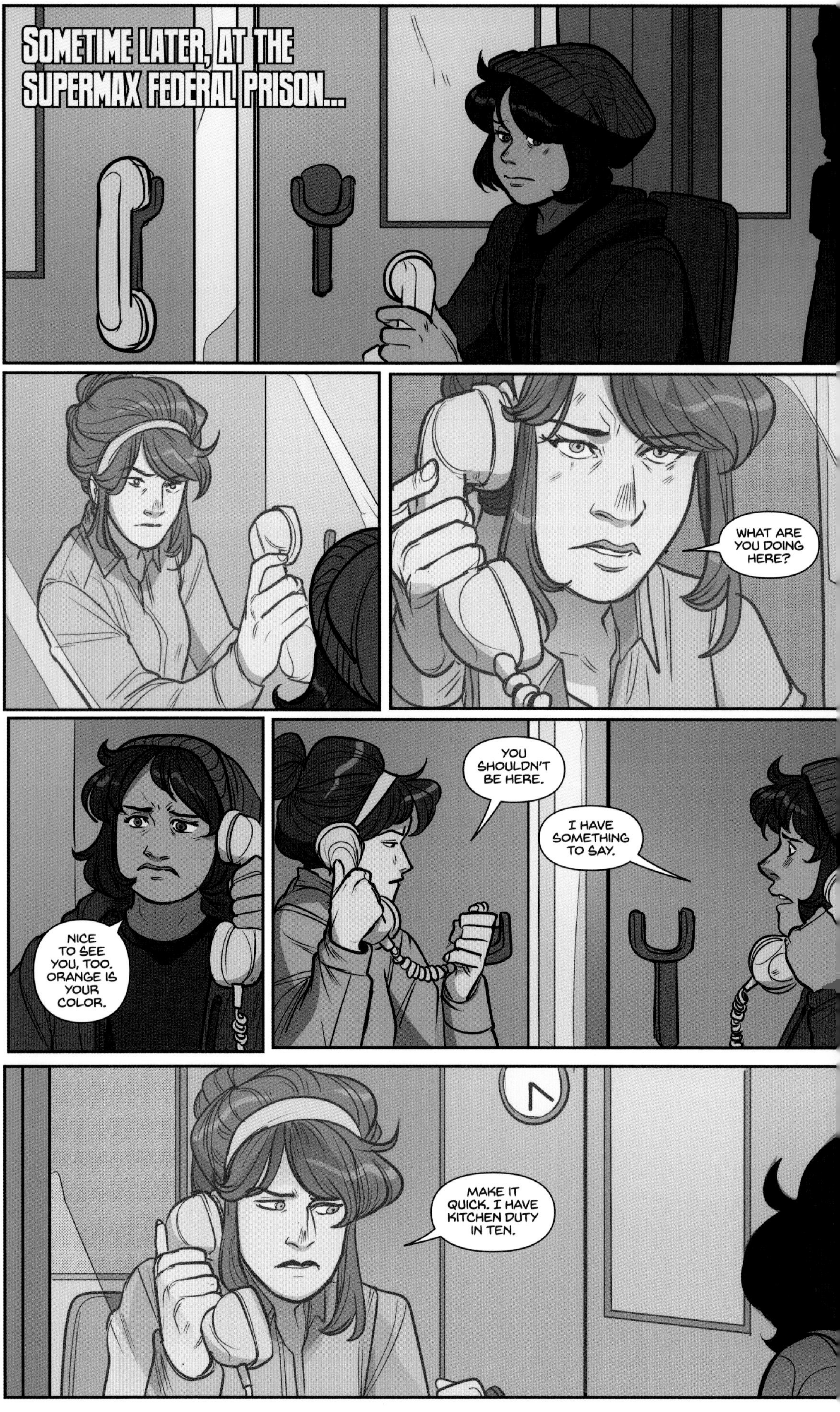
SOMETIME LATER, AT THE SUPERMAX FEDERAL PRISON...
WHAT ARE YOU DOING HERE?
NICE TO SEE YOU, TOO. ORANGE IS YOUR COLOR.
YOU SHOULDN'T BE HERE.
I HAVE SOMETHING TO SAY.
MAKE IT QUICK. I HAVE KITCHEN DUTY IN TEN.

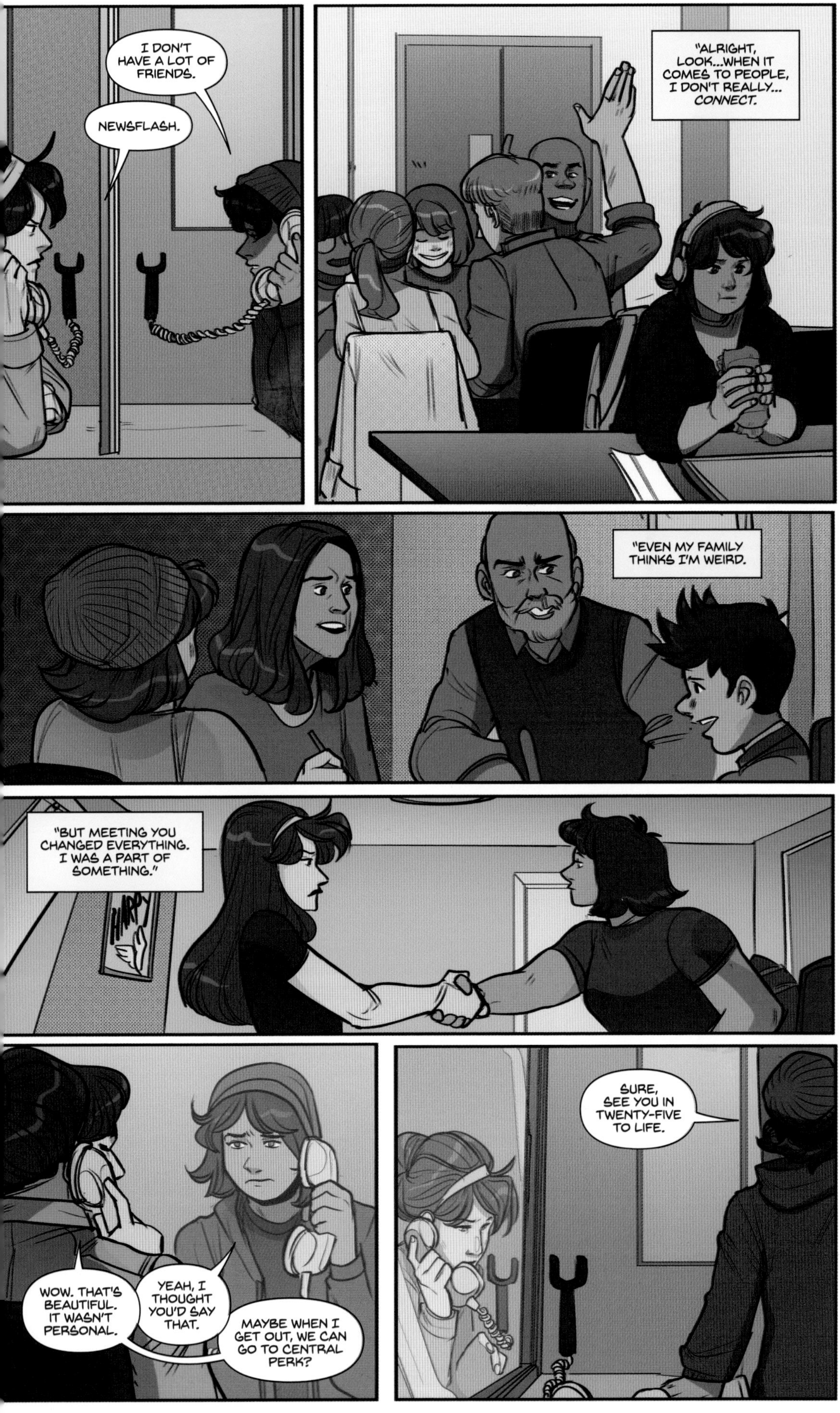
I DON'T HAVE A LOT OF FRIENDS.
NEWSFLASH.
"ALRIGHT, LOOK...WHEN IT COMES TO PEOPLE, I DON'T REALLY... CONNECT.
"EVEN MY FAMILY THINKS I'M WEIRD.
"BUT MEETING YOU CHANGED EVERYTHING. I WAS A PART OF SOMETHING."
HAPPY
WOW. THAT'S BEAUTIFUL. IT WASN'T PERSONAL.
YEAH, I THOUGHT YOU'D SAY THAT.
MAYBE WHEN I GET OUT, WE CAN GO TO CENTRAL PERK?
SURE, SEE YOU IN TWENTY-FIVE TO LIFE.

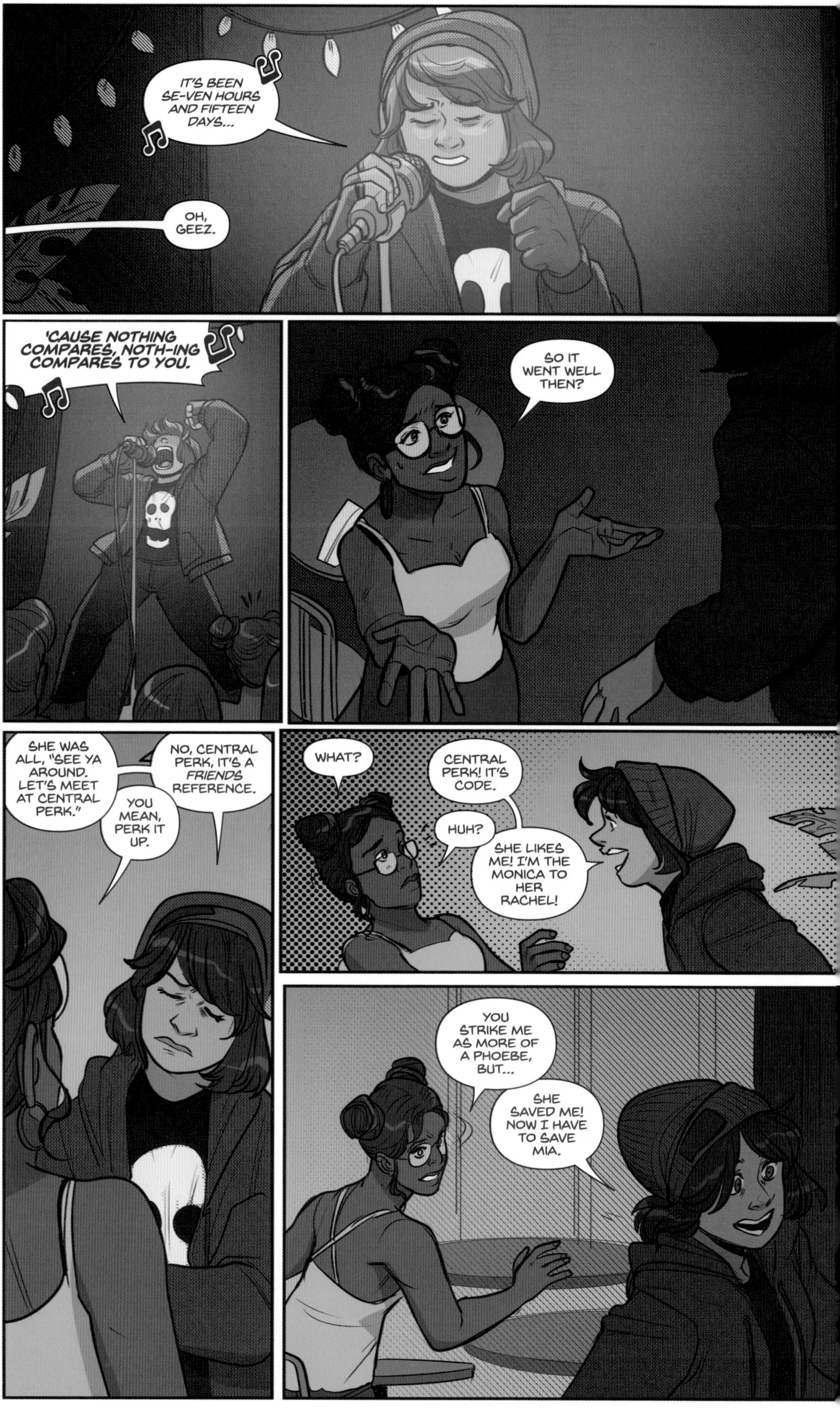
IT'S BEEN SE-VEN HOURS AND FIFTEEN DAYS...
OH, GEEZ.
'CAUSE NOTHING COMPARES, NOTH-ING COMPARES TO YOU.
SO IT WENT WELL THEN?
SHE WAS ALL, "SEE YA AROUND. LET'S MEET AT CENTRAL PERK."
YOU MEAN, PERK IT UP.
NO, CENTRAL PERK, IT'S A *FRIENDS* REFERENCE.
WHAT?
CENTRAL PERK! IT'S CODE.
HUH?
SHE LIKES ME! I'M THE MONICA TO HER RACHEL!
YOU STRIKE ME AS MORE OF A PHOEBE, BUT...
SHE SAVED ME! NOW I HAVE TO SAVE MIA.

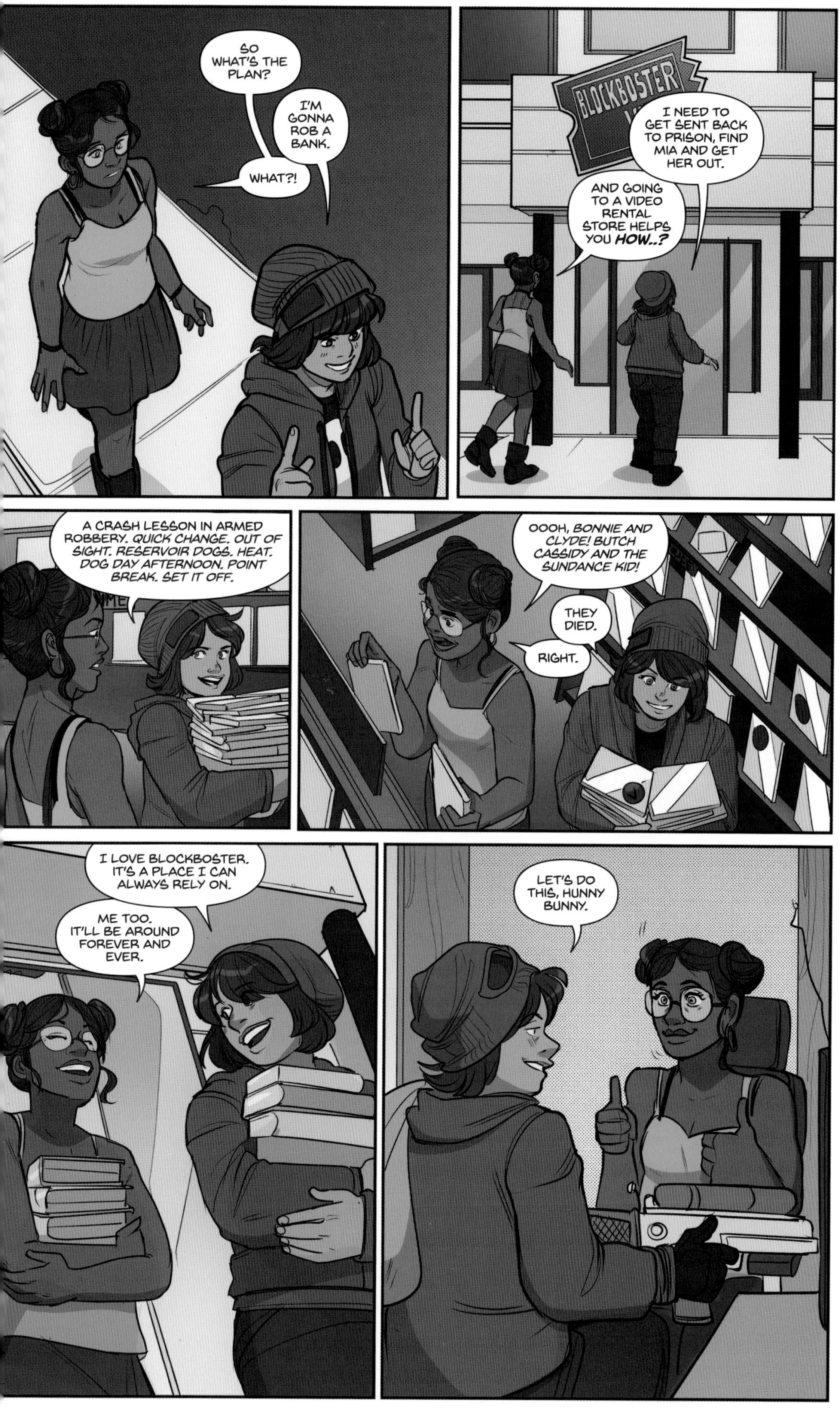
SO WHAT'S THE PLAN?
I'M GONNA ROB A BANK.
WHAT?!
BLOCKBOSTER
I NEED TO GET SENT BACK TO PRISON, FIND MIA AND GET HER OUT.
AND GOING TO A VIDEO RENTAL STORE HELPS YOU *HOW..?*
A CRASH LESSON IN ARMED ROBBERY. *QUICK CHANGE. OUT OF SIGHT. RESERVOIR DOGS. HEAT. DOG DAY AFTERNOON. POINT BREAK. SET IT OFF.*
OOOH, *BONNIE AND CLYDE! BUTCH CASSIDY AND THE SUNDANCE KID!*
THEY DIED.
RIGHT.
I LOVE BLOCKBOSTER. IT'S A PLACE I CAN ALWAYS RELY ON.
ME TOO. IT'LL BE AROUND FOREVER AND EVER.
LET'S DO THIS, HUNNY BUNNY.

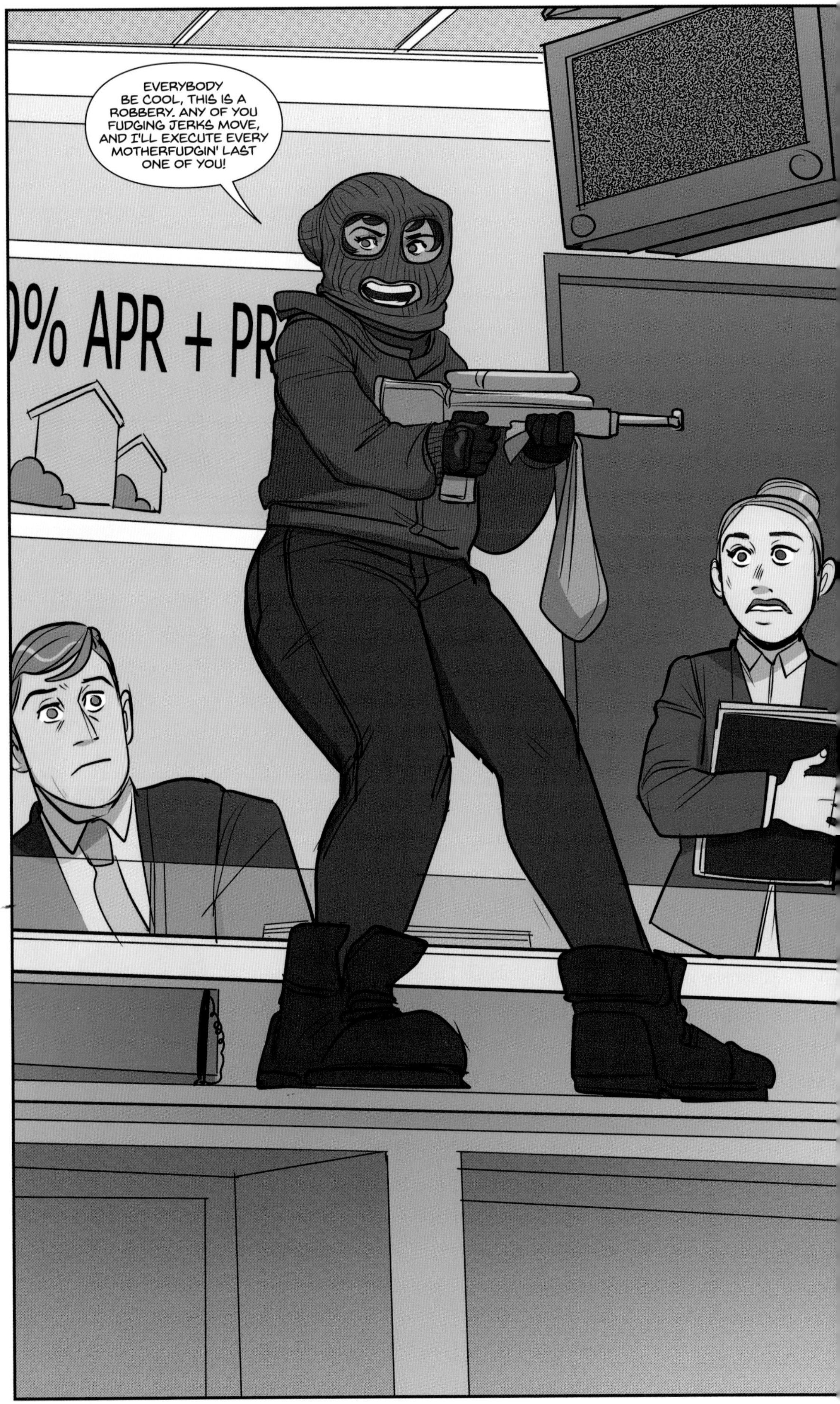
EVERYBODY BE COOL, THIS IS A ROBBERY. ANY OF YOU FUDGING JERKS MOVE, AND I'LL EXECUTE EVERY MOTHERFUDGIN' LAST ONE OF YOU!
0% APR + PR

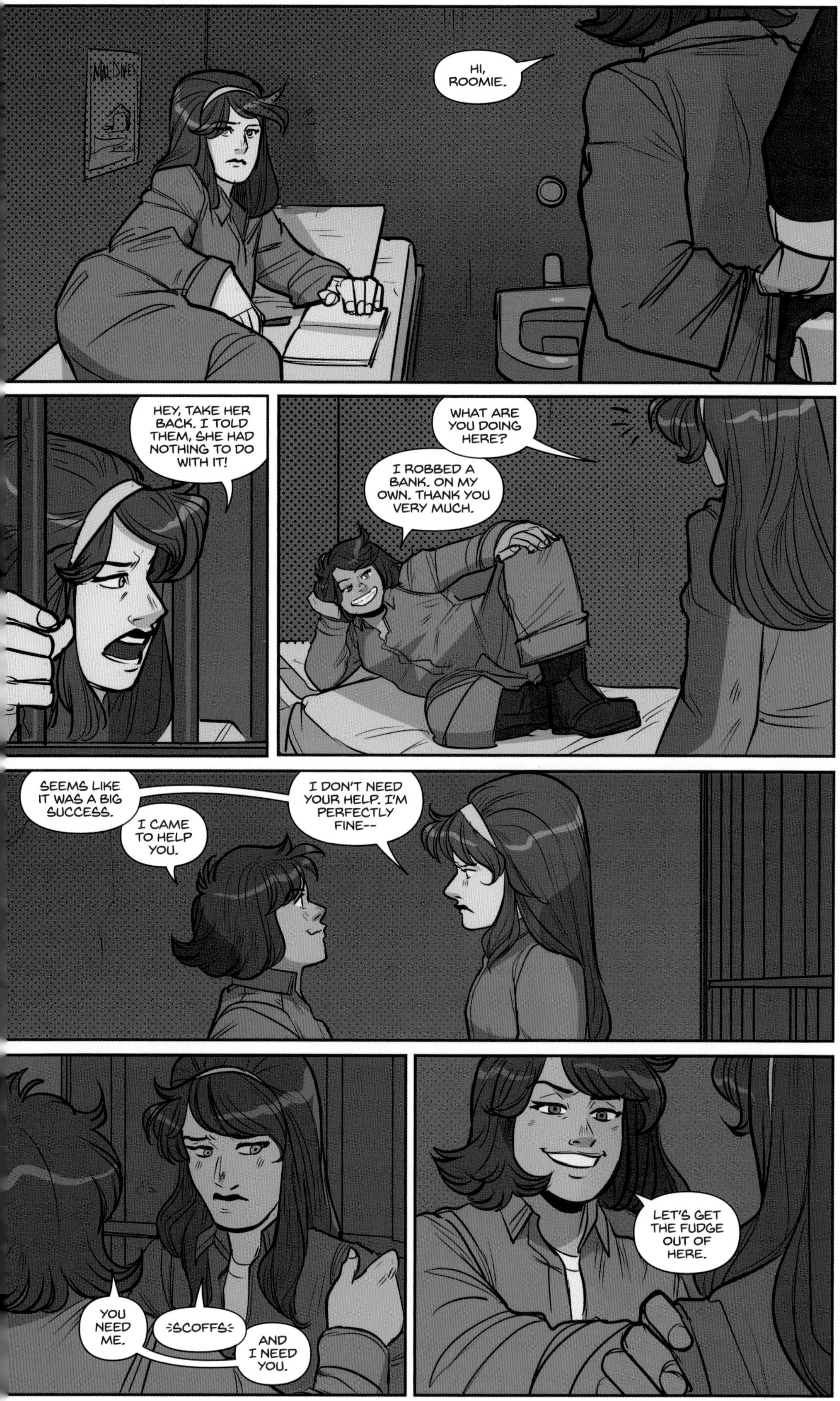
HI, ROOMIE.
HEY, TAKE HER BACK. I TOLD THEM, SHE HAD NOTHING TO DO WITH IT!
WHAT ARE YOU DOING HERE?
I ROBBED A BANK. ON MY OWN. THANK YOU VERY MUCH.
SEEMS LIKE IT WAS A BIG SUCCESS.
I CAME TO HELP YOU.
I DON'T NEED YOUR HELP. I'M PERFECTLY FINE--
YOU NEED ME.
SCOFFS
AND I NEED YOU.
LET'S GET THE FUDGE OUT OF HERE.

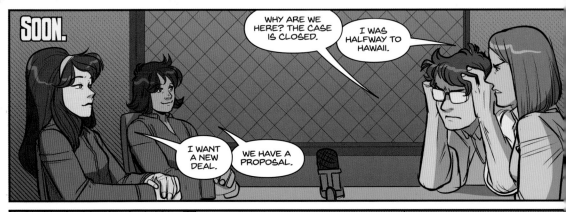

SOON.

WHY ARE WE HERE? THE CASE IS CLOSED.

I WAS HALFWAY TO HAWAII.

I WANT A NEW DEAL.

WE HAVE A PROPOSAL.

NO WAY! YOU MADE A FULL CONFESSION.

ACTUALLY, I DIDN'T CONFESS TO ANYTHING.

I DON'T HAVE THE NET. BUT WE KNOW WHO DOES.

WE'LL GET IT BACK. HELP YOU AVOID AN INTERNATIONAL PUBLIC RELATIONS SCANDAL. AND WE BOTH WALK. SCOT FREE. NO CHARGES.

AND MY MOM, SHE GOES FREE, TOO.

NO WAY.

FORGET IT!

THEN NO DEAL.

...

COULD YOU TWO BE MORE CONSPICUOUS?

PIPE DOWN BACK THERE.

OOOH, CAN WE ORDER TAKE OUT?

PIZZA!

NO ONE'S ORDERING FOOD!

I COULD GO FOR SOME MOZZ STICKS.

YAY. EXTRA RANCH, PLEASE.

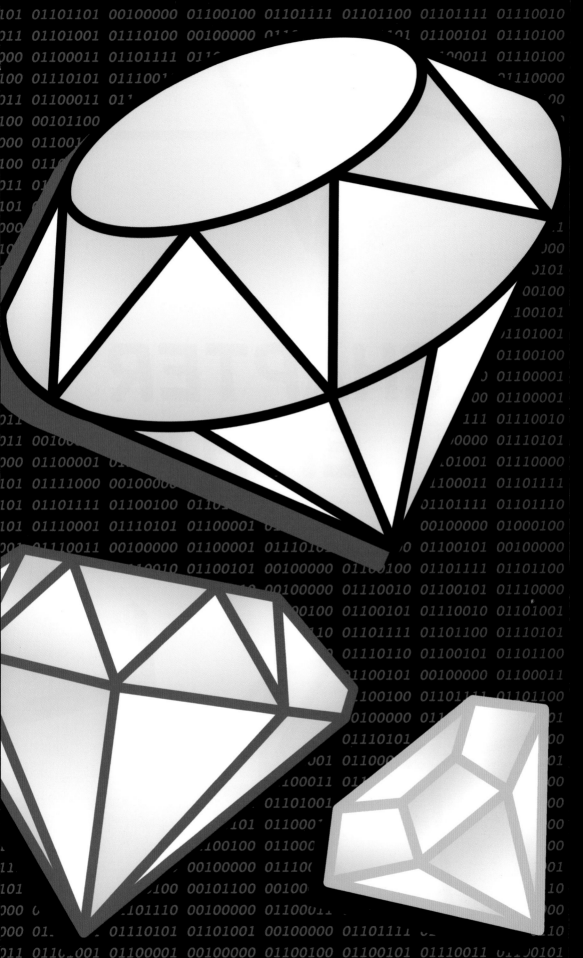

CHAPTER EIGHT

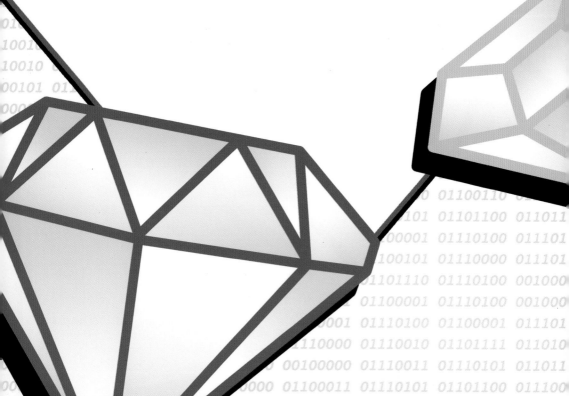

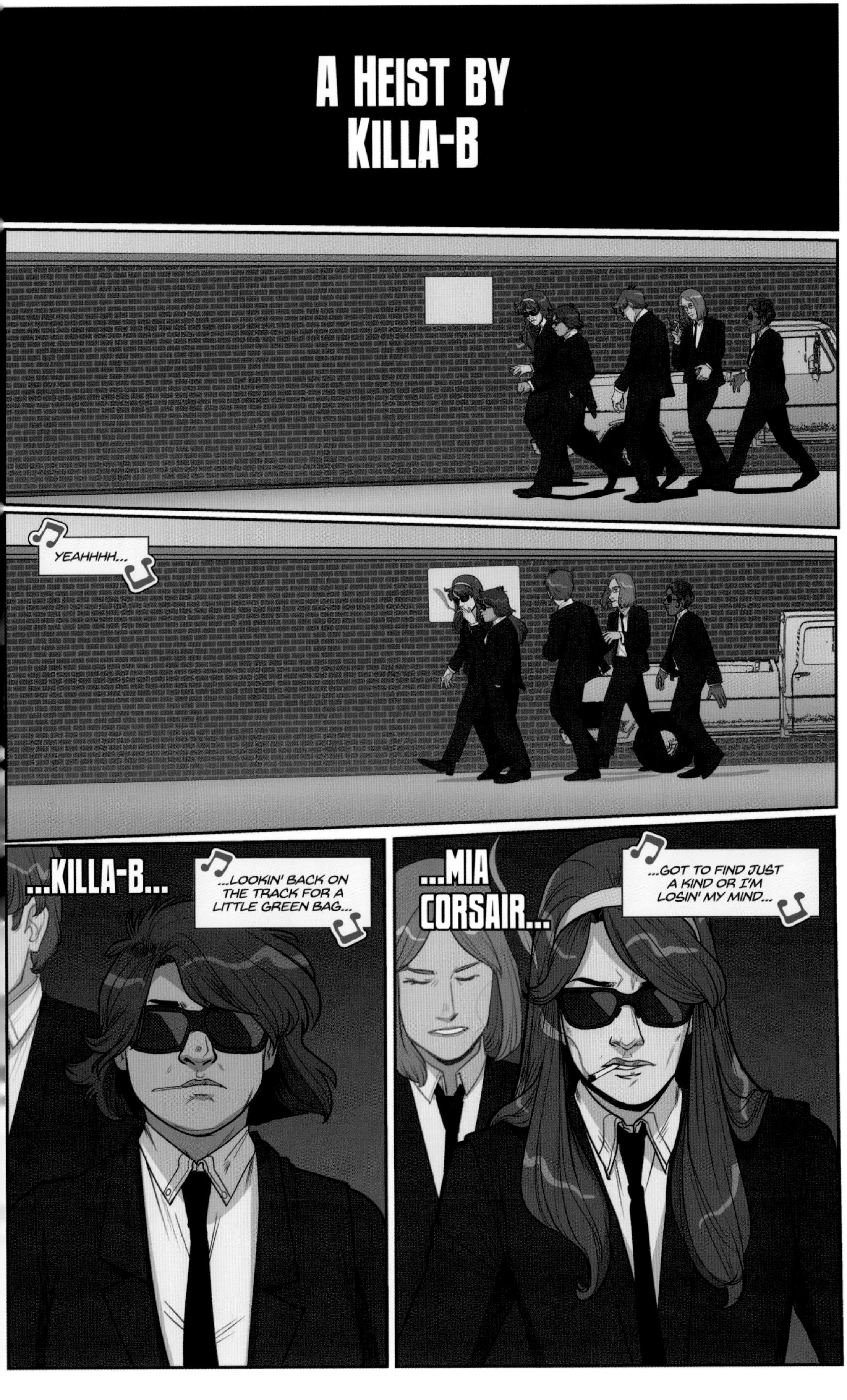
A HEIST BY
KILLA-B
YEAHHHH...
...KILLA-B...
...LOOKIN' BACK ON THE TRACK FOR A LITTLE GREEN BAG...
...MIA CORSAIR...
...GOT TO FIND JUST A KIND OR I'M LOSIN' MY MIND...

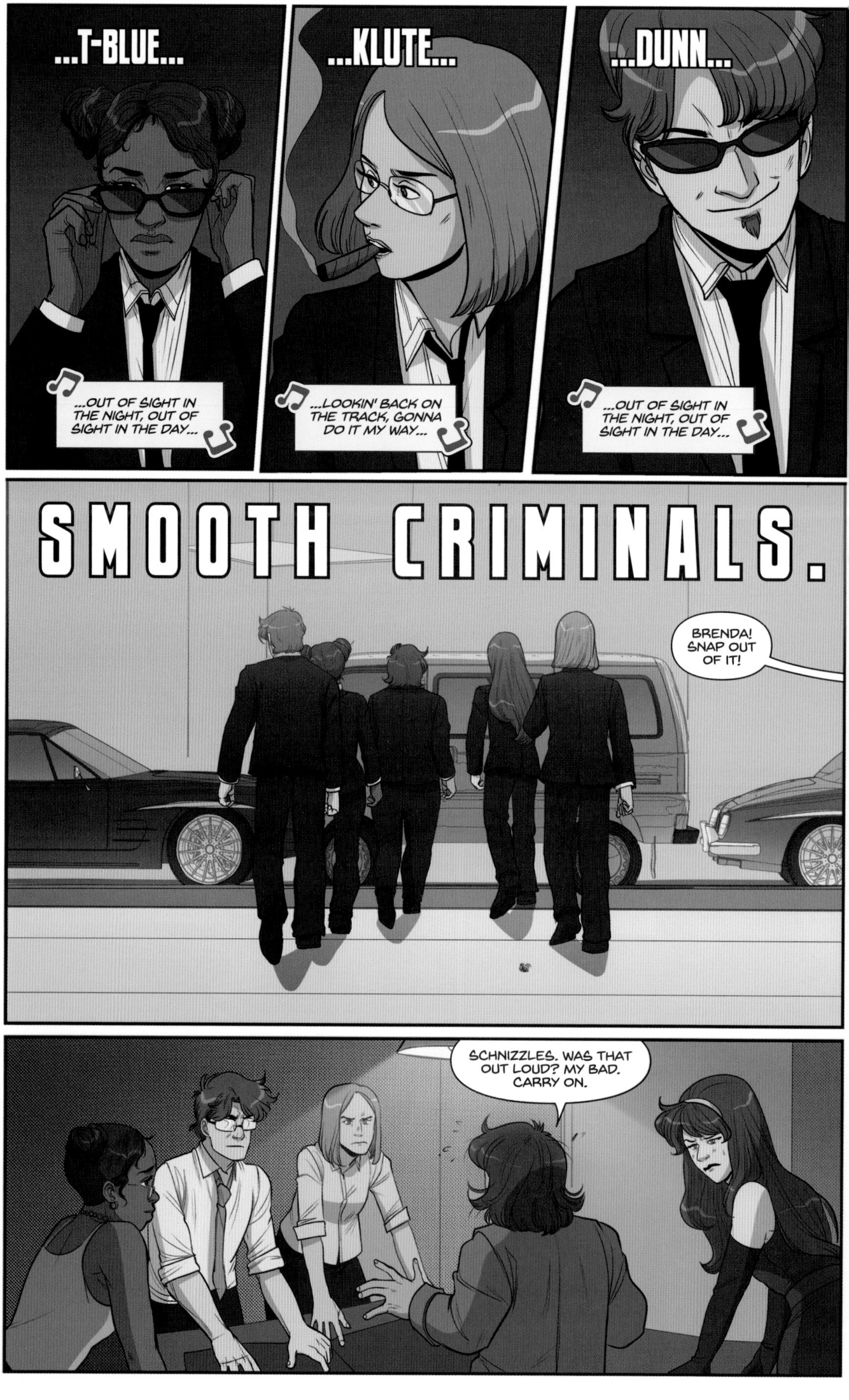
...T-BLUE...
...OUT OF SIGHT IN THE NIGHT, OUT OF SIGHT IN THE DAY...
...KLUTE...
...LOOKIN' BACK ON THE TRACK, GONNA DO IT MY WAY...
...DUNN...
...OUT OF SIGHT IN THE NIGHT, OUT OF SIGHT IN THE DAY...
SMOOTH CRIMINALS.
BRENDA! SNAP OUT OF IT!
SCHNIZZLES. WAS THAT OUT LOUD? MY BAD. CARRY ON.

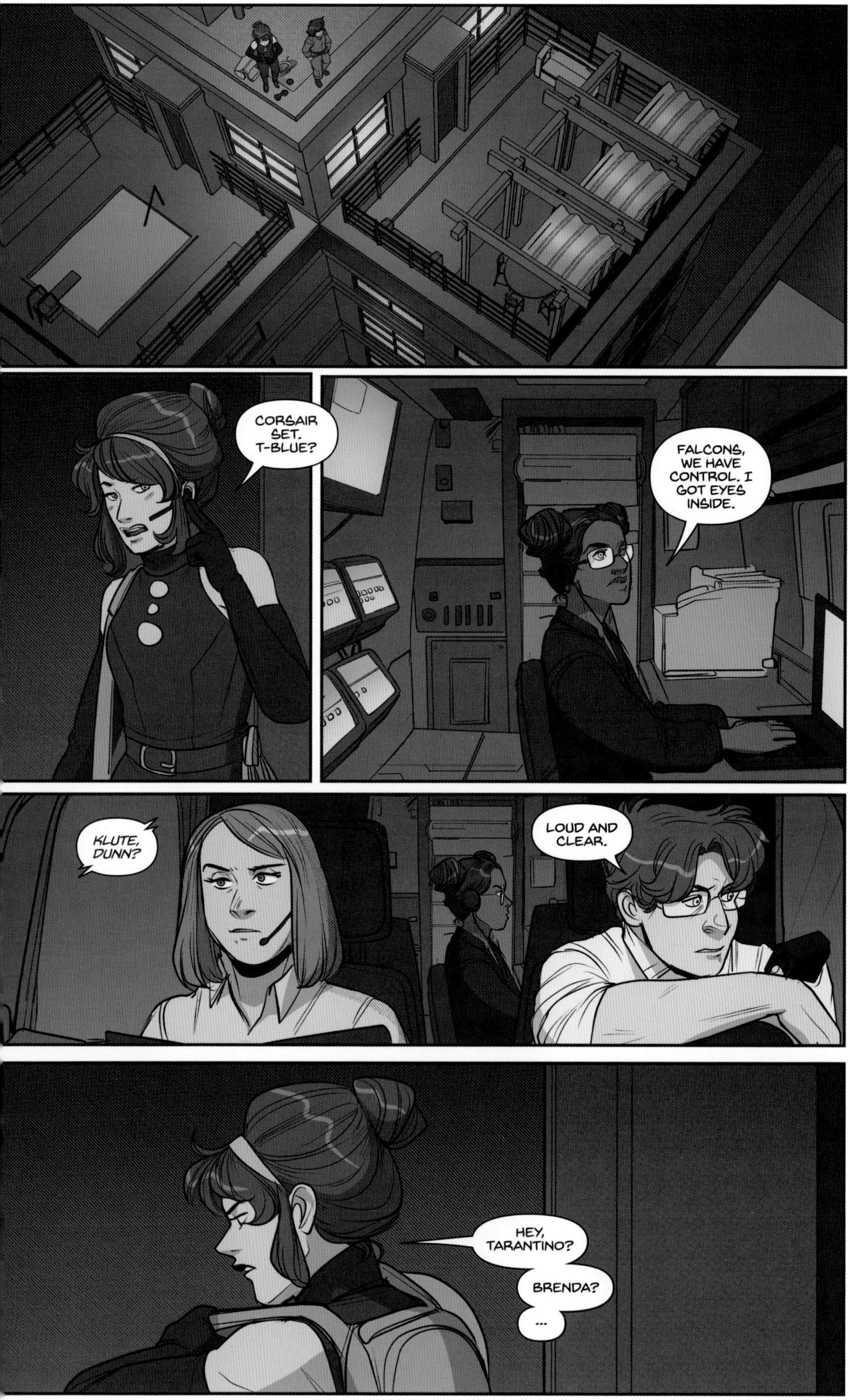
CORSAIR SET. T-BLUE?
FALCONS, WE HAVE CONTROL. I GOT EYES INSIDE.
KLUTE, DUNN?
LOUD AND CLEAR.
HEY, TARANTINO?
BRENDA?
...

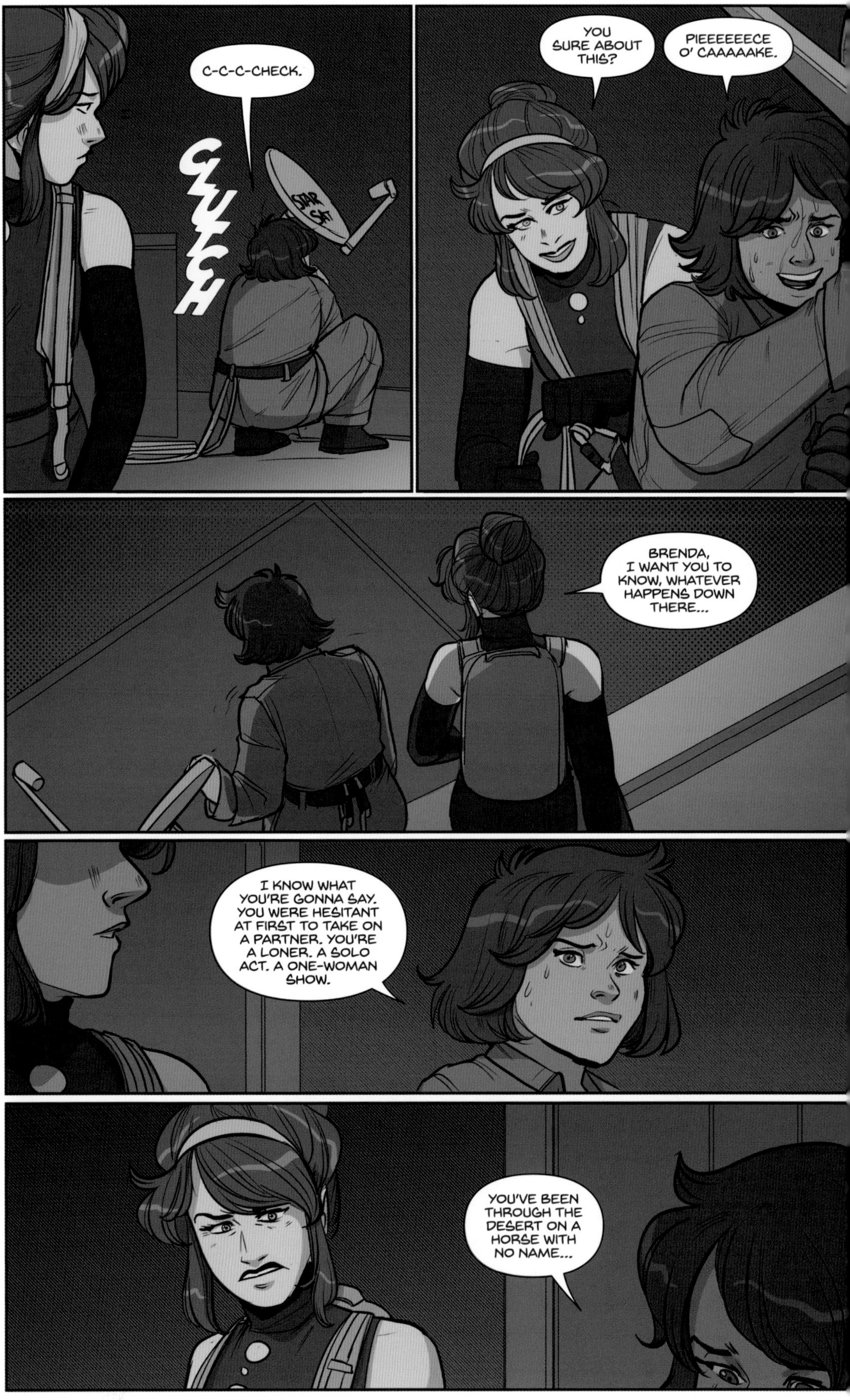

C-C-C-CHECK.
CLUNCH
YOU SURE ABOUT THIS?
PIEEEEEECE O' CAAAAAKE.
BRENDA, I WANT YOU TO KNOW, WHATEVER HAPPENS DOWN THERE...
I KNOW WHAT YOU'RE GONNA SAY. YOU WERE HESITANT AT FIRST TO TAKE ON A PARTNER. YOU'RE A LONER. A SOLO ACT. A ONE-WOMAN SHOW.
YOU'VE BEEN THROUGH THE DESERT ON A HORSE WITH NO NAME...

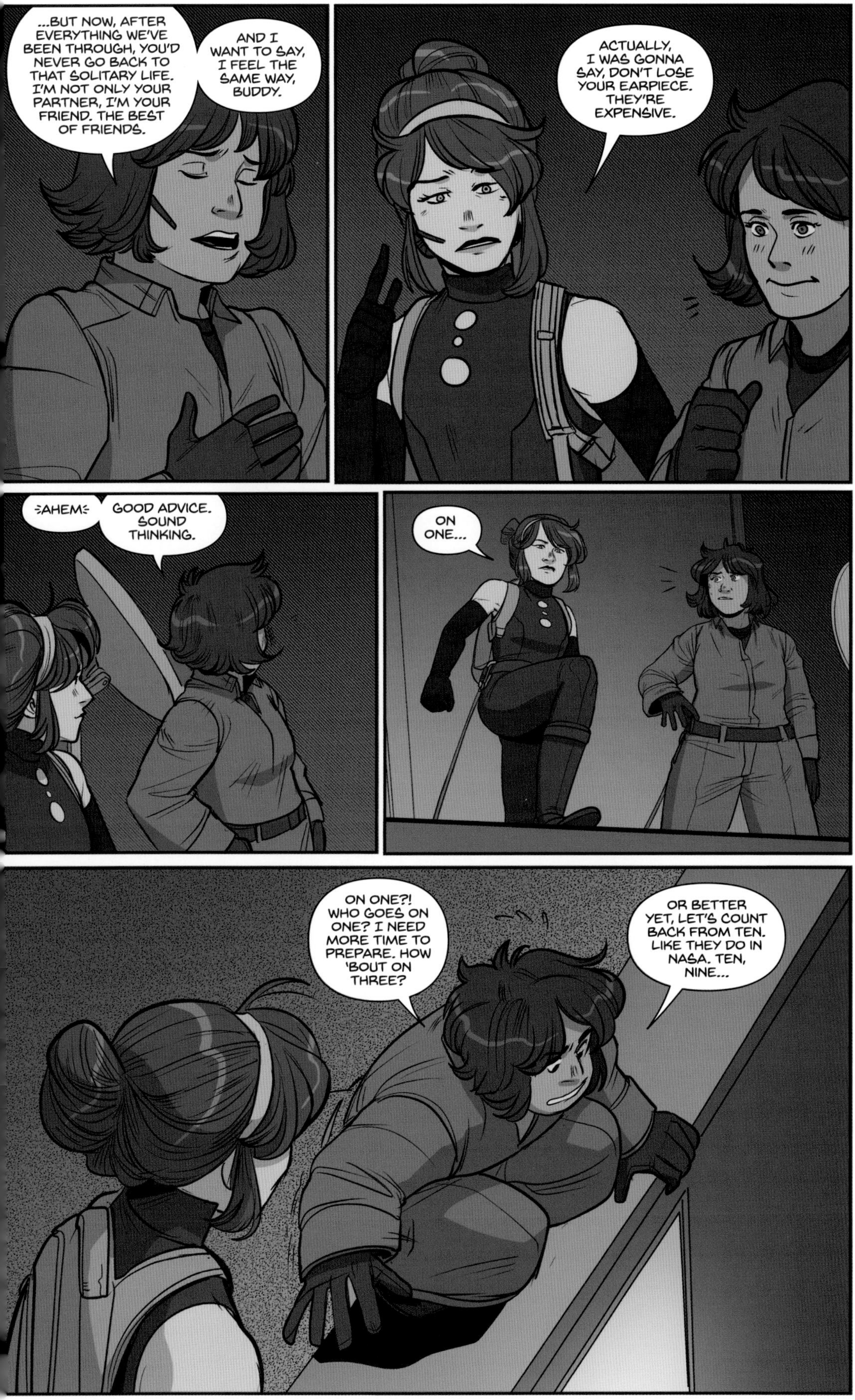

...BUT NOW, AFTER EVERYTHING WE'VE BEEN THROUGH, YOU'D NEVER GO BACK TO THAT SOLITARY LIFE. I'M NOT ONLY YOUR PARTNER, I'M YOUR FRIEND. THE BEST OF FRIENDS.
AND I WANT TO SAY, I FEEL THE SAME WAY, BUDDY.
ACTUALLY, I WAS GONNA SAY, DON'T LOSE YOUR EARPIECE. THEY'RE EXPENSIVE.
AHEM
GOOD ADVICE. SOUND THINKING.
ON ONE...
ON ONE?! WHO GOES ON ONE? I NEED MORE TIME TO PREPARE. HOW 'BOUT ON THREE?
OR BETTER YET, LET'S COUNT BACK FROM TEN. LIKE THEY DO IN NASA. TEN, NINE...

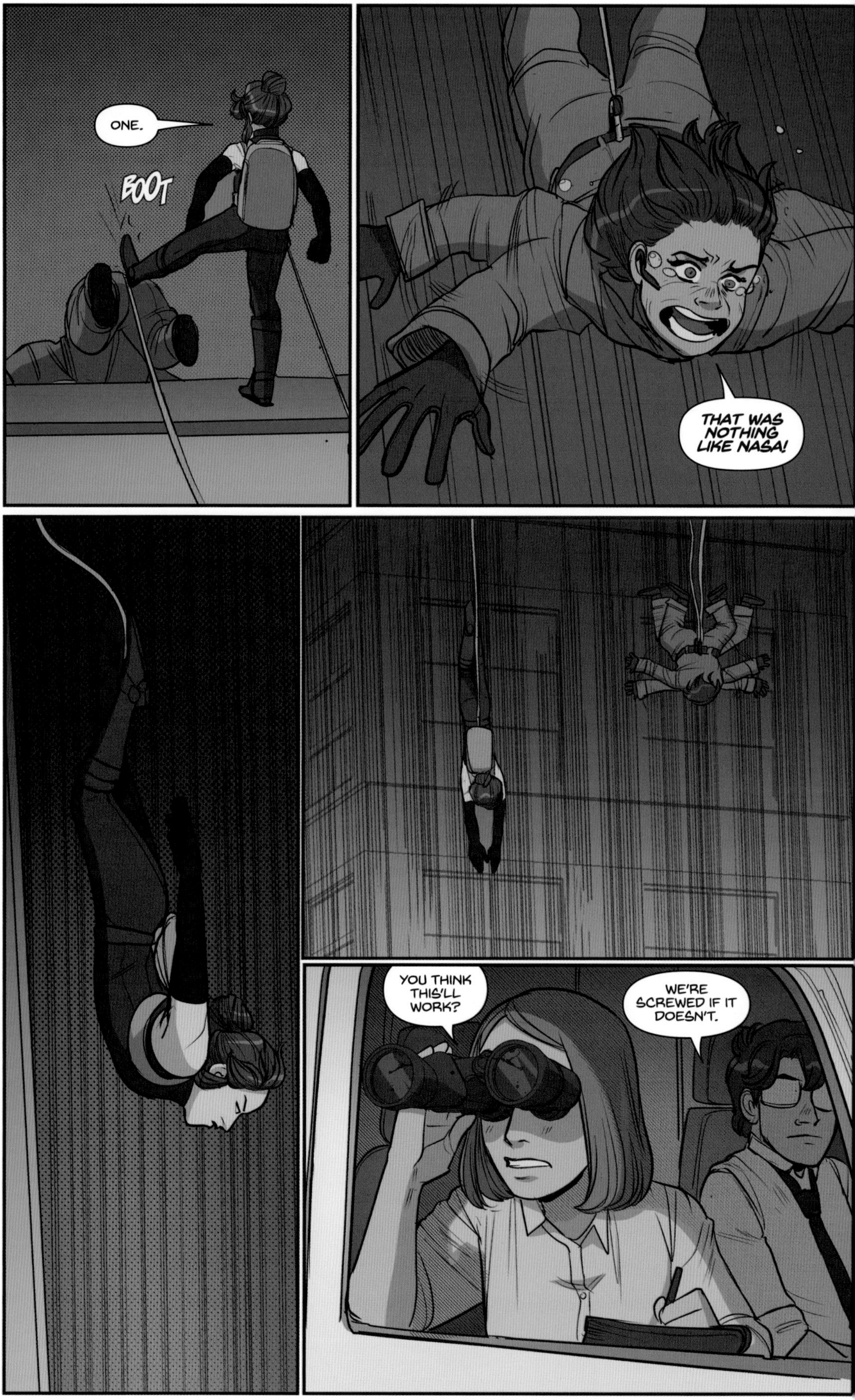
ONE.
BOOT
THAT WAS NOTHING LIKE NASA!
YOU THINK THIS'LL WORK?
WE'RE SCREWED IF IT DOESN'T.

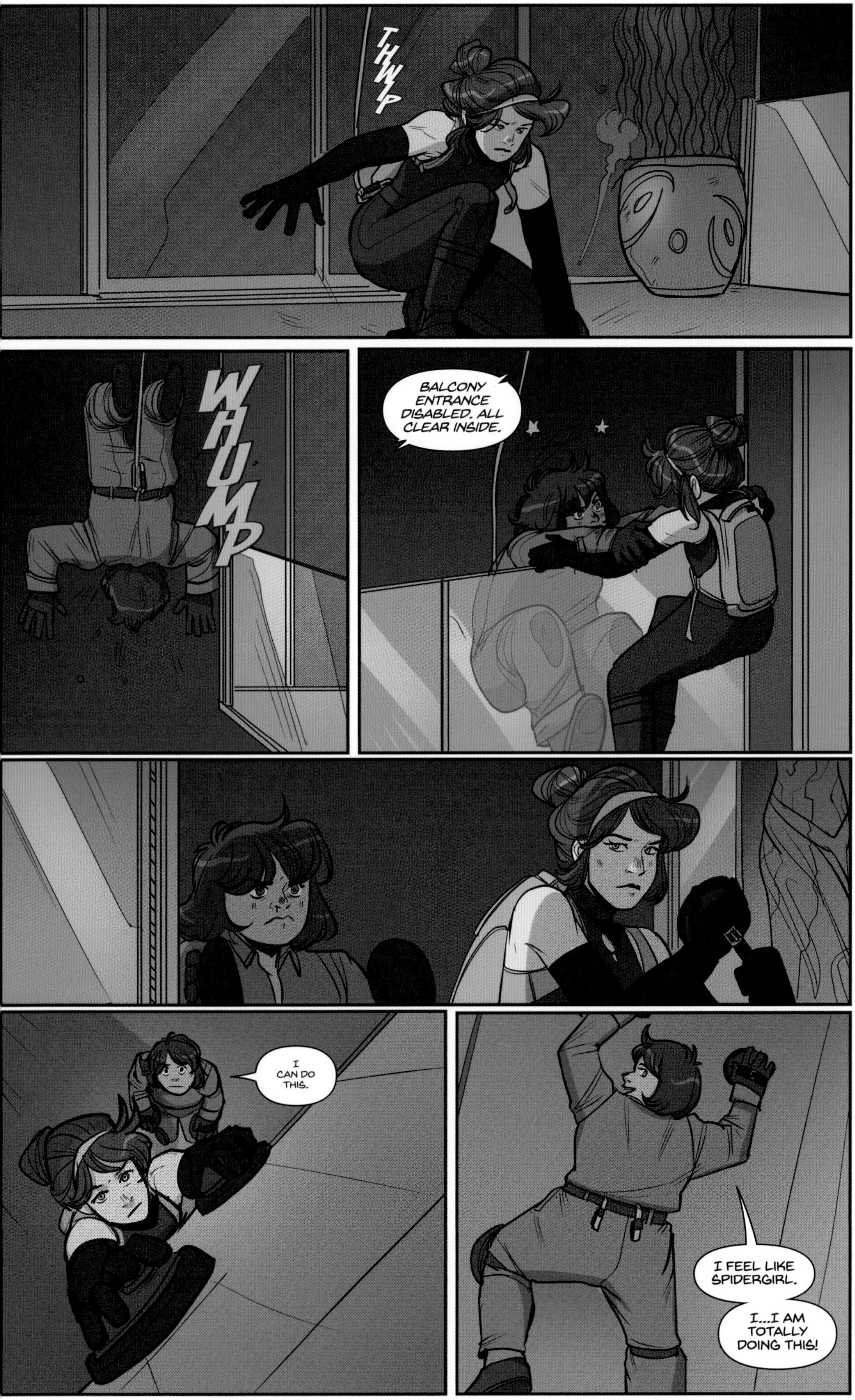
THWIP
WHUMP
BALCONY ENTRANCE DISABLED. ALL CLEAR INSIDE.
I CAN DO THIS.
I FEEL LIKE SPIDERGIRL.
I...I AM TOTALLY DOING THIS!

RICH PEOPLE, MAN. THIS IS THE LIFE.

A FRUIT FIT CRUSHER 5000! THIS GUY REALLY IS LOADED.

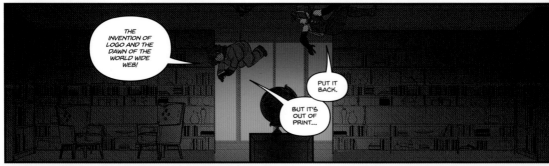

THE INVENTION OF LOGO AND THE DAWN OF THE WORLD WIDE WEB!

PUT IT BACK.

BUT IT'S OUT OF PRINT...

OOOOH, I BET TOMB RAIDER IS EPIC ON THIS.

MOVE ALONG.

ONE GAME?!

I'M A WORLD-CLASS POOL SHARK.

WHY DOESN'T THAT SURPRISE ME?

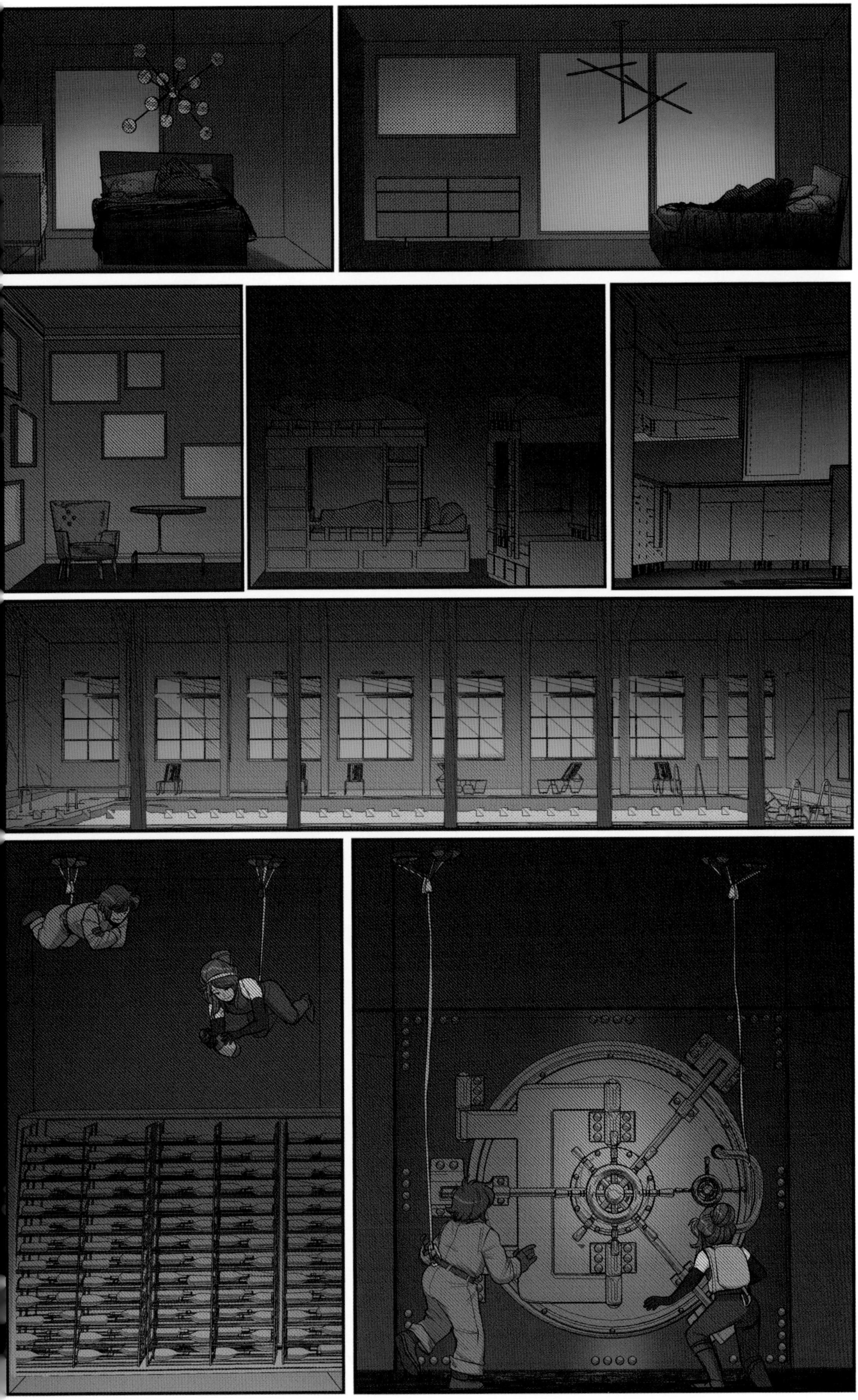

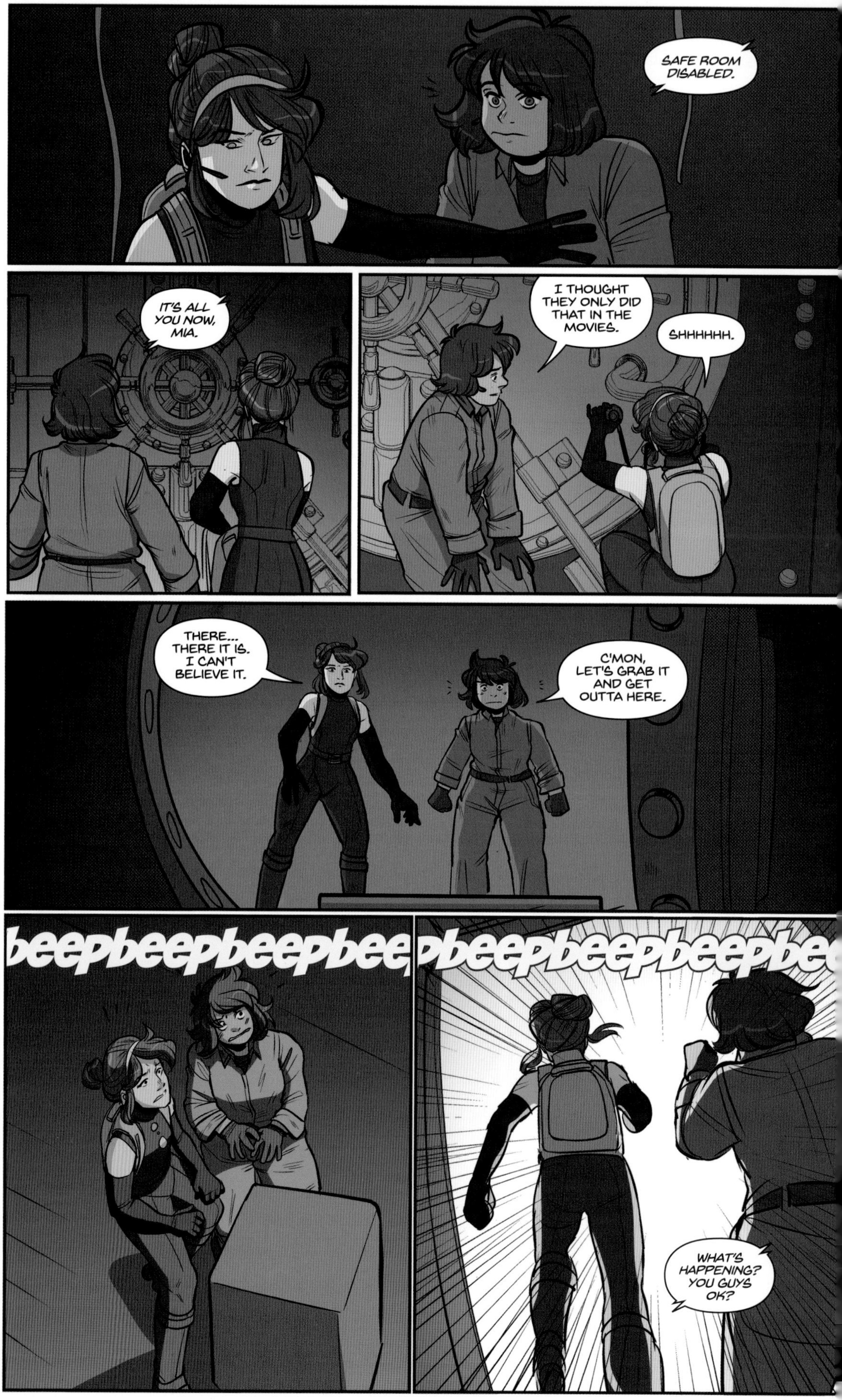
SAFE ROOM DISABLED.
IT'S ALL YOU NOW, MIA.
I THOUGHT THEY ONLY DID THAT IN THE MOVIES.
SHHHHHH.
THERE... THERE IT IS. I CAN'T BELIEVE IT.
C'MON, LET'S GRAB IT AND GET OUTTA HERE.
beepbeepbeepbee
pbeepbeepbeepbe
WHAT'S HAPPENING? YOU GUYS OK?

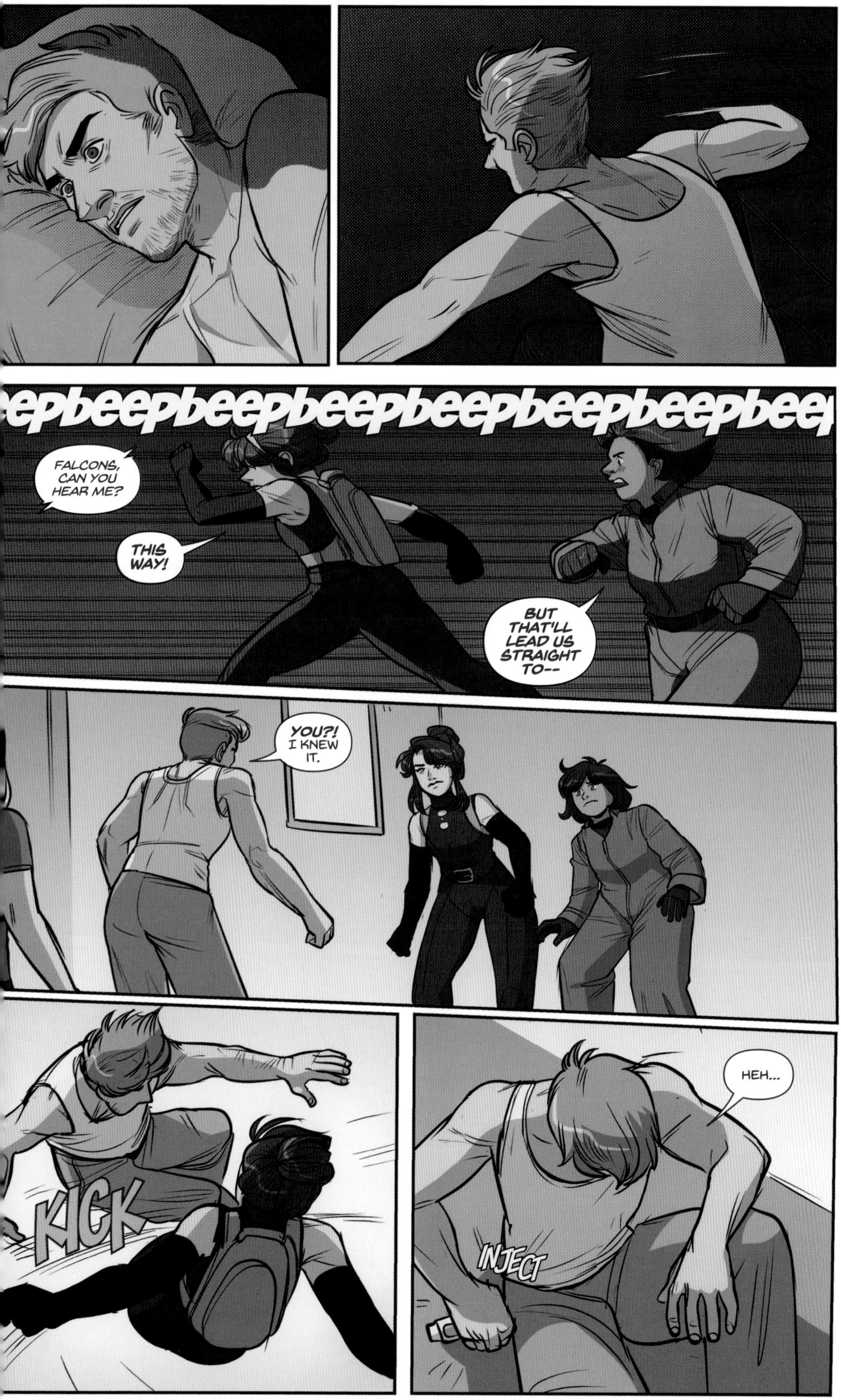
epbeepbeepbeepbeepbeepbeepbeepbeep
FALCONS, CAN YOU HEAR ME?
THIS WAY!
BUT THAT'LL LEAD US STRAIGHT TO--
YOU?! I KNEW IT.
KICK
HEH...
INJECT

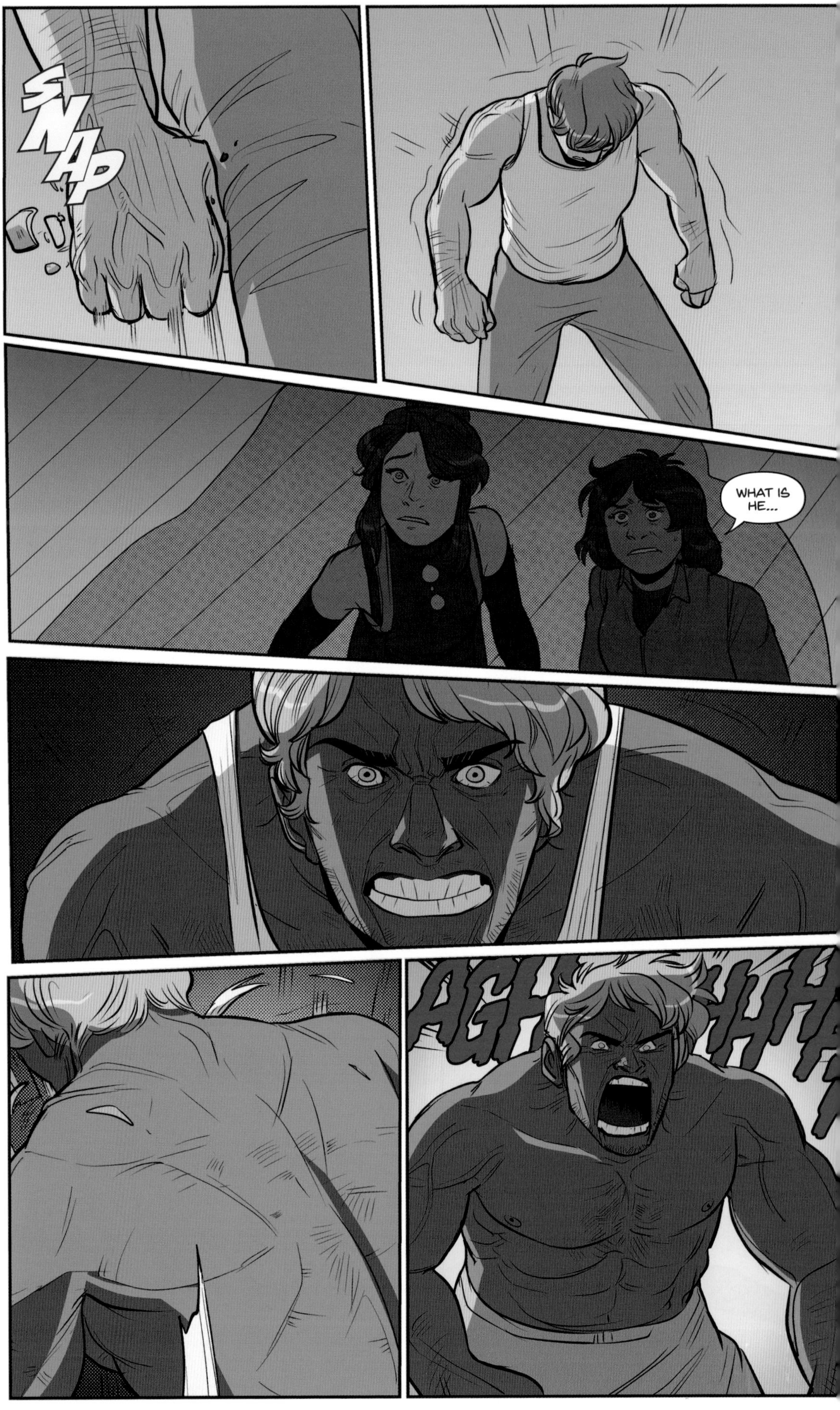
SNAP
WHAT IS HE...

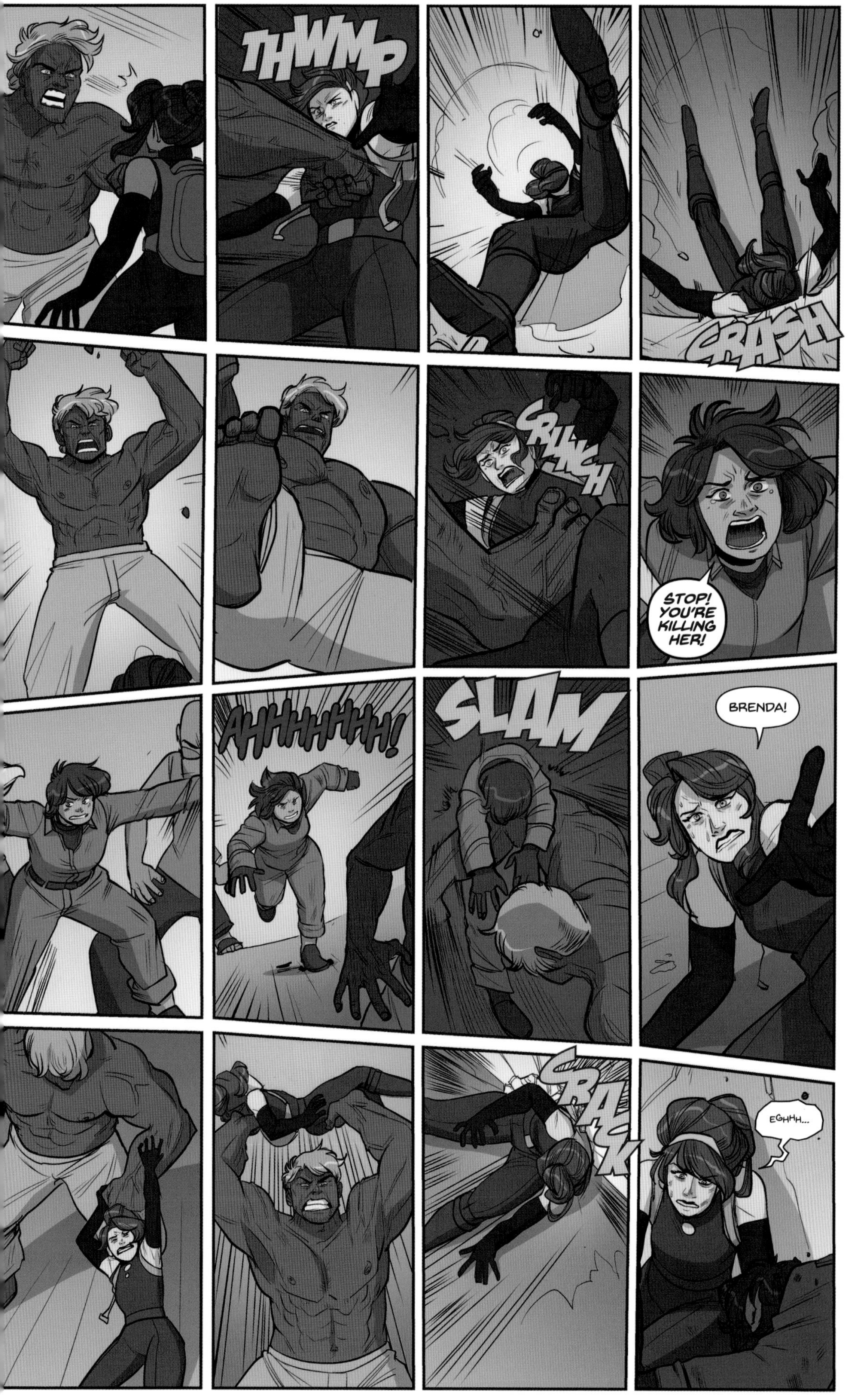
THWMP
CRASH
CRUNCH
STOP! YOU'RE KILLING HER!
AHHHHHHH!
SLAM
BRENDA!
CRAK
EGHHH...

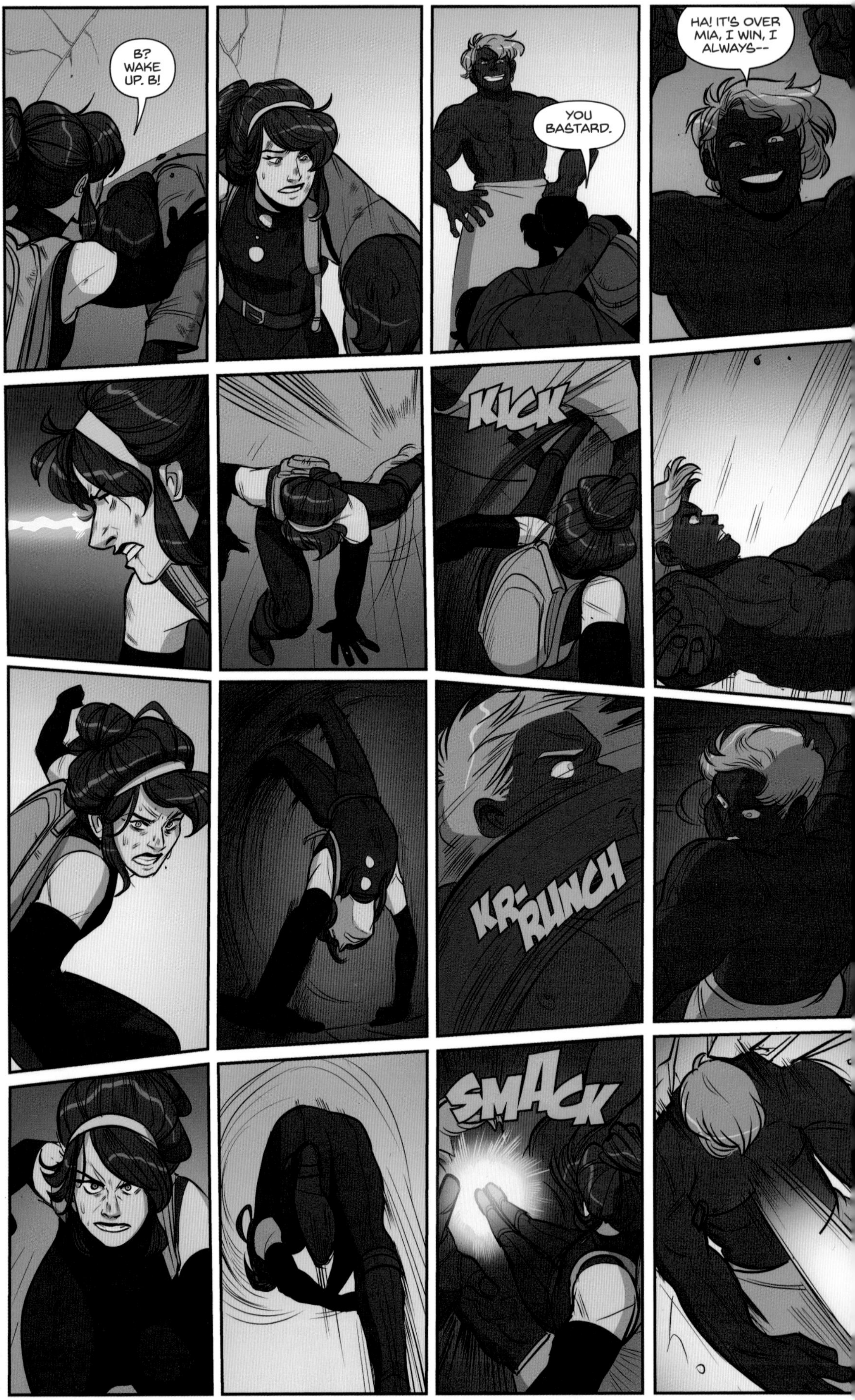
B? WAKE UP. B!
YOU BASTARD.
HA! IT'S OVER MIA, I WIN, I ALWAYS--
KICK
KR-RUNCH
SMACK

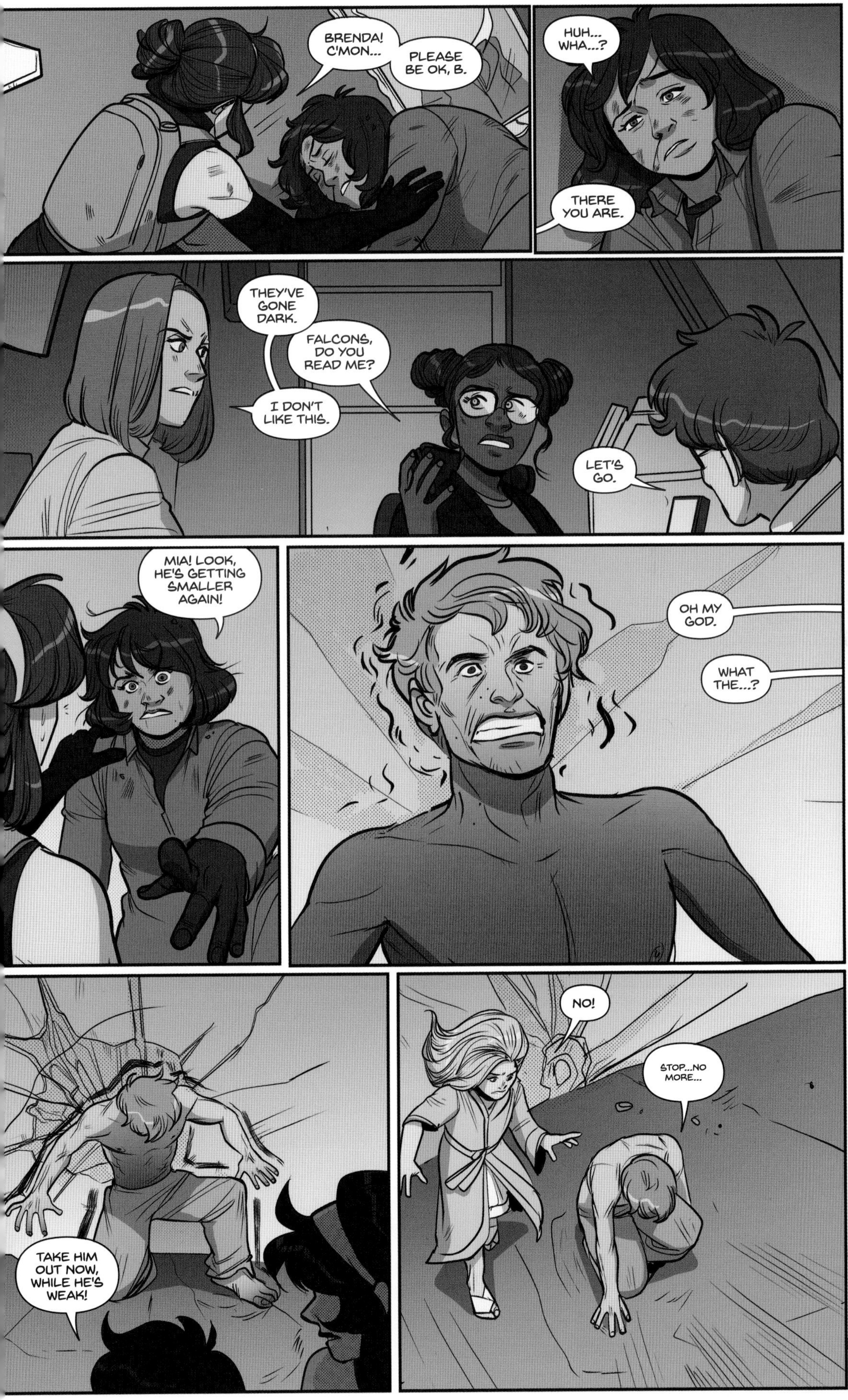
BRENDA! C'MON...
PLEASE BE OK, B.
HUH... WHA...?
THERE YOU ARE.
THEY'VE GONE DARK.
FALCONS, DO YOU READ ME?
I DON'T LIKE THIS.
LET'S GO.
MIA! LOOK, HE'S GETTING SMALLER AGAIN!
OH MY GOD.
WHAT THE...?
TAKE HIM OUT NOW, WHILE HE'S WEAK!
NO!
STOP...NO MORE...

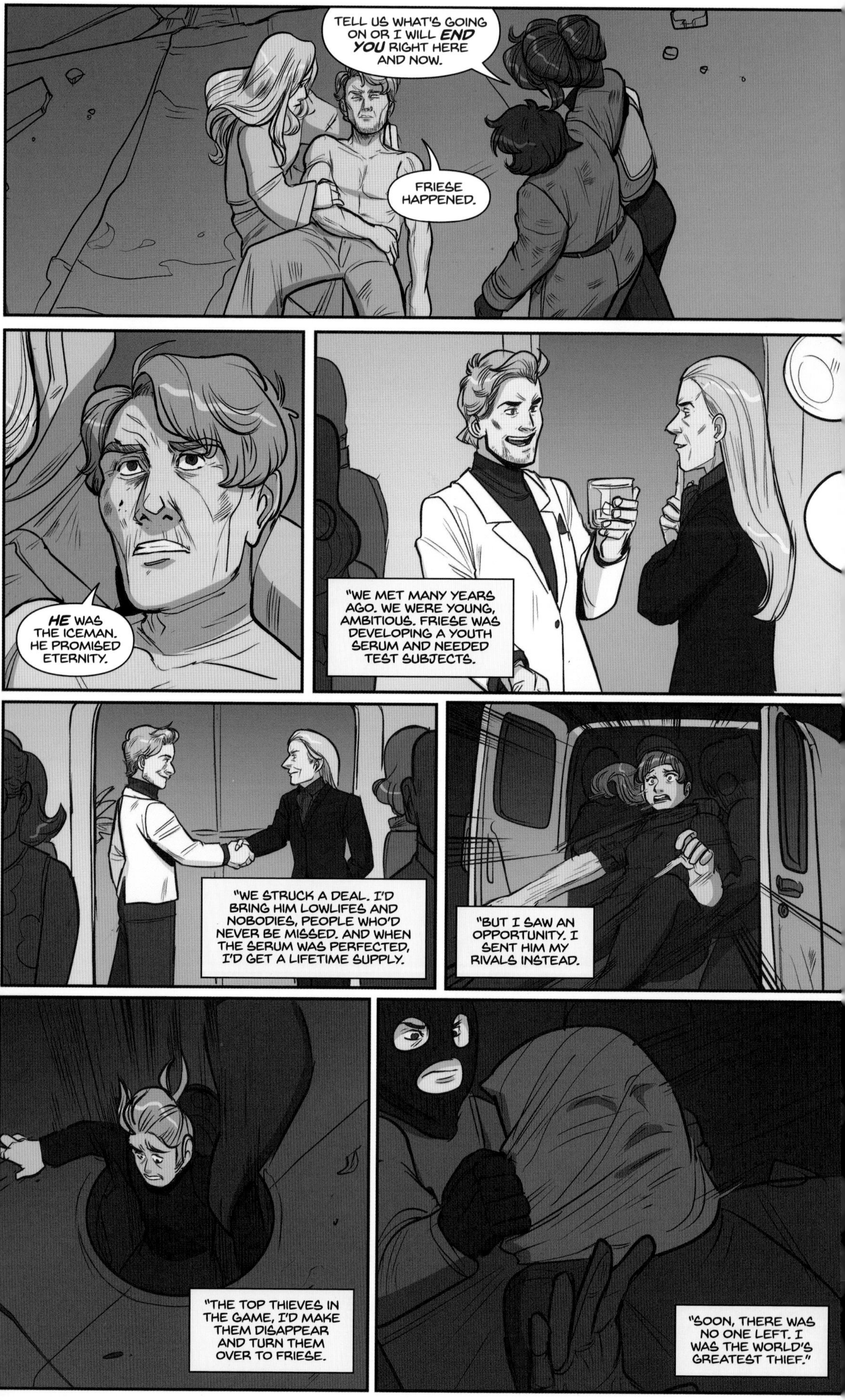
TELL US WHAT'S GOING ON OR I WILL END YOU RIGHT HERE AND NOW.
FRIESE HAPPENED.
HE WAS THE ICEMAN. HE PROMISED ETERNITY.
"WE MET MANY YEARS AGO. WE WERE YOUNG, AMBITIOUS. FRIESE WAS DEVELOPING A YOUTH SERUM AND NEEDED TEST SUBJECTS.
"WE STRUCK A DEAL. I'D BRING HIM LOWLIFES AND NOBODIES, PEOPLE WHO'D NEVER BE MISSED. AND WHEN THE SERUM WAS PERFECTED, I'D GET A LIFETIME SUPPLY.
"BUT I SAW AN OPPORTUNITY. I SENT HIM MY RIVALS INSTEAD.
"THE TOP THIEVES IN THE GAME, I'D MAKE THEM DISAPPEAR AND TURN THEM OVER TO FRIESE.
"SOON, THERE WAS NO ONE LEFT. I WAS THE WORLD'S GREATEST THIEF."

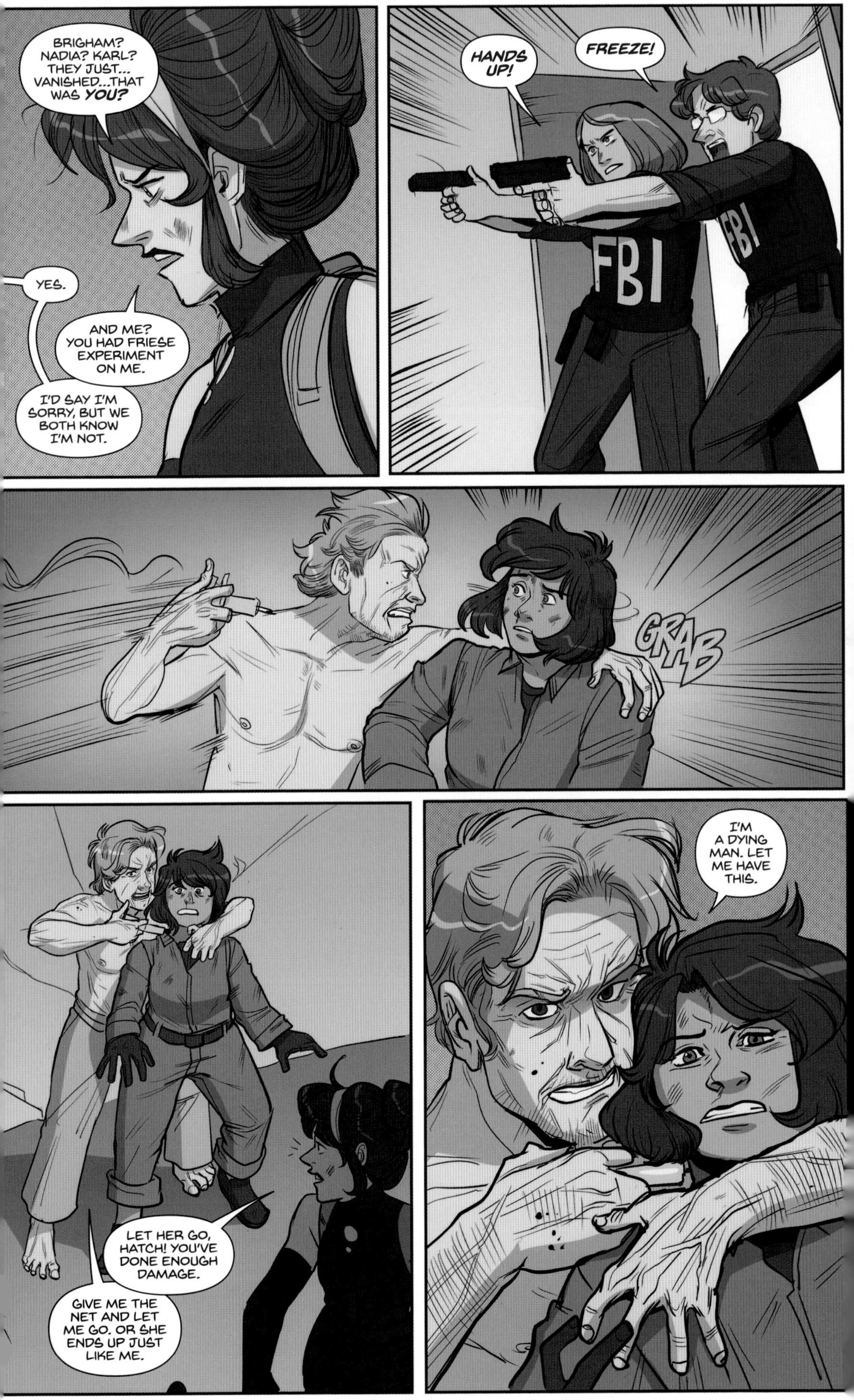
BRIGHAM? NADIA? KARL? THEY JUST... VANISHED...THAT WAS YOU?
YES.
AND ME? YOU HAD FRIESE EXPERIMENT ON ME.
I'D SAY I'M SORRY, BUT WE BOTH KNOW I'M NOT.
HANDS UP!
FREEZE!
FBI
FBI
GRAB
LET HER GO, HATCH! YOU'VE DONE ENOUGH DAMAGE.
GIVE ME THE NET AND LET ME GO. OR SHE ENDS UP JUST LIKE ME.
I'M A DYING MAN. LET ME HAVE THIS.

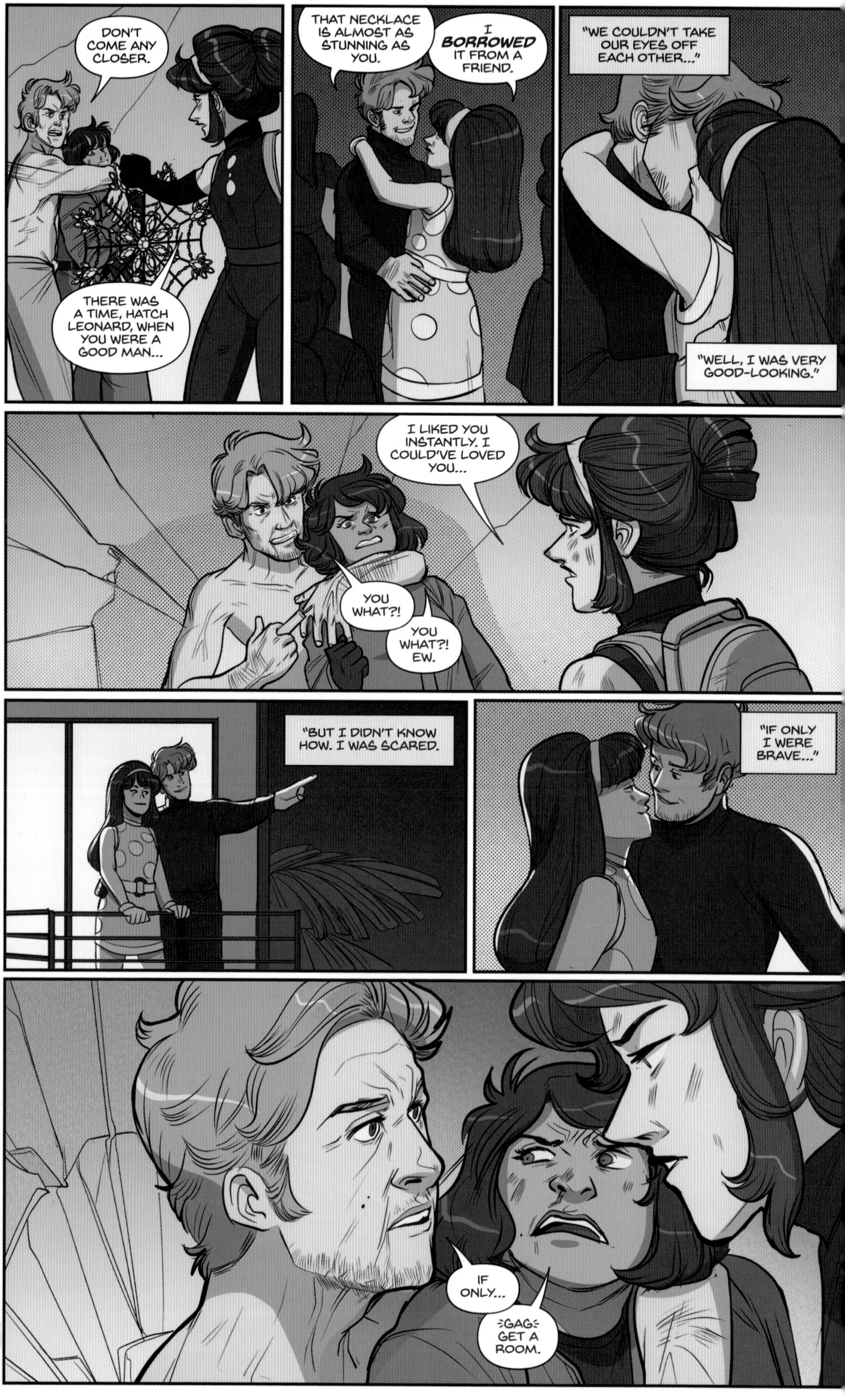
DON'T COME ANY CLOSER.
THERE WAS A TIME, HATCH LEONARD, WHEN YOU WERE A GOOD MAN...
THAT NECKLACE IS ALMOST AS STUNNING AS YOU.
I BORROWED IT FROM A FRIEND.
"WE COULDN'T TAKE OUR EYES OFF EACH OTHER..."
"WELL, I WAS VERY GOOD-LOOKING."
I LIKED YOU INSTANTLY. I COULD'VE LOVED YOU...
YOU WHAT?!
YOU WHAT?! EW.
"BUT I DIDN'T KNOW HOW. I WAS SCARED.
"IF ONLY I WERE BRAVE..."
IF ONLY...
GAG GET A ROOM.

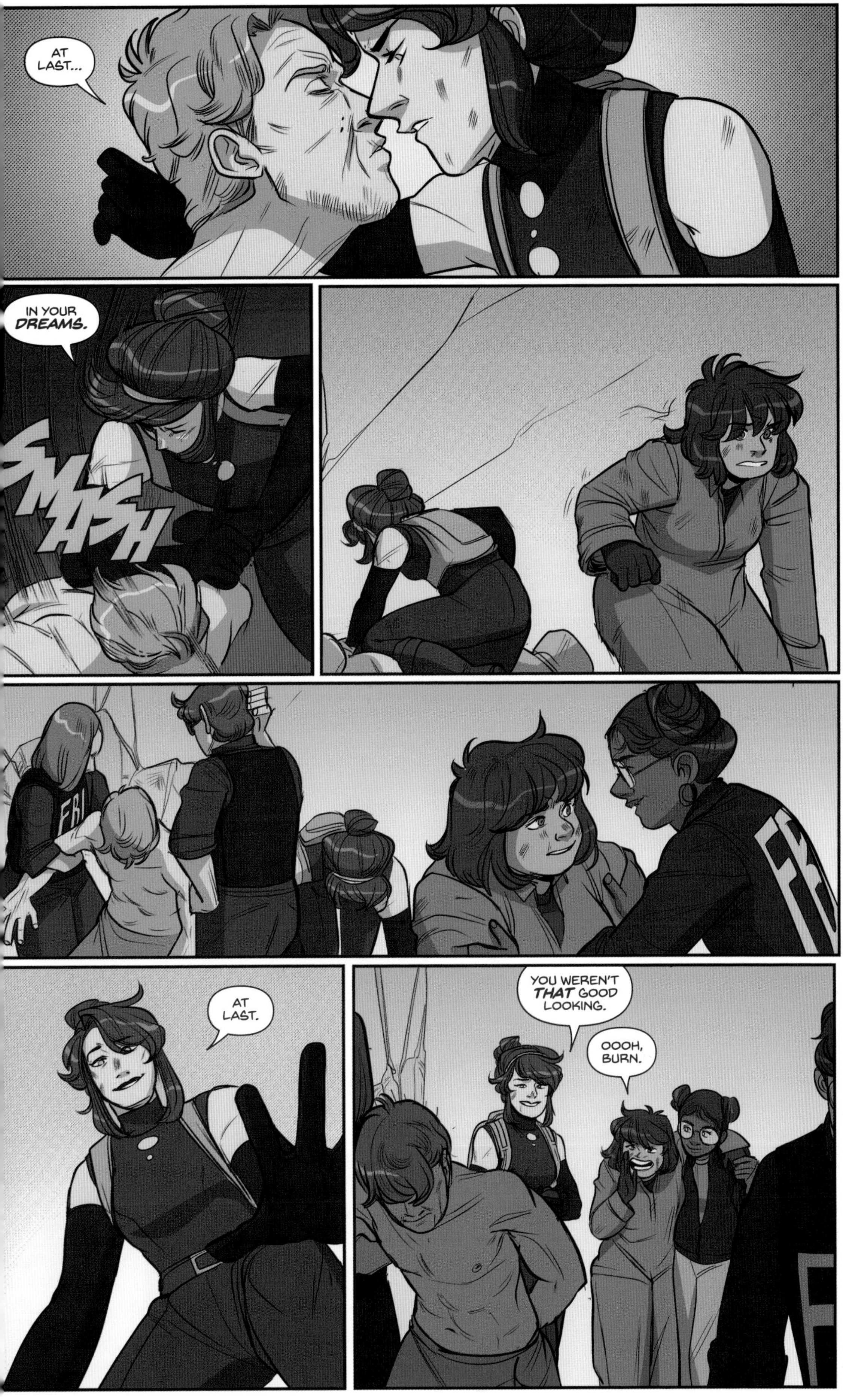
AT LAST...
IN YOUR DREAMS.
SMASH
FBI
AT LAST.
YOU WEREN'T THAT GOOD LOOKING.
OOOH, BURN.

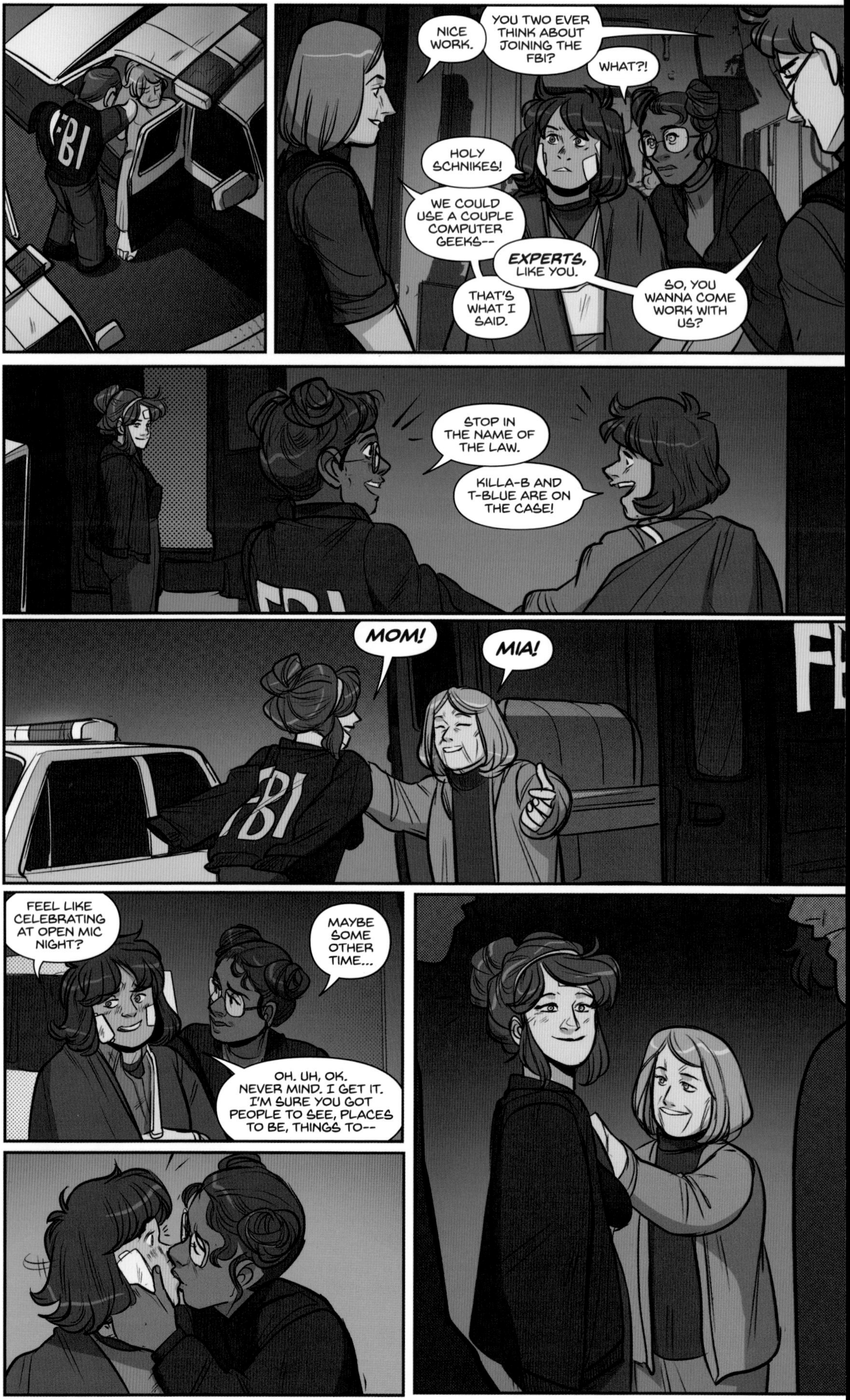
NICE WORK.
YOU TWO EVER THINK ABOUT JOINING THE FBI?
WHAT?!
HOLY SCHNIKES!
WE COULD USE A COUPLE COMPUTER GEEKS--
EXPERTS, LIKE YOU.
THAT'S WHAT I SAID.
SO, YOU WANNA COME WORK WITH US?
STOP IN THE NAME OF THE LAW.
KILLA-B AND T-BLUE ARE ON THE CASE!
MOM!
MIA!
FEEL LIKE CELEBRATING AT OPEN MIC NIGHT?
MAYBE SOME OTHER TIME...
OH. UH, OK. NEVER MIND. I GET IT. I'M SURE YOU GOT PEOPLE TO SEE, PLACES TO BE, THINGS TO--

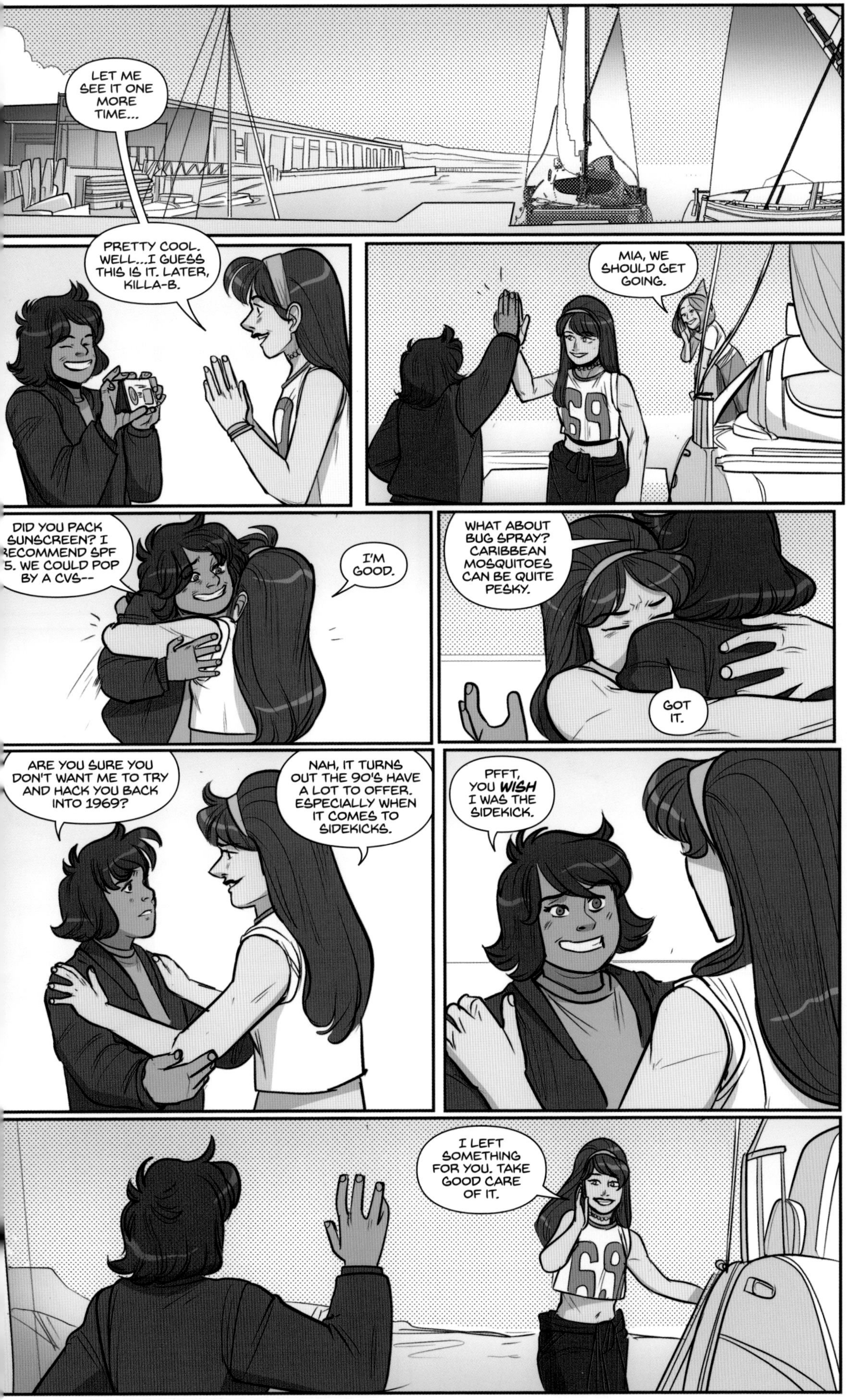
LET ME SEE IT ONE MORE TIME...
PRETTY COOL. WELL...I GUESS THIS IS IT. LATER, KILLA-B.
MIA, WE SHOULD GET GOING.
DID YOU PACK SUNSCREEN? I RECOMMEND SPF 5. WE COULD POP BY A CVS--
I'M GOOD.
WHAT ABOUT BUG SPRAY? CARIBBEAN MOSQUITOES CAN BE QUITE PESKY.
GOT IT.
ARE YOU SURE YOU DON'T WANT ME TO TRY AND HACK YOU BACK INTO 1969?
NAH, IT TURNS OUT THE 90'S HAVE A LOT TO OFFER. ESPECIALLY WHEN IT COMES TO SIDEKICKS.
PFFT, YOU WISH I WAS THE SIDEKICK.
I LEFT SOMETHING FOR YOU. TAKE GOOD CARE OF IT.

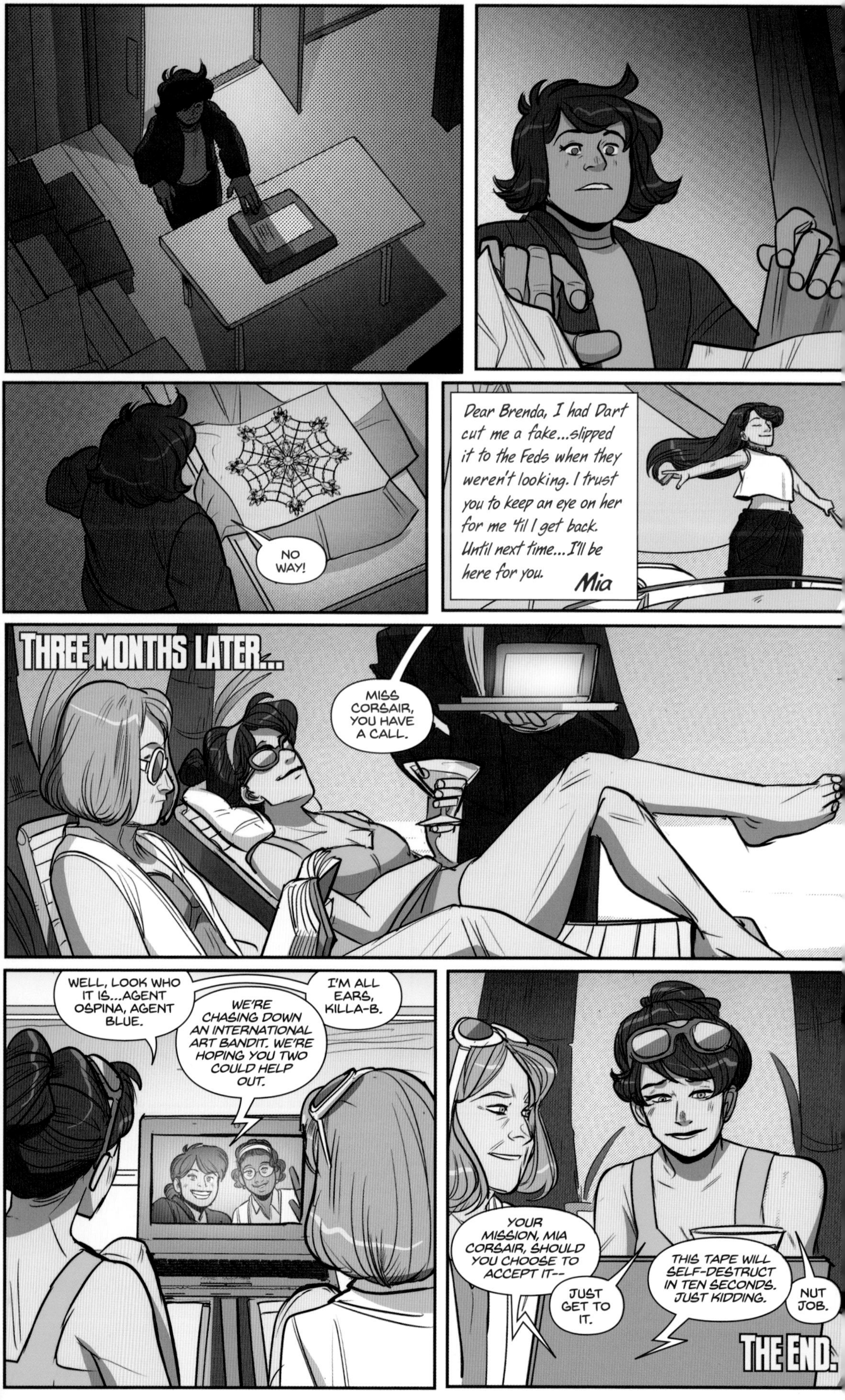
NO WAY!
Dear Brenda, I had Dart cut me a fake...slipped it to the Feds when they weren't looking. I trust you to keep an eye on her for me 'til I get back. Until next time...I'll be here for you. Mia
THREE MONTHS LATER...
MISS CORSAIR, YOU HAVE A CALL.
WELL, LOOK WHO IT IS...AGENT OSPINA, AGENT BLUE.
I'M ALL EARS, KILLA-B.
WE'RE CHASING DOWN AN INTERNATIONAL ART BANDIT. WE'RE HOPING YOU TWO COULD HELP OUT.
YOUR MISSION, MIA CORSAIR, SHOULD YOU CHOOSE TO ACCEPT IT--
JUST GET TO IT.
THIS TAPE WILL SELF-DESTRUCT IN TEN SECONDS. JUST KIDDING.
NUT JOB.
THE END.

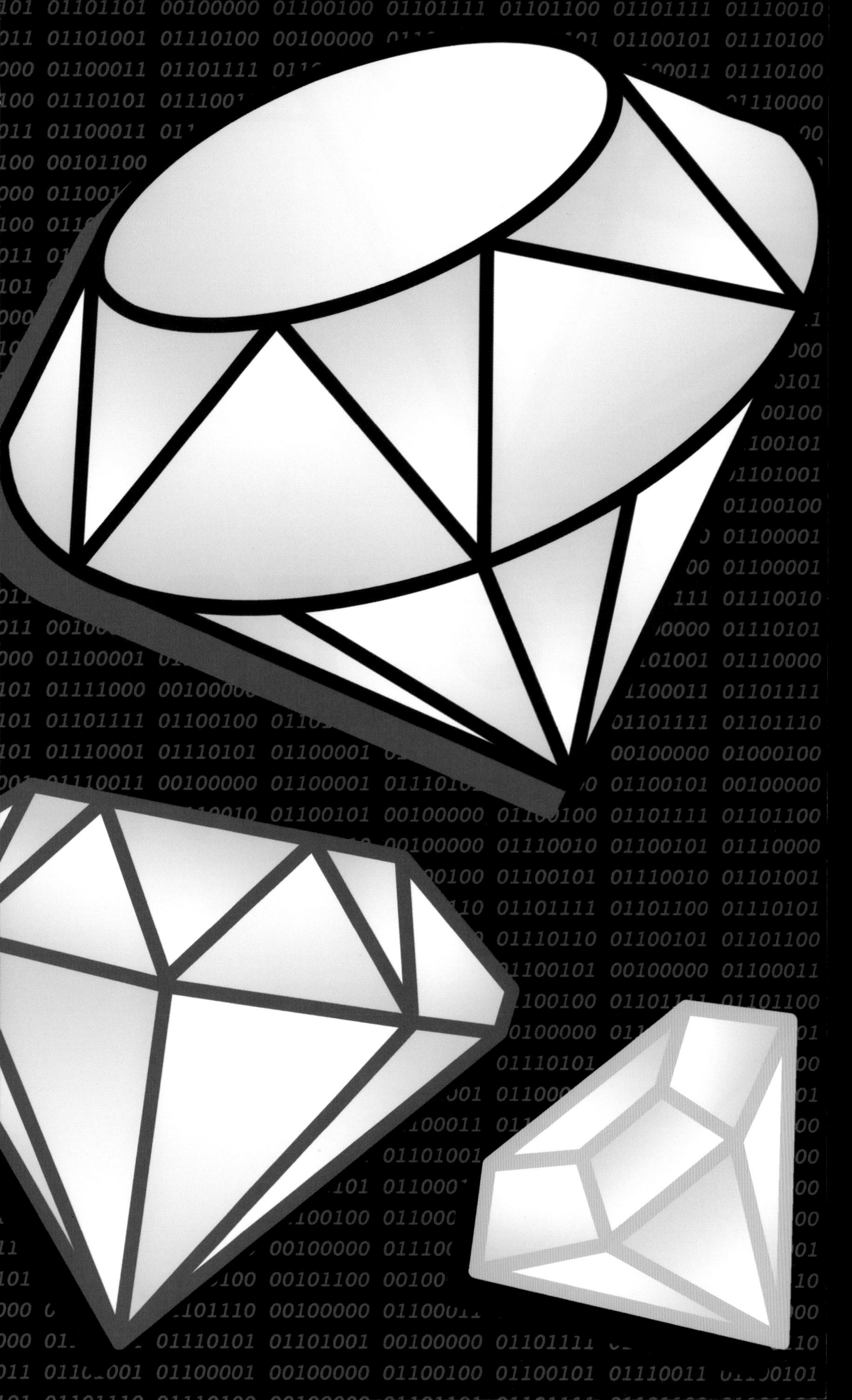

COVER
GALLERY

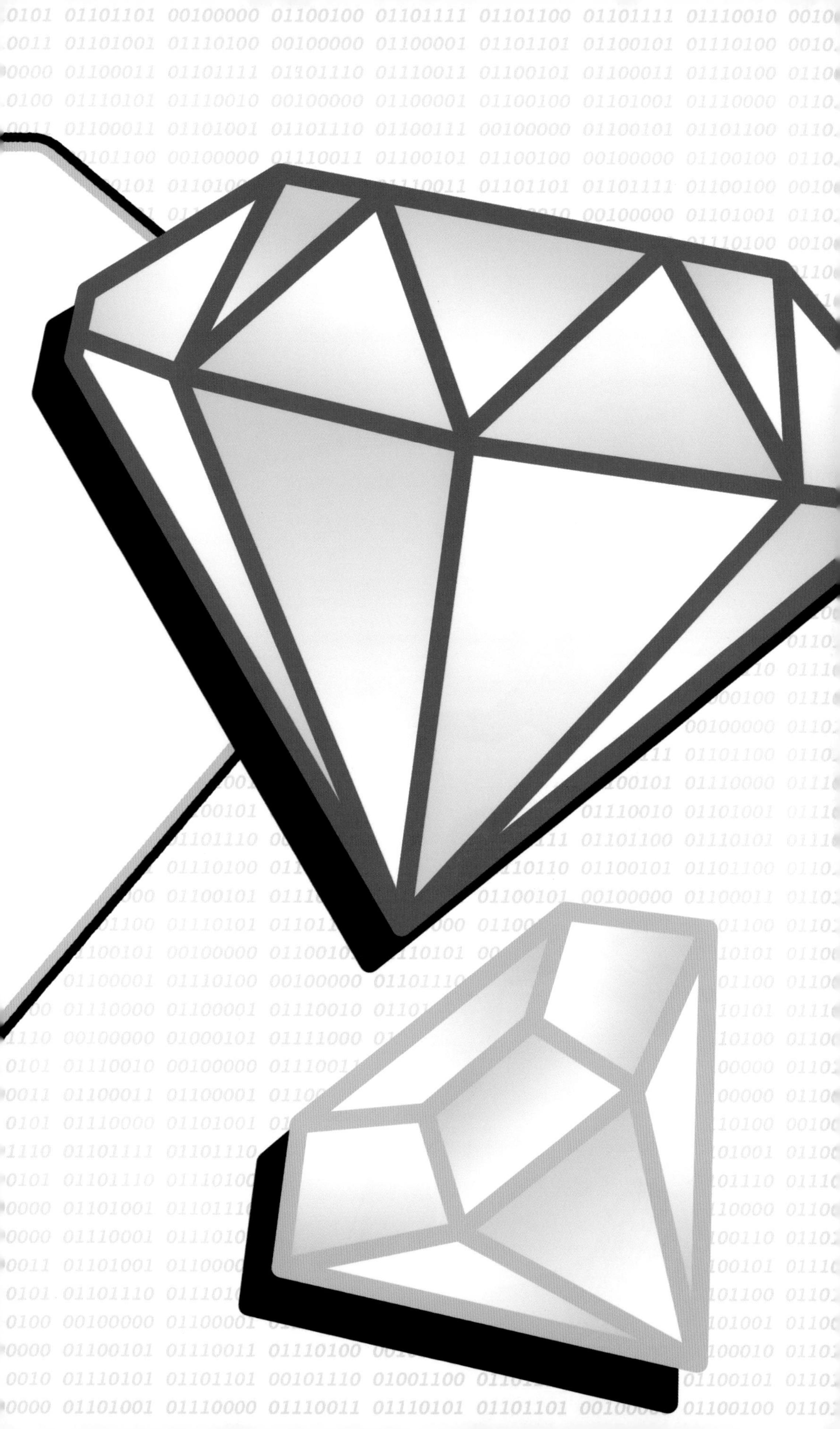

ISSUE 5 COVER
AUDREY MOK

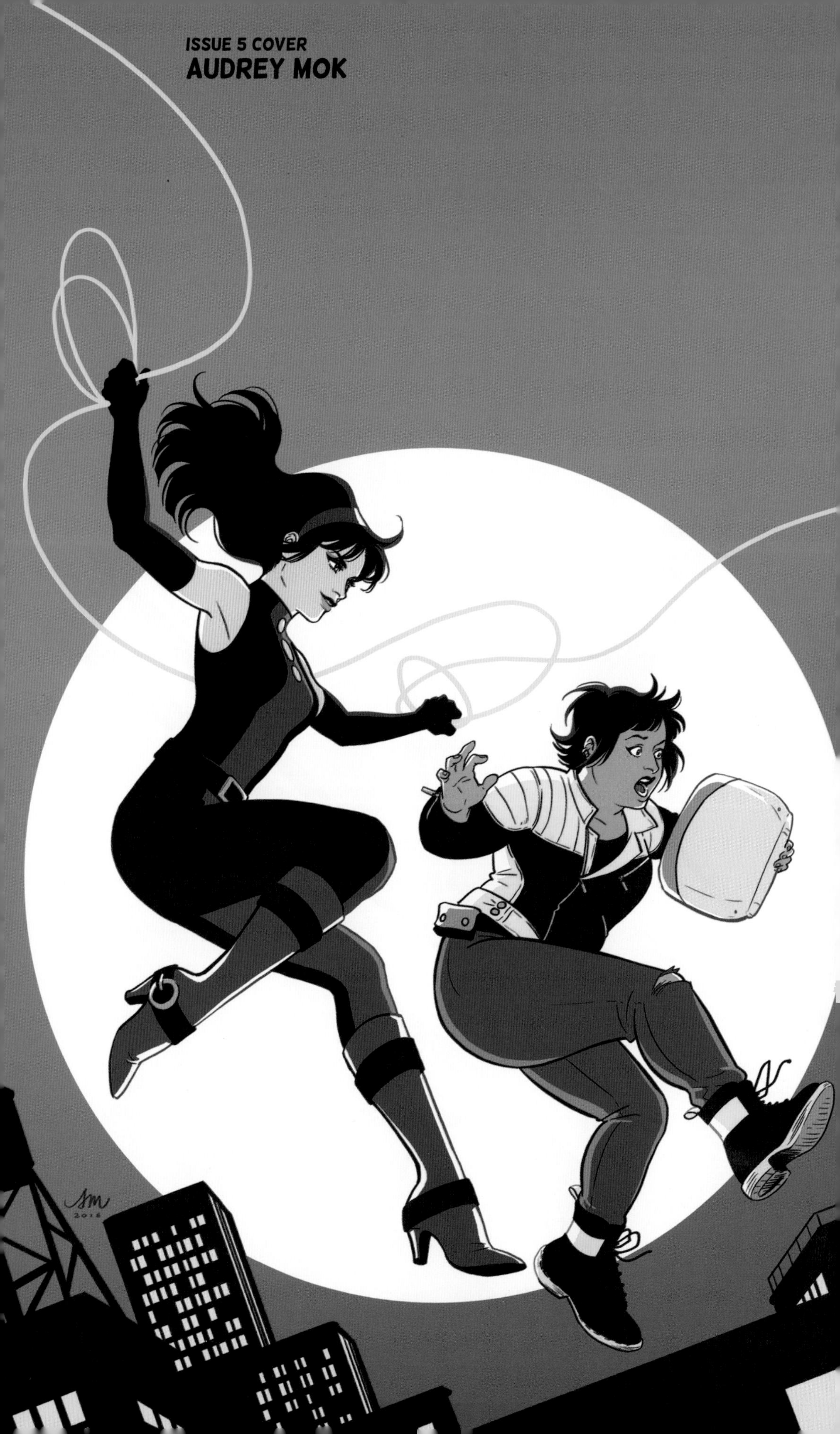

ISSUE 6 COVER
AUDREY MOK

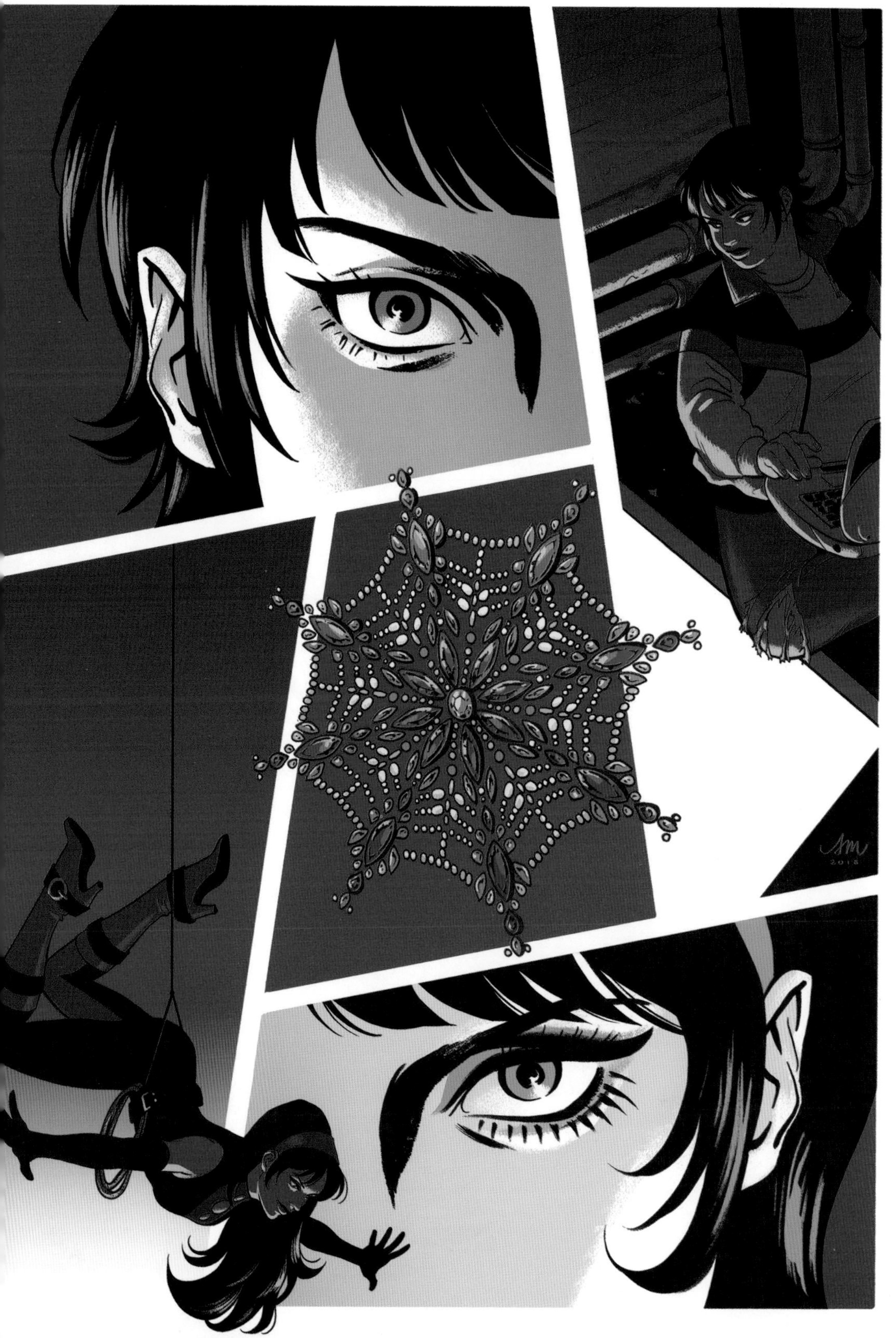

ISSUE 7 COVER
AUDREY MOK

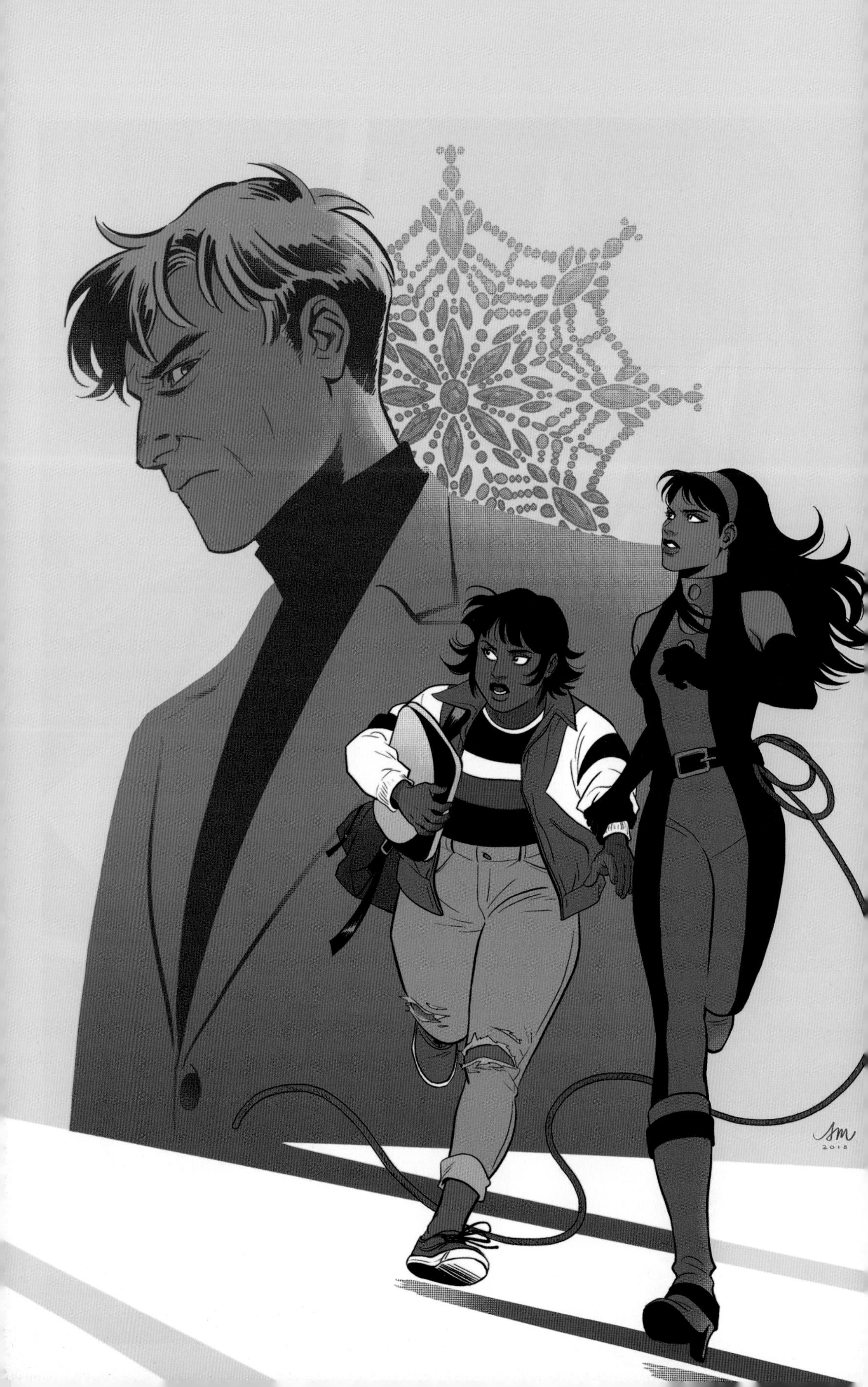

ISSUE 8 COVER
AUDREY MOK

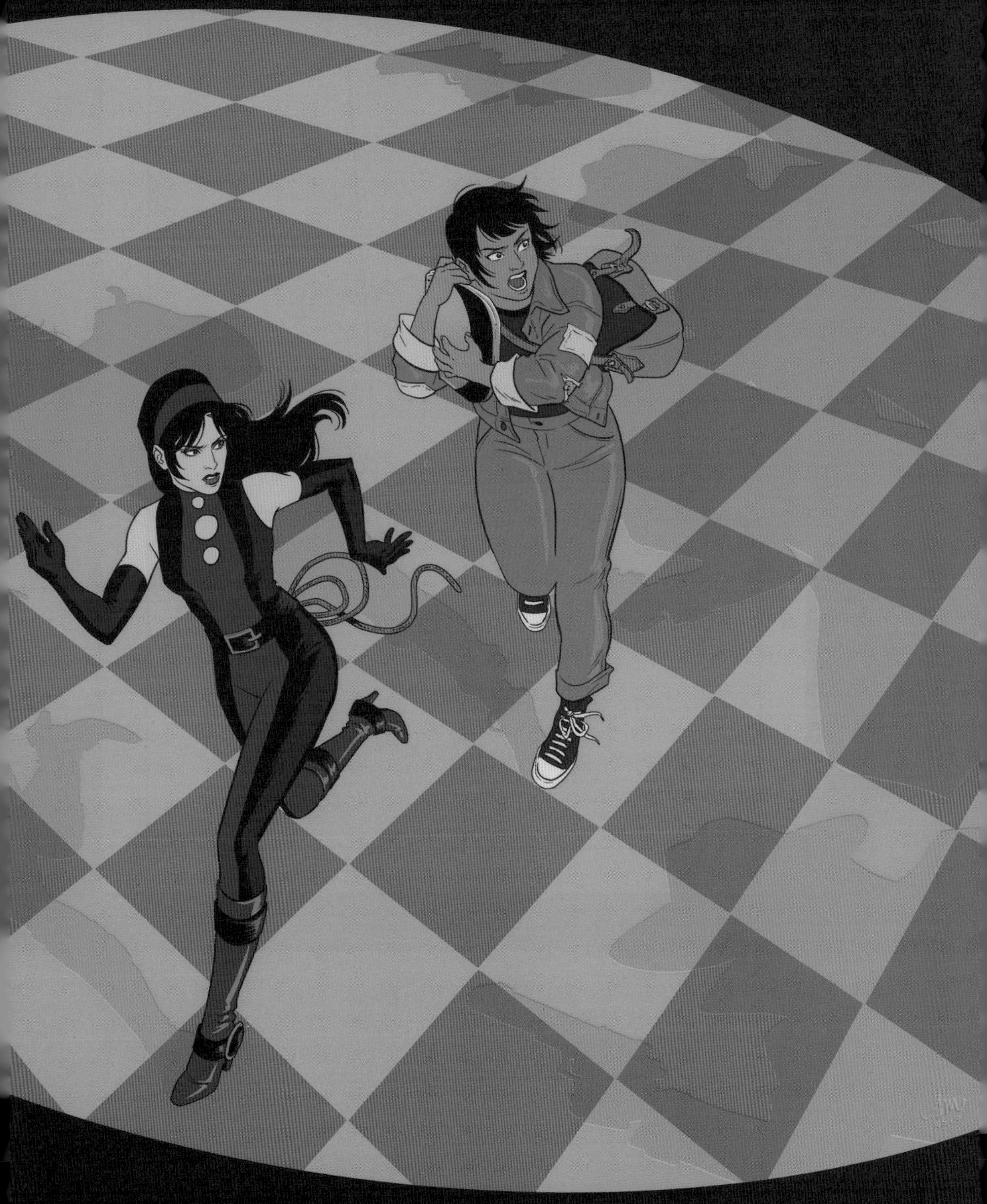

SCRIPT-TO-PAGE ISSUE #6, PAGE 17

PENCILS BY **LEISHA RIDDEL**

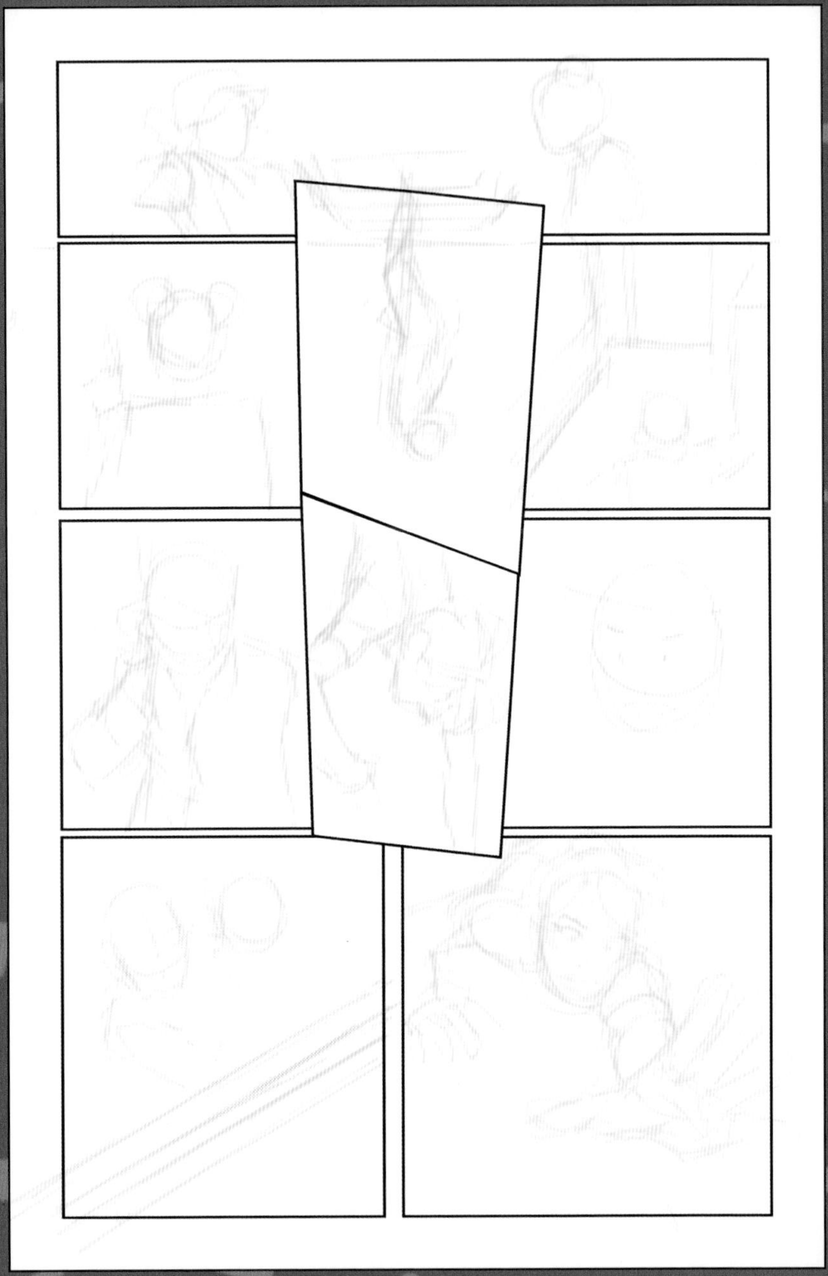

PANEL ONE: Tallulah regards Brenda curiously.

TALLULAH BLUE: Begin what?

BRENDA: Uh…Singing. Obviously.

TALLULAH BLUE: You want me to sing? Now? Here?

BRENDA: Well, of course not. You need your guitar. Duh. Another time, then. Bye-bye.

PANEL TWO: Mia twirls gracefully from the ceiling, moving through the security web.

PARTIAL INKS BY
LEISHA RIDDEL

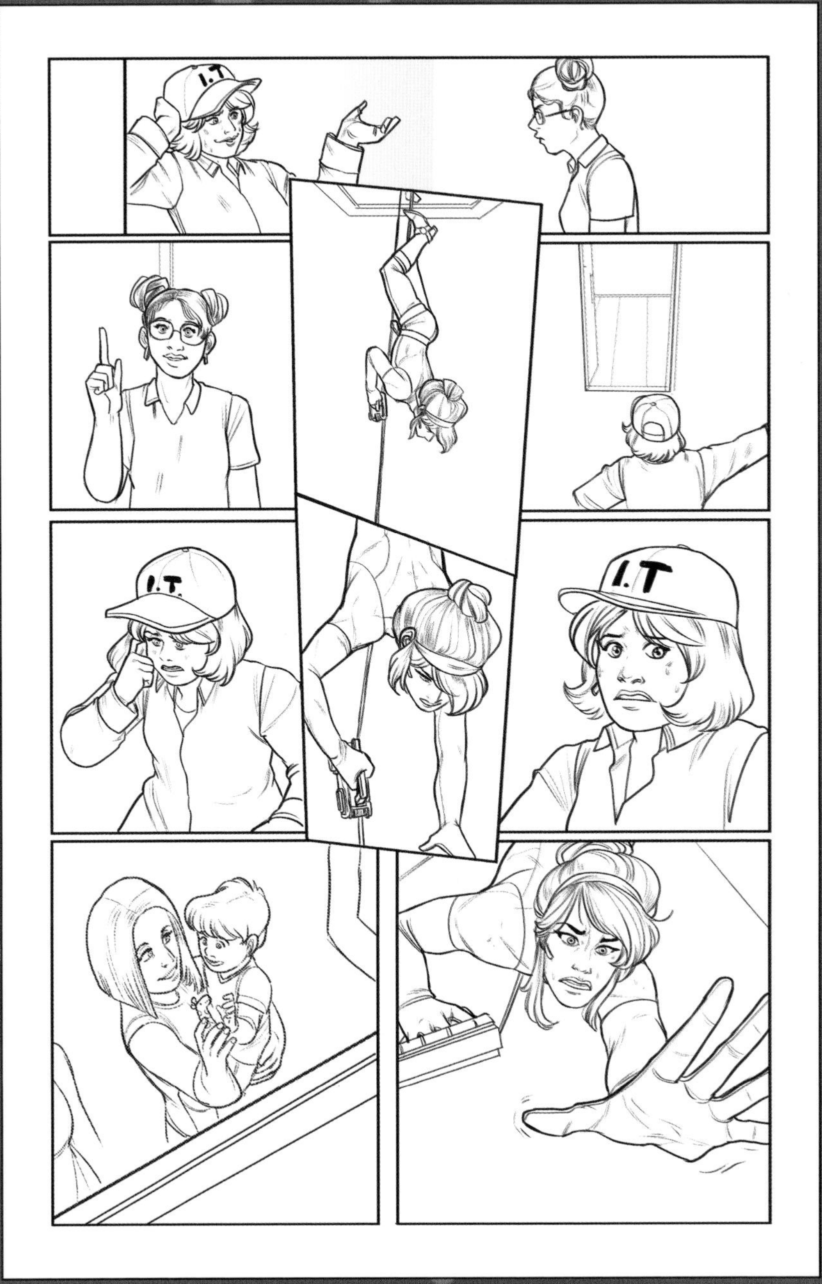

PANEL THREE: Tallulah Blue heads for the door, Brenda breathes a sigh of relief.

TALLULAH BLUE: It's in my locker.

BRENDA: What?

TALLULAH BLUE: My guitar. Be back in a nanosec.

BRENDA: Take your time!

PANEL FOUR: Mia dangles from one leg, wrapped around the rope, her hands free to maneuver through the security web.

BRENDA(OS): How's it going?

FINAL INKS BY

LEISHA RIDDEL

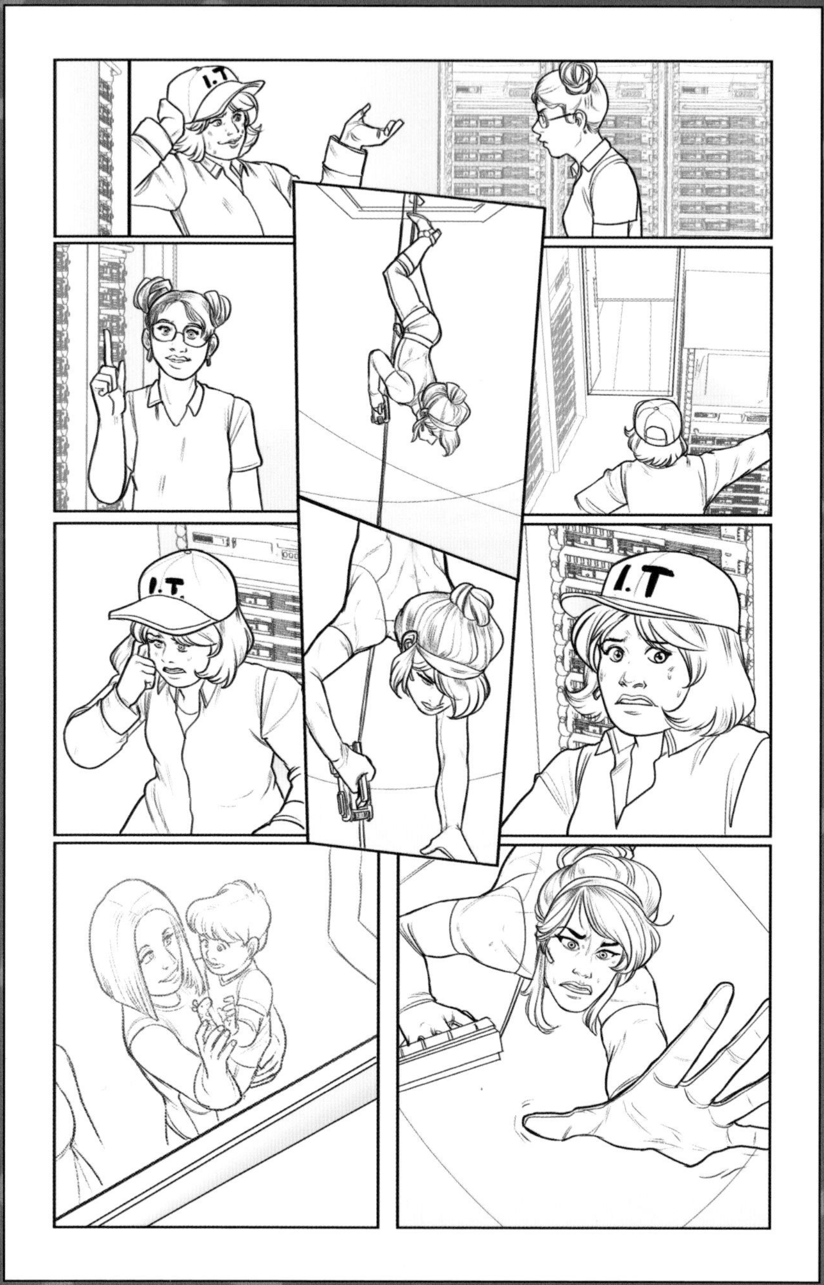
I.T
I.T.
I.T

PANEL FIVE: Mia weaves through the web confidently.

MIA: What the hell happened?

PANEL SIX: Mia flips over gracefully.

BRENDA(OS): T-Blue happened.

MIA: What?

BRENDA(OS): She runs the IT department!

MIA: What?!

BRENDA: I know! This is a nightmare--

COLORS BY
BRITTANY PEER

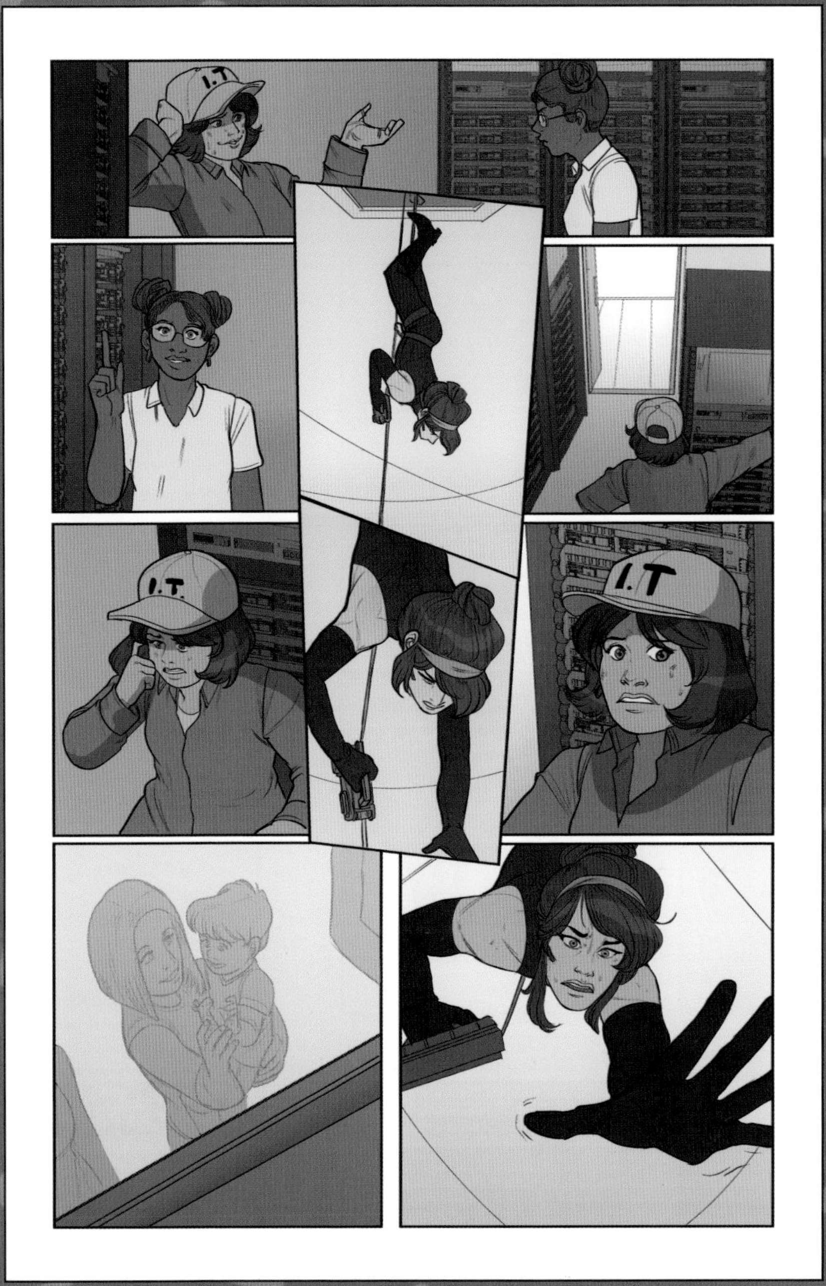
I.T.
I.T.
I.T
I.T

PANEL SEVEN: Mia reaches out for The Net, so close. The audience is enthralled by the presentation. When a voice pipes up…

MIA: Well, we've gotta improvise. I'm almost there--

CHILD IN AUDIENCE BELOW: I love you.

DISCOVER
ALL THE HITS

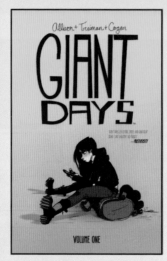

Lumberjanes
Noelle Stevenson, Shannon Watters, Grace Ellis, Brooklyn Allen, and Others
Volume 1: Beware the Kitten Holy
ISBN: 978-1-60886-687-8 | $14.99 US
Volume 2: Friendship to the Max
ISBN: 978-1-60886-737-0 | $14.99 US
Volume 3: A Terrible Plan
ISBN: 978-1-60886-803-2 | $14.99 US
Volume 4: Out of Time
ISBN: 978-1-60886-860-5 | $14.99 US
Volume 5: Band Together
ISBN: 978-1-60886-919-0 | $14.99 US

Giant Days
John Allison, Lissa Treiman, Max Sarin
Volume 1
ISBN: 978-1-60886-789-9 | $9.99 US
Volume 2
ISBN: 978-1-60886-804-9 | $14.99 US
Volume 3
ISBN: 978-1-60886-851-3 | $14.99 US

Jonesy
Sam Humphries, Caitlin Rose Boyle
Volume 1
ISBN: 978-1-60886-883-4 | $9.99 US
Volume 2
ISBN: 978-1-60886-999-2 | $14.99 US

Slam!
Pamela Ribon, Veronica Fish, Brittany Peer
Volume 1
ISBN: 978-1-68415-004-5 | $14.99 US

Goldie Vance
Hope Larson, Brittney Williams
Volume 1
ISBN: 978-1-60886-898-8 | $9.99 US
Volume 2
ISBN: 978-1-60886-974-9 | $14.99 US

The Backstagers
James Tynion IV, Rian Sygh
Volume 1
ISBN: 978-1-60886-993-0 | $14.99 US

Tyson Hesse's Diesel: Ignition
Tyson Hesse
ISBN: 978-1-60886-907-7 | $14.99 US

Coady & The Creepies
Liz Prince, Amanda Kirk, Hannah Fisher
ISBN: 978-1-68415-029-8 | $14.99 US

BOOM! BOX™

**AVAILABLE AT YOUR LOCAL
COMICS SHOP AND BOOKSTORE**
To find a comics shop in your area, visit www.comicshoplocator.com
WWW.**BOOM-STUDIOS**.COM